# HEROES FOR GHOSTS

## TOM WALLACE

ENIGMA HOUSE PRESS

ISBN: 978-1-940466-70-5

Goshen, Kentucky 40026
www.enigmahousepress.com

# Dedication

*This book is dedicated to Marilyn Underwood, Julie Watson and Sarah Small, my three pillars of strength.*

And did they get you to trade
your heroes for ghosts . . .
And did you exchange
a walk-on part in the war
for a lead role in a cage?

*Wish You Were Here*
Pink Floyd

# Chapter One

M olly Jackson had never been happier in her life than she was at this moment. Or more in love. Sitting next to Bobby on the sofa, she wouldn't have cared if the world ended right then and there. In fact, deep down, that might be what she preferred. Being with Bobby, this man she adored and worshipped, throughout all eternity was the perfect dream come true. Being *without* him . . . well, that was another matter altogether, one she refused to entertain. That was the perfect nightmare.

Twenty-seven, born and raised in a small Iowa community, Molly met Bobby Conrad in Chicago a few weeks after he left the army. It was a magical moment, almost Hollywood-like. "Meet-cute" was how she'd heard it referred to in a movie she recently watched on TV. She was working as a receptionist for a dentist at the time. Bobby came in to have a painful wisdom tooth extracted, and while waiting to be taken to the back, he and Molly struck up a conversation. Their connection was immediate. Whatever constitutes that electrical spark a man and woman sometimes feel when they first meet was definitely present in that moment. Within a matter of minutes, Bobby asked her for a date and she quickly said yes.

"Meet-cute" to be sure, even if Bobby was in excruciating pain.

It was easy to see why she was so attracted to him. He was ruggedly handsome, and his body, not long removed from the army and a year in Afghanistan, looked as if it had been carved from marble by a great sculptor. He was lean and kind of scary looking, but he had gentle eyes and a soft voice. Maybe it was the contradiction between tough and tender that drew her to Bobby.

As for Molly, she accepted the reality that she was several notches below beautiful. Pretty, yes, in a conventional way, but more often than not, guys—and some gals—generally described her as sexy, whatever the hell that meant. Anyone would certainly say that now if they saw how she was dressed—cutoff jeans, tank top and no bra. She was a shade above five-four, had hair the color of pure gold, green eyes that would sparkle in a dark room, a figure any model would be proud to have, and a toned body that was the gift of genetics rather than the result of Pilates, running, or other forms of working out. Men didn't just do a double-take when they saw her; they stared. No man ignored her.

Molly moved closer to Bobby, put her hand on his inner thigh, and began messaging it. This was a ploy that never failed to work. It normally resulted in the two of them naked and in the sack within seconds. Not this time, though. He gently removed her hand without looking up from the paper he was studying. She scooted away, pouting, but both of them knew she was only pretending to be angry. Truth is, neither of them ever got genuinely angry with each other. Anger wasn't part of their relationship.

"Do you think you'll get to meet Nicole this afternoon?" Molly asked after turning down the TV volume several notches.

Bobby looked at her, shook his head, and said, "No, I don't. How many times have I explained it to you? What is being shot today will be with stand-ins or stunt doubles. Nicole Kidman is the star of this damn movie. She's the one who eventually solves the crime. She won't be there. Neither will the actress that my character is assassinating. They'll show up later when they film the close-up stuff."

"What's the actor's name you're filling in for? Tom . . . what is it? I forgot."

"Tom Hardy. And I'm not really filling in for him. I'm . . . actually I don't know what I'm doing, to be honest with you. Making movies is not a world I'm familiar with. The only thing I know about movies is I like to watch them."

"But didn't the director say you might have some screen time?"

"Maybe, but not likely."

"What did he tell you?"

"Basically, after firing the shot I pack up the rifle, hurry down the steps, and walk out into the alley. There will be a camera back there to record me coming outside. He said there's a slim chance they'll use that shot, depending of course on how things look once they view it. But according to him, it's more likely that they'll shoot a close-up of Tom Hardy coming out of the building. And that's what will end up in the movie."

"Will he be dressed like you are now?"

"Exactly the same."

"Where do you get the gun?"

"You mean, rifle?"

"Yes, Mr. Army guy, the rifle."

"I suppose a prop man will give it to me when I get to the location."

"And the bullets won't be real, will they?"

"No, dummy, they'll be dummies. Or blanks. Whatever they use in movies."

"How will you know when to shoot?"

"When my cell phone rings one time, my directions are to get the actress—my 'victim'—in sight, wait until my phone rings a second time, and then, Bam, I fire. She falls down, blood flies everywhere, and pandemonium breaks out. There will probably be half-a-dozen cameras rolling, capturing the scene from all angles and vantage points."

Molly thought about this for a few seconds, then said, "How do they do the blood? And is it real blood?"

"They use something called squibs, which are attached to the actor's body. When the bullet hits the victim the movie people have a way to make the squibs explode. I'm not clear on all the details. And no, it is not real blood."

She put her arms around him and gave him a big hug. "Aren't you excited?" she whispered. "Knowing you're part of a big movie?"

"I'm not excited about the movie, only the paycheck," he replied. "Twenty-five grand for, what? Maybe two hours' work? Three, at most? And for playing the role of a sniper? My job in the war? Are you kidding me? When will something like this ever happen again? Never, that's when."

"What are you going to do with all that money?"

"You mean, what are *we* going to do with all that money?"

"Okay, we."

"First, I'm going to buy you a big diamond ring and then we're gonna get hitched. I want to spend the rest of my life with you, Mols. You, and no one else. Once we're officially a married couple I want us to go on a vacation. A real one, to some place neither of us have ever been to. The Bahamas, maybe. Or Cancun. Wherever you want to go."

"Not Cancun. Too many drugs, too much violence in Mexico. The Bahamas sounds good, though. I could do that."

Well, think about it. I'll go anywhere so long as you are by my side."

"Think we could find a nicer place to live?" she asked. They rented a four-room, ground-level efficiency owned by a landlord with no interest in upgrading or improving the place. "This dump is too small, and Hank isn't going to spend any money to make it nicer."

"Yeah, most def. We'll move."

"God, I love you, Bobby."

"And I love you even more."

"That's not possible," she said after kissing him on the lips.

Bobby stood and smoothed his wrinkled Levis, then slipped on a gray hoodie given to him by the movie's producer. Although the outside temperature was warm, he had been ordered to wear the sweatshirt over a black T-shirt. The boots he wore in Afghanistan rounded out his "movie" ensemble.

"When do you get paid?" Molly asked as he headed for the door.

"Once the shoot is completed I drive to a warehouse, which is the movie headquarters." He showed her the address on a slip of paper. "Once I'm there, the person in charge of finance cuts me a check for twenty-five big ones. Then I come home to you and we celebrate. Maybe I'll stop along the way and buy a bottle of expensive champagne."

"Why would they shoot a movie in Chicago?"

"Good a place as any, I suppose."

"When do you think you'll be home?"

"Well, I don't know shit about how this movie stuff works, but if all goes well, and if I don't screw things up, I should be back by five, five-thirty."

"You won't screw things up, Bobby. You'll be perfect. Maybe you'll be so good they will tell Tom Hardy to hit the road."

"Yeah, I'm sure that's what will happen."

He opened the door, put on the red baseball cap with **Lone Assassin** in black letters on the front, turned back, and gave her a kiss. "I love you, Molly Jackson," he said. "More than you'll ever know."

"I love you more." She stroked his cheek after he was seated on his motorcycle. "Be careful, babe. And if you do see Nicole Kidman, tell her I said hello."

"That will be the first thing I say to her."

Molly had tears in her eyes and joy in her heart as she watched him speed away.

---

AT SIX O'CLOCK, Molly was getting antsy; by seven-thirty, she was absolutely panic stricken. This was very much out of character for her. She never lost control of her nerves. Never became frantic or seized by terror. She was cool under pressure, just like her police officer dad had been. In that way, she was a chip off the old block. But that wasn't the case right now. At this moment, as the minutes and hours ticked away, and with Bobby almost two hours late, she was a mess. Something had to be wrong.

*Where are you, Bobby,* she kept repeating, sometimes silently in her head, but more often than not out loud. *Why aren't you answering your phone?*

A dozen calls to his cell phone resulted in getting his answering machine. On five of those calls she left messages, begging, pleading with him to get back in touch with her, and to let her know what was happening. Finally, after concluding that he wasn't going to answer, she stopped leaving messages, more certain than ever that something bad had happened to him.

As she paced the small living room, wild thoughts raced through her mind with lightning speed, ranging from the probable (working on the scene took longer than expected), to the tragic (he's been killed or badly injured in an accident), to the one that hit her hardest of all (he never really loved me; it was all a lie, a pretense).

Those thoughts fought for the top spot, each one twisting and turning in an effort to grab the lead. She felt as though the Indy 500 was taking place inside her mind. Her stomach churned, and she feared that her heart, seized by fear and uncertainty, was about to explode. Her blood pressure was off the charts.

*Calm the hell down,* she whispered to herself.

But she couldn't; her thoughts wouldn't allow it. They continued to race forward at an ever-increasing speed. A mental three-card monte was being played in her tortured mind, each scenario being manipulated by an unseen dealer, the answer to her question hidden like a serpent beneath a rock. And despite her best efforts, despite her deep desire for one of the first two possibilities to be uncovered, she quickly realized that it was the third scenario that kept turning up.

Why that one and not one of the others? she asked herself, knowing full well what the answer would be. Bobby hadn't failed to return home because the damn scene took too long to shoot. Even if it did run longer than anticipated, it never would have taken *this* long. And if he had been involved in an accident, either the police or someone from the hospital would have informed her. She would've heard from somebody.

No, she silently admitted, the final scenario was the reason why he hadn't returned home.

*Bobby doesn't love me anymore.*

*He is in love with someone else.*

*My dreams are ashes, my life has been ruined.*

No, that simply wasn't possible, Molly screamed out loud. He dearly loves me. I saw it in his eyes, heard it in his voice. He wants to spend his life with me, and only me. We are meant to be together forever.

But . . . he wasn't home yet, which could only mean *something* had happened. Maybe he was involved in an accident. Or perhaps it's something more benign, like his motorcycle broke down, or he had a flat tire. And since he never remembers to charge his cell phone, that's why he hadn't called her, or why he didn't answer her calls to him.

Whatever the reason, good or bad, he wasn't home.

And the hands on the clock were not standing still.

Molly now faced two clear-cut choices: either stay where she was, which meant more worrying, fretting and pacing, or hop in the car and drive to the location where Bobby was to be paid. Given those options, the answer was a no-brainer:

*Go find Bobby.*

She remembered the name of the street written on the slip of paper Bobby showed her, but not the actual address. Lacking that information didn't concern her. The street was maybe two miles from the apartment. It was a street she knew very well, because she had to drive past it every day on her way to work. Unless traffic was really heavy, it shouldn't take her more than a few minutes to get there. Once she did, she would drive up and down the street looking for his motorcycle. Find the cycle, find Bobby.

Having made her decision, she grabbed her car keys off the kitchen table, picked up her purse, and went outside. After closing and locking the door, she quickly got in her car and started the motor, unaware that Chicago TV station WGN had interrupted regular programming with breaking news:

Senator Dana Shapiro had been shot dead while giving a speech in front of the Art Institute of Chicago.

---

IT TOOK MOLLY LESS than twenty minutes to arrive at the street where Bobby was to be paid for his work on the movie. It was a tree-lined street that featured a combination of old brick homes and more modern condominiums. This was one of those big city neighborhood areas where the old was rapidly giving way to the new. Progress in the eyes of some, loss of tradition the verdict of others.

Molly saw Bobby's motorcycle parked outside one of the older —if not the oldest—buildings on the block. The structure, located at the very end of the street, was in complete disrepair. Crumbling or missing bricks left gaping holes that gave the exterior a pock-marked look, while the many broken, shattered windows only added to the overall feeling that a once-impressive place had fallen victim to time and neglect. Bobby had described the place as a warehouse, but it didn't look like one. Molly's immediate thought was that the place had once been an apartment building, which the name carved into the brick above the front entrance seemed to confer. In its heyday, the place was known as the Continental Arms.

Molly parked, got out of the car, and slowly began walking toward the front entrance. It had now grown dark, and although there was no one around, she felt uneasy. Sometimes silence can be more frightening than loud noise, and this was one of those times. Adding to her unease was the open front entrance, a dark rectangular hole that seemed to beckon visitors into an even darker place. Molly started to call out for Bobby, but she didn't. Fear had silenced her voice.

Taking out her cell phone, she held it up, using it as a flashlight. Cautiously, she entered the building, moving slowly forward, her eyes sweeping from side to side, her heart going wild in her chest. A noise to her left caused her to jump, but the source of the noise was a large rat scurrying across the floor. Seeing the rodent did little to assuage her growing fear.

Creeping forward ever more slowly, she made her way through what had once been the apartment's main lobby and into a smaller second room, one she guessed that back in the old days had been the manager's office. More noise to her right caused her to flinch. But this time she didn't turn to check out the source of the noise. She had no desire to see another large rat.

Instead, she edged deeper into the room, holding the cell phone high in the air, waving it from left to right in an effort to win the battle against the darkness. Shadows danced across the walls like ghostly apparitions. This was, she felt, a place where ghosts would have felt at home.

Turning to her left, she looked down.

And that's when she saw it.

The body of a man lying face down, his head resting in a sea of blood.

She didn't need to see the dead man's face to know who he was.

Bobby.

Molly stood motionless, paralyzed by a combination of fear and disbelief. *This can't be Bobby*, she said to herself. *Who would want to harm him? That's not possible.* But as much as she tried to convince herself that the poor soul lying dead on a crumpled concrete floor wasn't the man she loved, all of her efforts failed.

She knew.

The dead man was Bobby, the love of her life.

But what if he's not dead? she wondered. What if it's only a head wound? If he's still alive maybe he can be saved. Should she check him for a pulse? No, call nine-one-one first, get help on the way, and then check to see if Bobby is still alive.

She pulled her phone close and started to dial the numbers. She had just punched in the nine when she heard another noise coming from behind her, a noise she recognized as one coming not from a rodent, but rather from a different and much larger animal.

A man.

Before she could punch in the two ones and complete the call, her head was violently yanked back, and she felt something cold and very sharp placed against her neck. And she instantly knew what the object was, and what was about to happen.

She was going to die.

Molly had one final thought before the knife began slicing her throat.

*I love you, Bobby.*

# Chapter Two

K evin O'Malley, bent at the waist, was sucking air as though oxygen had all but vanished from the earth, convinced that each breath he took might be his last one ever. He was gulping it in like a man given his first drink of water after wandering for days in the desert. His lungs screamed, burned like fire, and the pain in his side was close to excruciating. It felt like he was constantly being jabbed in his ribcage by a dagger.

And yet, he still had another thirty minutes of pain to suffer through.

"If you want to be an exceptional tennis player, Kevin, this is what you have to do," Jack Dantzler said from the other side of the net. "You gotta keep pushing against the wall, against the pain, keeping in mind always that those guys you might have to play sometime down the road aren't about to give in. They're willing themselves to keep moving forward even when their body is screaming that it's time to quit. They're doing whatever it takes to beat your ass. And they will if they have more stamina, more desire, more guts than you have. So, you either suck it up, pay the price now, or you lose later on."

"I know, I know, you're right, Mr. Dantzler," Kevin said, still struggling to fill his red-hot lungs. "But, man, you aren't making it easy."

"You want easy, find another coach. You want to win, do what I say."

"I want to win, so I'm sticking with you."

"Good choice."

Thirty minutes later, practice session completed (Kevin would call it a torture session), Kevin's entire body glistened with perspiration, giving him the appearance of a medieval knight whose armor was wet from heavy rains, and he was once again drinking in the oxygen. But when he walked off the court and sat in one of the chairs next to where Dantzler was sitting, Kevin wore the look of a conqueror, a sixteen-year-old warrior who had faced off against a mighty foe and come away victorious. Somewhere on his sweaty, tired face was the look of pride. A sense of accomplishment. He had gone one-on-one with the monster known as fatigue and kicked it in the ass.

After grabbing his water bottle and taking a long drink, he said, "Think I could ever be as good as Roger Federer?"

"Somebody has to be. Might as well be you."

This was Dantzler's standard reply when one of his male students hit him with that question, or when one of the females wondered if she could ever rival Serena Williams or Maria Sharapova. It wasn't a lie, but it certainly wasn't the truth, either. No, none of them would ever come close to matching Roger or Serena; their skill and talent level was beyond these kids' ability to comprehend. But it was an acceptable answer, Dantzler felt, because it offered encouragement rather than unreasonable promises or false hope. It landed somewhere on the middle ground. Equally important, there was no hint of negativity. A kid could take this answer and run with it, at least until reality eventually slapped him or her in the face.

Which it would, sure as the sun would rise in the east tomorrow morning.

But that was a hard truth they didn't need to hear at this point in their young lives. Time would hand it to them soon enough.

Dantzler was a hundred times better than any of these kids would ever be, but even he, on his best day in his prime, would have had no chance against Roger Federer. There are the good, the great and the exceptional. Dantzler judged himself to be somewhere on the very high end of good, or on a good day, perhaps on the low end of great. Exceptional was way out of reach. Exceptional resided in a far-off galaxy, home to a blessed few.

"What do I need to work on the most?" Kevin asked after using his towel to wipe sweat from his face.

"Everything."

"Everything?"

"You want to have a complete game, don't you? Well, to do that you need to improve in all areas. Footwork and racket preparation are the keys to success. Along with mental toughness. Those three areas should always be your primary focus."

"My dad says you are the best player to ever come out of Lexington," Kevin said. "Maybe even in all of Kentucky."

"Your dad is being overly generous in his assessment. I was pretty good, yeah, but good ain't good enough at the highest levels."

"Dad said if you had concentrated on tennis rather than becoming a detective you might have captured one of the Grand Slams."

Dantzler laughed, said, "How much was your dad drinking when he said that?"

"Dad doesn't drink." Kevin took another sip of water. "You played John McEnroe, didn't you?"

"Yeah, and I lost."

"Three sets, right? Seven-five in the third set, right? That's damn close. And he went on to become number one in the world. You don't think you could have done that had you focused on tennis?"

"No, Kevin, I don't. McEnroe had the hands of an artist. He could do shit with a tennis racket that I could never do. Ever. I played exceptionally well that day, managed to make it close and interesting. Had we played the next day I doubt it would have been so close. He was just better and more gifted than I was. Johnny Mac was special, I wasn't. And that's it in a nutshell."

"Truthfully, do you think I can be at least as good as you, Mr. Dantzler?"

"Kevin, you would need to be far superior to me if you hope to be anywhere close to Roger Federer."

Dantzler left the court a few minutes after Kevin had departed, went into the locker room, put his equipment into his locker, undressed, and took a shower. The hot water did its job, loosening his tight muscles and easing those aches that were a grim reminder that he wasn't as young as he'd once been. Time was the unbeatable opponent; the body understood this much sooner than the mind did. His mind said, "You can still do this," but his body told him, "Don't even think about trying it."

After showering and dressing, he went up to the counter in the lounge area, ordered a Diet Pepsi, then sat at a table close to the big-screen TV mounted on the wall. Dantzler had come to the lounge hoping to find David Bloom or Sean Montgomery, but neither man was there.

Dantzler, Bloom, and Sean owned the Tennis Center, having purchased it almost a dozen years ago. Bloom, a psychiatrist, was Dantzler's former college teammate, while Sean was an ex-cop who went back to law school and was now a defense attorney. They were Dantzler's closest friends, and the two men he trusted most.

Sitting alone, eyes staring ahead, Dantzler let his thoughts drift in different directions. Primarily, he focused on this past year, and the changes that had taken place. Big, substantial, life-altering changes. After twenty-seven years as a homicide detective, he handed in his gold shield. He did so for no other reason than a desire to do something different. To travel an unknown path. To see what else was out there on the distant horizon waiting for him to discover.

For the past twenty-seven years, every path he took began with the discovery of a dead body and ended with the apprehension of—and sometimes the death of—a murderer. Putting away the worst society had to offer was a noble cause. Even a necessary cause. He knew this in his deepest heart. But it wore on you. Seeing so much death and suffering and grieving and ugliness claimed a bit of your soul.

It nibbled away at your faith in humanity.

Too much nibbling and your humanity could be gone altogether.

Better to walk away before that happened.

After giving his notice, Dantzler stayed on the job a few extra months while Eric Gamble settled in as the new head of the Homicide Unit. Eric took the job after Richard Bird, long-time head of the department, called it quits. Eric handled his new task exactly the way Dantzler knew he would—competently and professionally. In a brief span of time, Dantzler's early prediction proved to be dead-on —that Eric would be better at the job than Richard Bird had been.

And Richard had been damn good.

Some of the higher-ups on the police force felt the Homicide Unit would be greatly weakened by Dantzler's departure. After all, they argued, he had never failed to solve a case. How do you top perfection? With him gone, the solve rate was sure to take a hit, they said. But that dire prediction hadn't yet proved to be accurate. Dantzler knew of six homicides that had been reported since he quit the department, and all six had been solved. Thus far at least, there had been no fall-off in performance levels since he retired.

Regardless of what the naysayers said, the Homicide Unit was still very solid. Eric was a superb in-the-field investigator—unlike Bird, who was better suited for administrative work than actively chasing down murderers—and he had strong support from Jake Thomas, who, in Dantzler's opinion, had the talent to become an even better homicide detective than he'd been. Jake, a local kid, joined the Marines after 9/11 and fought with distinction in Iraq and Afghanistan, earning a slew of medals and commendations for his battlefield actions. In his four years as a homicide detective, Jake had performed exactly as he had while in the military—with honor and bravery.

Victoria Jefferson, Eric's cousin, was now officially a team member, as was Jason Ford, a Lexington native who had returned to his hometown after spending a decade working homicide cases in Knoxville. With that quartet firmly in place—and performing admirably—Dantzler walked away, confident in their ability to keep the unit running at the highest level possible.

Since leaving the police force, Dantzler had met all the requirements necessary to become a private investigator, filling out paperwork, taking—and easily passing—all the required tests. Prior to doing any of those things, he had rented a small office in a building owned by Sean. He purchased a desk, chair, laptop, file cabinet, and a table for his printer. The bare basics. If he needed more later on, he'd buy it. This would be his new headquarters. Once he had settled in, he made contact with two people who might send clients his way—Grace West, a famous defense attorney in Chicago, and Mike Brennan, a Manhattan district attorney. Both promised to help in any way they could. The irony wasn't lost on Dantzler—working with Grace would likely mean trying to get a guilty scumbag off the hook, while aiding Mike would translate into trying to put an individual behind bars. Oh well, he reasoned, life is full of weird contradictions. But in the end, who he worked for didn't matter, be it a prosecutor or a defense attorney. Who signed the paycheck was irrelevant. The only thing that concerned him was uncovering the truth, regardless of which party was handing him his paycheck. That was his job, his only job. Anything beyond that belonged in other hands. That was no different from his days as a detective.

Thus far, Dantzler's experience as a private investigator consisted of turning down five jobs and saying yes to exactly none. He'd paid seven months' worth of rent and utilities for his office, and collected not one single nickel in income. Not what you would call a sound business model.

But he wasn't worried. He had an advantage over many others who decided to change careers in mid-stream, especially those whose new job offered no guaranteed income. He was fortunate to have plenty of money. Between his pension, his savings, the income from the Tennis Center, and tennis lessons, if he chose to give them, he had the luxury of not having to worry financially.

What this meant was that he had the option to accept only those cases that were interesting and challenging. After spending the past twenty-seven years matching wits with cold-blooded killers, he wasn't about to waste precious time spying on cheating husbands, or unhappy wives on the prowl for new and exciting sexual adventures.

No, if it wasn't a big case, let someone else handle it.

But . . . he was a man of action, and for men like that, boredom came easily and quickly. Giving the occasional tennis lesson was fine. He had no qualms about that, and it did serve to keep him busy and active. But he needed something new, exciting.

Most of all, what he needed was a challenge.

And little did he know he was about to get what he wished for.

## Chapter Three

Having never been to Chicago, Danny Kafka possessed no real knowledge of the city. He knew the Cubs captured the World Series in 2016, and Michael Jordan won a boatload of NBA championship rings with the Bulls, and that the water in the river that cuts through the city was somehow colored green each St. Patrick's Day. Oh yeah, and as a kid he'd heard that more than one-hundred years ago the city burned to the ground. Something about an old woman's cow knocking over a lantern in a barn. He wasn't sure if that story was factual or not, just as he questioned whether Nero actually fiddled while Rome was being swallowed up by flames. Maybe they were, maybe they weren't. Who could ever know for sure? Either way, true or false, they both made for legendary tales.

Danny arrived in the Windy City around nine in the morning and went straight to his hotel. He was pleased but not surprised when the taxi pulled to a stop in front of the Blackstone Renaissance Hotel on South Michigan Avenue. One look at the place was all it took for Danny to know that staying in this joint didn't come cheap. Prices here were way out of his range. He couldn't afford to stay in this hotel's bathroom, much less a big suite, which is what he'd been booked into. He didn't even want to know how much it cost per night to stay here. A bundle of cash, to be sure. But he wasn't going to worry about it, because cost was something that didn't bother movie people. They had loads of cash to spend, and they obviously weren't shy about spending it.

If they wanted to put him up in one of Chicago's finest and ritziest hotels, who was he to argue or complain? And why shouldn't he be accorded special treatment? After all, he was one of the stars of their movie.

*The movie?*

Danny still had a difficult time accepting the realization that he had been chosen to play a key role in a big-budget movie, a thriller titled *Lone Assassin*. And not just any role either. He was, in fact, playing the part of the assassin. The centerpiece of the movie.

It had happened so fast, like a bolt of lightning streaking across the night sky. Finally, at long last he had been handed that big break every struggling actor dreams of. And Danny had definitely been struggling. Since arriving in New York City three years ago, his entire acting resume consisted of a single TV commercial for a local mattress store. His role: lie back on a mattress, fake a big yawn, and utter what had to be the most inane line ever conceived – "sleep on one of these babies and you'll never have to count sheep again."

That's a long way from speaking lines written by Shakespeare or Tennessee Williams. It's doubtful that any actor, even one as skilled as De Niro, could make that bullshit line sound good.

Other than that one-day gig, which earned him four-hundred bucks, there had been nothing else. He'd auditioned for half-a-dozen plays on and off-Broadway, and seven or eight TV commercials, but he hadn't landed a single role. Adding to Danny's frustration, no one from the movie world had come calling. Danny hadn't heard a peep from anyone.

Until . . .

Eight days ago, as he was leaving an acting class, he got a call from Abe Pearlstein, his eighty-eight-year-old agent, saying he had some terrific news to share. A producer wanted Danny to read for a part in an upcoming movie. Danny was blown away when he heard those words from Abe. Blown away didn't accurately describe

Danny's feelings at that moment. What Abe told him sounded almost too good to be true.

"Are you sure about that, Abe?" Danny inquired, skepticism clinging to his every word. "He asked for me specifically?"

"Would I make such a claim if it weren't true?" Abe answered. "And yes, he asked for you. He wants Danny Kafka."

"Jesus, I don't know what to say. I'm beyond shocked."

"You shouldn't be. From their perspective, you're the perfect choice to play the role of a sniper."

"But I was never a sniper."

"Come on, kid, think about it. So what if you were never a sniper. You have the ideal credentials to play that role."

Danny had to admit that Abe's last statement was true. He had what many gangsters and singers like to refer to as "street creds." Having street creds signified importance, status. In reality, Danny had a credential shared by only a handful of individuals, living or dead. The highest credential of them all.

The Medal of Honor.

———

THE PRODUCER, his name was Carson Welles, scheduled the audition for the following afternoon. It would take place in Danny's second-floor East Village apartment. Abe warned Welles that the apartment was small, but the producer said that shouldn't be a problem. It wasn't. Welles and another man showed up at the apartment on time with a camera, some lights, and a large case carrying a couple of rifles. After placing the weapons on a table, the two men went to work getting things ready to film the scene. As they were going about their tasks, Danny studied the one-page script he'd been given, working furiously to commit it to memory. Welles also suggested that Danny check out the two weapons so he could get a comfortable feel for them. Danny did as told, although he knew plenty more about weapons than the two movie folks did.

The audition lasted approximately an hour, with Danny filming the scene three times. When filming concluded, Welles and his partner, who hadn't uttered a single word the entire time, quickly packed up their things and departed. Neither man spoked to Danny—not even a thank-you—nor did either one offer a handshake. They simply left.

From his perspective, Danny felt good about how the audition had gone. The way he viewed it, he'd knocked it out of the park. But Welles's silence indicated otherwise. Danny really didn't know what to think. Perhaps this was how all movie producers act. Maybe there were worse things than silence. At least Welles didn't say Danny stunk it up, or that he wasn't right for the part. Hearing either of those assessments would have been much worse than hearing nothing at all.

All Danny could do was keep his fingers crossed and hope for the best.

The next day Abe phoned to let Danny know the part was his. He also provided Danny with further details. On Friday of next week, Abe said, Danny was to leave New York and fly into Chicago's O'Hare Airport. His flight would be arriving around nine in the morning. A suite had been reserved for him at the Blackstone Renaissance Hotel in downtown Chicago. After settling into his suite, Danny was to wait for a phone call from one of the movie's producers. That caller would give him further instructions. Before ending the call, Abe had one final bit of news for Danny.

"Your salary for this gig is a million-four. Them ain't small potatoes, kid."

No, a million-four sounded good to Danny. Maybe even too good to be true.

---

ON FRIDAY MORNING, after a week that seemed to last a month, Danny made the flight from The Big Apple to The Windy City. He checked into his suite and unpacked, a task that took him less than five minutes. Among the instructions he'd been given was to remain in his room and wait for a phone call, which came seconds after he had finished unpacking. The caller, a woman who identified herself as an assistant to the producer, informed Danny that an Uber driver would be out front to pick him up in fifteen minutes. The reason for the trip, she said, was for Danny to get a look at the place where he would be shooting his initial scene, which would be filmed first thing Monday morning. After ending the call, Danny went straight down to the lobby to wait for the Uber vehicle.

While waiting, Danny picked up a brochure detailing the Blackstone's story and began leafing through it. Seems the hotel had a long history of famous—and infamous—celebrities who frequented the place over the past decades. Virtually every president from Taft to Teddy Roosevelt to Dwight Eisenhower to Jimmy Carter stayed here at one time or another. Hence the nickname "the Hotel of Presidents." The Vanderbilts, Rockefellers, Spencer Tracy, and Bette Davis were among the famous, while mob bosses Lucky Luciano and Al Capone topped the infamous roster.

The Uber driver showed up on time and Danny climbed inside. After introducing himself and getting the driver's name (Brian), the vehicle pulled away from the hotel. Danny asked Brian if he knew the destination and Brian said he did. He informed Danny that a man named Carson Welles had given him orders to drive down South State Street and point out the building where Danny was to film his first scene. The trip didn't do much to enlighten Danny. All he learned was that the street was extremely busy, and that the building where the scene was to be shot was just one in a long row of tall structures. Danny asked Brian if they could stop so he could go inside and check out the building, but was told that that wasn't part of the plan. Less than an hour after leaving the hotel, Danny was back in his suite, staring out the window, thinking about heading outside and grabbing an early lunch.

Instead, with fatigue overriding his hunger, Danny flopped down on the huge bed, closed his eyes and tried to grab some shuteye. He couldn't; he was way too wired to sleep. Thoughts kept crashing into the sheep he was supposed to be counting. For Danny, those thoughts sometimes tended to feel more like movie flashbacks than anything else. They showed up, stayed around for a second or two, and then floated away, to be quickly replaced by the next flashback.

One by one they flashed by.

The memory of his father telling him that trying to be an actor was a colossal waste of time. Him dragging two wounded comrades back to safety despite having been shot in the leg. Him firing the machine gun at a group of charging Taliban soldiers. Him standing at attention in the White House as Barack Obama put the Medal of Honor around his neck. His initial meeting with Abe Pearlstein.

That flashback always brought on a big smile.

The afternoon Honest Abe strolled into his life.

Within days after Danny landed in New York, word quickly spread that a former war hero was in town hoping to become an actor. Agents came out of the woodwork, intent on landing Danny as a client. They came in a steady stream, like vultures, each agent offering a greater promise of glory. It would be a cinch, they all claimed, because every Broadway or Hollywood producer would view any play or movie featuring a genuine war hero as box office gold. They also said Danny's last name, same as the famous writer, would be yet another plus in his favor. Here Danny, they intoned. Sign this contract and the world will be your oyster.

Danny always felt the need to take a shower after one of those sleazy bastards walked away.

And then late one afternoon Abe rumbled in. Looking older than Moses, breathing hard from a walk up two flights of stairs, the remains of a cigar firmly clamped in the corner of his mouth, he nodded as Danny opened the door, walked straight to the kitchen sink, filled a glass with tap water, and downed the entire contents without removing the cigar.

Danny liked this man immediately. He just knew instinctively that this old dude was going to be a straight shooter. Here at last was a no-bullshit guy. He wasn't going to promise Danny the world and all those oysters that supposedly come with it. This was a tell-it-like-it-is kind of guy, and as it turned out, a world-class storyteller. Abe had tales to tell about virtually every famous person who had been in Manhattan during the past sixty years. There seemingly wasn't anyone he hadn't met. Danny also liked the fact that Abe's blue suit and white shirt looked as if they'd been worn for a week, which wasn't beyond the realm of possibility. Topping it off, Abe was a dead ringer for Danny Devito's Penguin character in that *Batman* movie.

Danny talked with Abe longer that evening than he had with all the other agents combined. Abe was in every regard a true New York character. Born and raised in Brooklyn (where he still resided), he had never driven an automobile, and on only three occasions during his eighty-eight years had he ventured outside the five boroughs that comprise New York City. He had a small office in Manhattan, but spent most of his time hanging out at Katz's Deli with a group of life-long friends. By his own admission, it had been years since he had a client that hit it big in the theatre or movie world. Early in his career, in the fifties, he did represent several young actors who were fortunate to have some success. However, after seeing their name in lights, they left Abe for other more-prominent agents, or in some cases, to sign on with one of the bigger talent agencies. Despite losing them—and the money they would have earned him—Abe was utterly lacking in either anger or resentment. He took it all in stride.

That night, after their three-hour conversation, Danny agreed to let Abe become his agent. Since Abe had brought no contract with him, the two men sealed the deal in the old-fashion way—with a firm handshake. As Danny watched Abe waddle down the stairs, he was pleased with himself for putting his fate in the hands of an ancient and honest New York Jew rather than one of those smooth-talking younger dudes who promised him the moon and all the stars that surrounded it.

Regardless of the outcome of this adventure, whether it ended in success or failure, Danny felt good about his decision to go with the man he always referred to as Honest Abe.

---

DANNY WOKE up feeling groggy and slightly disoriented. Grabbing his cell phone off a table next to his bed, he checked the time and saw that it was almost six o'clock, meaning he'd been asleep for more than five hours. He had known he was tired, but he didn't realize he was that tired. He slowly got out of bed, went into the bathroom and splashed cold water on his face. The cold worked its magic, quickly bringing him back to life. He then walked over to the window, opened the curtains, and looked out at Lake Michigan. Dusk was closing in but the street below the hotel was still buzzing with activity. Chicago, like New York, never really shut down.

Standing there, Danny's stomach reminded him that he hadn't had a bite to eat since very early in the morning. And that hadn't amounted to much. A stale bagel and a glass of orange juice was all he had prior to leaving for the airport. He needed to refill his empty stomach.

Danny spied an area directory on a large table and began thumbing through it, looking for a place close by where he could get some food. His top choices were a hamburger and fries, or spaghetti and meatballs. But being unfamiliar with the area, he had no clue what restaurants were nearby, or what type of food they might serve. His best bet was to ask someone down in the lobby for a recommendation. He'd inquire about the places they frequented, not where they normally send tourists. The locals know where to find the really good food. That's where he wanted to go.

First, he needed to take a shower. The flight and the longer-than-expected nap had him feeling grubby. He wanted to feel refreshed before he went in search of chow. A shower and fresh clothes should do the trick. But first he wanted to see what was happening in the world. He picked up the TV remote and hit the ON button.

And saw his face on the large screen.

*What the fuck?*

Danny couldn't believe what he was seeing. But there he was, bigger than life, on CNN, with Wolf Blitzer informing the viewing audience that U.S. Senator Dana Shapiro had been gunned down two hours ago while making a speech, and that a former Medal of Honor recipient named Danny Kafka had taped a statement in which he announced that he was going to assassinate her.

Danny felt dizzy with disbelief as Wolf warned his audience that some of the language on the tape might be disturbing. As for Danny, he knew exactly what the words were going to be. He'd spoken them about a hundred times while committing them to memory.

"Dana Shapiro is a disgrace as a United State senator," Danny said, standing behind a table, a rifle in hand. "More important, the bitch is a friend of Russia who wants nothing more than to help that totalitarian country destroy our American way of life. She is like a rabid dog that must be put down. And for the sake of our beloved country, which I proudly fought for and bled for, using this weapon, I will rid us of such a dangerous and un-American individual. That's my solemn pledge to you. God bless the United States of America."

Danny's initial reaction was that this had to be some kind of a joke being played on him by the movie folks. An initiation of some sort. He was being punked. But that couldn't be true. You don't get Wolf Blitzer and CNN to join in on a prank, especially one informing the public that a senator had been shot dead, and a Medal of Honor recipient was the person who fired the killing shot. No reputable news organization would take part in something that unflattering, that incriminating, that damaging to someone's reputation. You just don't do shit like that.

What about other cable channels? Were they also showing the tape, or was it only being seen on CNN? Curious, Danny switched to Fox, then MSNBC. Same story, same tape, different TV hosts.

Having been in his share of life-threatening situations, Danny knew what it was like to be under fire. He knew fear, and he knew how to deal with it. How to handle himself when everything was on the line. But he'd never felt fear like this in the past. This fear was something entirely new and unfamiliar to him. And he had no clue how to handle it.

Before he could even begin to assemble his thoughts, much less devise a plan of attack, he heard loud noises coming from outside his suite. A man with a deep voice barked an order for someone to "open the door and stand aside."

Less than twenty seconds later, Danny was on the floor being handcuffed by an **FBI** agent, while six fellow agents surrounded him with weapons drawn.

After the cuffs were securely fastened, Danny was yanked roughly to his feet by the agent, who then rattled off the Miranda warning as they headed for the door.

Danny didn't hear a word the man said.

# Chapter Four

Dantzler and Sean Montgomery spent Saturday morning painting lockers in the men's dressing room in the Lexington Tennis Center. They had hoped to be done by noon but that didn't happen. It was nearing two in the afternoon and they were still slapping on the fresh coat of paint, knowing they had only themselves to blame for spending five hours on what should have been a three-hour job at best. The mistake they made was plain and simple—beginning the job so early in the day. There was far too much traffic coming and going in the locker room to get anything done in a timely manner. Had they been wiser, they would have held off doing the job until late at night, after the Tennis Center closed for the day. That's exactly what they would do when it came time to work on the women's lockers.

At the present time, only Doug Norman, a math professor at Transylvania University was in the room. A longtime regular, he had played some doubles with three fellow professors, taken a shower, and was now in the finishing stages of getting dressed.

"Did you and Burt win?" Dantzler asked.

"Easily," Doug Norman replied, adding, "Lenny and Bob aren't much competition, to be honest with you. Both of them are having knee problems, so they aren't nearly as good as they once were. But we have fun and that counts for plenty. Plus, it's great exercise. So we keep punishing ourselves twice a week."

Dantzler's cell phone buzzed. He put the paint brush down, wiped his hands with a canvas rag, and picked up the phone. He listened for a few seconds, then said, "Sorry to hear that. Tell her I hope she gets to feeling better. Not a problem. We can get together one day next week. Just let me know when it's convenient for her. Sure. And thanks for giving me a heads-up. Bye."

"Who was that?" Sean asked.

"The very Honorable Mayor Elizabeth Anderson. I was scheduled to give her daughter Lindsey a lesson at three-thirty. But Lindsey is in bed suffering from a severe migraine."

"Is Lindsey any good?"

"Big dreams, small talent. But she does work at it, I'll give her that."

"Migraine, huh?" Sean said. "Never had one of those babies. Had an uncle who did, and he said they're brutal. Hey, Jack. Question: migraine or gout?"

"Neither."

"Come on, you gotta pick one."

"Hey, Sean. Question: Roy Cohn or F. Lee Bailey?"

"I refuse to answer until you give me your pick. Migraine or gout?"

Doug Norman laughed out loud, said, "Sean, you're an attorney, Jack, you have a Ph. D in Philosophy, and this is the intellectual level of your discourse? I'm shocked and appalled."

"Well, Doug, my friend, we can't all be math wizards," Sean answered. "And for the sake of accuracy, Jack did not earn his doctorate. There's this pesky little thing called a dissertation that he failed to turn in. What was the proposed title of that unfinished work of art, Jack? 'Why Kierkegaard Would Have Been a Lousy Tennis Player?' Wasn't that it?"

"Nah. It was Spinoza, not Kierkegaard."

"My bad," Sean said. "So you see, Doug, Jack's not as educated as you thought he was."

Grinning, Doug picked up his equipment bag, headed for the door, and said, "You two have turned this locker room into an intellectual wasteland."

"Hey, Doug," Sean shouted. "Newton or Einstein?"

"Hey, Sean," retorted Doug. "Jennifer Lopez or Charlize Theron?"

Sean spread his arms, said, "See how easy it is to sink to our level, Doug? Took you no time at all to land in our little intellectual wasteland, did it?"

Doug's response was to give Sean the finger on his way out the door.

"He's a great guy," Sean said after Doug was gone. "Be nice if more people around here were like him."

"Yeah, he's one of the good ones, no doubt about it." Dantzler picked up the paint brush and a can of paint. "I'm done for the day. Let me make a sign that says Wet Paint and we're out of here."

"You plan on going to the big shindig?"

"Of course. Wouldn't miss it for the world."

The big shindig, as Sean called it, was a get-together at the police station honoring Bruce Rawlinson, the longtime desk sergeant who was retiring after thirty years on the job. A true relic, Rawlinson had been on the force before Dantzler put on a uniform. He was a piece of work, a legendary gossip, and a world-class ball-buster. He was also an excellent cop, and an even better human being. Everyone liked and appreciated Bruce, even when he did occasionally get on your nerves.

"What time do the festivities kick off?" Sean asked.

"Five. But I want to get there early, drop in and see how Eric is holding up."

"When was the last time you were in his office?"

"Been at least a couple of months. Why do you ask?"

"Be prepared for a big surprise."

"How so?"

"The lad now has a 48-inch flat-screen TV in his office. Had it installed about a month ago. There is also one in the break room. How's that for progress?"

"It's not all that surprising. We both know Rich was tight with a buck and something of a Luddite."

Sean said, "Eric will have that TV tuned to ESPN all day. He loves that NBA, NFL stuff. He'll never get any work done."

"Let me make a sign and put it up. Then we'll go see what Eric is watching."

---

DANTZLER AND SEAN were joined by David Bloom, who also wanted to pay his respects to Rawlinson. The trio rode downtown in Bloom's Lexus and found a place to park a block away from the police station. Bloom used a credit card to pay for the privilege of parking his car without having to worry about being ticketed, or worse, getting towed.

The celebration, still an hour or so away from getting started, would take place in the break room. Already, several early birds were there, no doubt having arrived in advance for the purpose of securing one of the few chairs that surrounded the table. A box obviously filled with a cake rested in the middle of the table, alongside two-liter bottles of Diet Pepsi, Diet Coke and ginger ale. Dantzler recognized the early arrivals, nodded at them as he passed by the break room, but didn't stop and chat. That would come later. For now he wanted to see Eric and the big TV in his office.

Eric was sitting behind the desk looking like a man who had been born to occupy that chair. He simply had the look of a natural-born leader. Dantzler realized this within days after Eric joined the Homicide team, and he had been among the loudest voices in favor of Eric replacing Captain Bird in the top spot. Although Eric was now in his late thirties, he was still more handsome than Denzel Washington on his finest day. And he was certainly far better dressed than Denzel. Some would argue that he was better dressed than everybody. Eric always looked as if he had just come from a GQ Magazine shoot, where he was likely the classiest-attired guy there.

But Eric wasn't alone. Sitting across from him were Captain Bird and Milt Brewer, another retired veteran of the Homicide

Unit. When Dantzler, Sean, and Bloom entered the room, Bird and Brewer stood. As per today's new standards, greetings were exchanged in the form of fist bumps rather than handshakes.

"Nice TV, Eric," Sean noted. "How'd you manage it? Some kind of a minority thing?"

"Want to know how I got it, Sean? I paid for the damn thing, that's how."

"No shit?"

"I said if one was installed in my office, paid for by the department, then I would cough up the cash for one in the break room. The higher ups agreed. Now everyone is happy, and I'm the big hero."

"You've always been my hero, Eric," Sean said.

Sean had been right about the TV being a doozy but he was wrong about what station Eric would be watching. No ESPN at the moment. Rather, it was tuned to CNN, where the murder of Senator Dana Shapiro by a Medal of Honor recipient was still dominating coverage. Although the incident happened yesterday afternoon, according to CNN (and the competing cable news networks), it was still being classified as "Breaking News."

"You guys keeping up with this story?" Eric asked.

"Impossible not to," Bloom answered. "It has just about everyone glued to the tube. That's all folks are watching at the Tennis Center."

Milt said, "Hard to believe the kid did something that crazy."

"That's because he didn't do it," Jake Thomas said, moving quickly into the room. As he drew nearer to the TV, he pointed at the screen, and loudly proclaimed, "There is no fucking way Danny Kafka committed that murder. No way in hell."

All six men were startled by the ferocity of Jake's outburst, but none more so than Dantzler. He had *never* seen Jake this emotional, this upset. His face was a mask of anger, his voice that of a true believer. This wasn't the Jake that Dantzler was familiar with. That Jake was always cool, calm, and collected. He didn't rattle, didn't lose his composure, regardless of the circumstances. He had served in Iraq and Afghanistan, was wounded a couple of times, then came home with a half-dozen medals awarded for bravery, including the Silver Star, the Bronze Star, and the Legion of Merit. You don't collect hardware like that unless you keep your emotions in check.

The room remained quiet, save for the conversation on CNN. All eyes were fixed on Jake, the intensity of his statements having taken everyone by surprise. His outburst seemed to freeze their tongues.

Finally, Bloom, the psychiatrist, broke the silence, saying, "It can happen, Jake. Considering all the nasty shit he saw over there, PTSD is not out of the realm of possibility. Something, who knows what, caused him to crack."

"Guys like Danny Kafka don't *crack*, Doc. Sorry, but that diagnosis is bullshit. Just like what they're saying Danny did is complete and utter bullshit." Jake pointed at the TV screen, which was once again showing Danny Kafka, rifle in hand, announcing his intention to assassinate Dana Shapiro. "Want to know why I'm right about this?"

The answer to Jake's question came in the form of silent head nods.

"Do any of you know what type of weapon Danny is holding?" Jake asked.

"Not positive, but my guess would be an AK47," answered Dantzler.

"Close, but not accurate. It's an AKM, which is an updated version of the AK47. And trust me, the AKM is a terrific assault weapon, a real killing machine. It's capable of wiping out a crowd in a matter of seconds. As good a combat weapon as you'll ever find. But you know what it's not good for? Being used by a sniper. It doesn't have the range, let alone the accuracy to pull off the shot that killed the senator. With that rifle, even the most well-trained and experienced shooter would be lucky to hit a target from more than four-hundred, five-hundred meters, at best. And they are claiming Danny made that shot from a distance of maybe two-thousand meters? Impossible."

"Could be there was another rifle, Jake," Eric said. "No one is saying that's the one he used."

"Danny said it on the tape. Want to know another reason why I'm certain he didn't do it? Danny wasn't a trained sniper. I was. And I was a damn good one, too. But there is no way in hell that I could have made that shot with the rifle he's holding. No one could."

"Jake, you sound as if you know Danny Kafka," Dantzler said. "Did you guys serve together in the army?"

"Danny was in the Marines, but, yeah, I knew him. We were in the hospital at the same time recuperating from our wounds. Spent a lot of time together, talking and bitching about the war. You know, just hanging out. We must've played a hundred chess matches while we were there. This was before he did the things that earned him the Medal of Honor. By the time I was ready to be released from the hospital my time in service was up, so I came home and left the military. Danny went back into the sandbox."

"Damn, Jake, I'm truly sorry your buddy is in such hot water," Milt said, "but I gotta tell you, it doesn't look good for him. Not with him confessing to the crime. That's tough evidence to overcome."

"That tape is bogus," Jake responded, anger still clinging to every word. "I don't know how it was done, or who did it, but it's not real. I'd stake my life on it."

"It's a tragedy, no doubt about it," Milt said. "For the senator's family, and for the Kafka kid. Guy wins the Medal of Honor and then this? Sad."

"You don't *win* the Medal of Honor, Milt. It's not a trophy they give you at the end of the game. You *earn* the Medal of Honor. You're a Vietnam vet. You should know that."

"You're absolutely right, Jake. Sorry I misspoke. But . . . the bottom line is, medal or not, he's gonna need one helluva lawyer."

---

THE CELEBRATION LASTED a little more than two hours and went off with only one slight hitch—the cake was gone before much of the crowd showed up. That problem was solved when Eric ordered five large pizzas with various toppings. Not surprisingly, they vanished almost as fast as the cake had.

As the honoree, Rawlinson had to endure plenty of razzing, hugs, jokes, back slaps, and genuine good wishes. He took it all in stride, mostly giving off the awe-shucks-I-don't-deserve-this vibe. But he didn't fool anyone; it was all an act. He loved every second of being the center of attention.

After hanging around for the better part of two hours, Dantzler, Sean, and Bloom left the party, walked down the street, turned a corner, and went into McCarthy's. Dantzler and Sean each ordered a pint of Guinness, Bloom his usual Maker's Mark neat. In a change from standard procedure, they chose to drink outside on the back patio.

Dantzler was quieter than normal, a fact Bloom quickly picked up on.

"You seem to be a little out of sorts, Jack," Bloom stated. "My hunch is it has to do with Jake."

"Never seen him like that. He was genuinely upset by what happened."

"Jake refuses to accept the fact that his friend could have committed such an act. It's a classic example of denial. Chances are he'll never accept it, regardless of what the evidence proves."

"Thing is, Jake is convinced the evidence *doesn't* exist."

Sean said, "The Kafka kid is on tape declaring his intention to kill the senator. Then she gets gunned down. I'd say that's pretty damn strong evidence."

"I can't argue with you, Sean," Dantzler said.

# Chapter Five

D antzler got home around nine p.m., went straight to the kitchen, opened a can of Pepsi, and then settled in to watch some TV, either a baseball game, or a decent movie if he could land one that interested him. Turns out he didn't even search for a game or a movie. When he clicked the TV on, there was Anderson Cooper and the CNN panel discussing what was now being billed as "the Tragedy in Chicago," a B-movie title for a serious event. Joining Anderson and the panel regulars were a pair of retired U.S. Marine generals, both of whom said they needed to gather more information before passing judgment on Danny Kafka's guilt or innocence.

A reasonable request, Dantzler felt, although the two ex-military men were certainly in the minority. It was pretty obvious that they were in no hurry to condemn one of their own. The panel members, along with virtually every talking head on rival cable news channels, had already found Danny Kafka guilty of the crime, and were prepared to hand down a sentence of life behind bars.

It was easy to see why they were convinced Danny Kafka was the shooter. By this stage of the investigation, Chicago PD had released further details of the shooting, stating that the killing shot was fired from the window of a twelve-story building two blocks from where Dana Shapiro was giving her speech. According to the Chicago detectives, the building was empty at the time, having been closed due to a gas leak. Dantzler found that to be an intriguing tidbit.

However, it was what Anderson Cooper said next that may have driven home the final nail in Danny Kafka's coffin.

"During a search of the area surrounding the building, detectives discovered a rifle hidden behind a large Dumpster. It is also being reported that Danny Kafka's fingerprints were found on the weapon, and that ballistics testing proved that it was the rifle used to murder Dana Shapiro."

Fingerprints and ballistics, when combined with that self-incriminating tape, were virtually impossible barriers to get past.

By midnight, Dantzler had given up listening to the endless noise streaming from the TV, opting instead for the quiet of his back deck, which overlooked the small lake that bumped up against his backyard. This was his own personal fortress of solitude, the one place where he could sit alone and let his mind wander in whatever direction it wanted to go. On numerous occasions during his years as a detective, thoughts he had on this deck ended up helping him solve difficult homicide cases. The answer he was looking for had a habit of showing up like a surprise guest in the dead of night.

Tonight, however, his thoughts weren't on a homicide. Well, in a matter of speaking, they were. He was thinking about Jake, and how adamantly he held to the belief that Danny Kafka was innocent of the crime he was being accused of committing. Jake had not simply stated his belief; he'd shouted it from the mountaintop. His passionate words echoed and rattled in Dantzler's head.

*There is no fucking way Danny Kafka committed that murder. No way in hell.*

Dantzler was wading so deep in the stream of his own thoughts that he almost didn't hear his phone buzzing. The sound practically startled him out of a trance. He rubbed his eyes, then picked up the phone. The number wasn't familiar, but the caller's voice certainly was.

It was Grace West, the beautiful, famous, and highly successful Chicago-based defense attorney with whom he shared a brief history in the not-too-distant past. Brief, with a mix of good tossed in with the not so good. She had been his sparring partner during a murder trial in which she defended a local woman accused of committing the crime. She grilled him hard while he was on the witness stand.

"This is quite the unexpected call," Dantzler said. "You must be really bored."

"Me, bored? Come now, Jack. You know better than that. I'm never bored." Grace laughed, said, "I didn't wake you, did I? Not that I give a shit if I did. Why? Aren't you happy to hear from an old girlfriend?"

"I don't think a girlfriend would up and leave without saying goodbye."

"I said goodbye, Jack. Short and sweet, I will admit, but I did bid you a fond farewell."

"Same old Grace. Still as cocky and arrogant as I remember."

"I can tell from your tone that you're still upset because I eviscerated you on the witness stand two years ago. You need to man up and move past that. I eviscerate every witness I cross examine."

"Maybe so, Grace. But you lost that case, remember? The woman you were defending is sitting in a prison cell at this very moment. And she'll be in prison for the remainder of her natural life. Hate to burst your bubble, Grace, but even you don't win them all."

"Lighten up, Jack, and forget about that damn trial. We had some fun, didn't we? Had some happy times, shared a few nice moments. And I have to admit, the sex was good too."

"Apparently it wasn't good enough to keep a relationship going. Or to even give the relationship a chance."

"There's always tomorrow, Jack. Who knows what might happen?"

"Why are you calling, Grace?"

"I have a client who is innocent. I want you to help me prove it."

"You say that about all your clients, Grace. You're a broken record when it comes to that my-client-is-innocent line. According to you, everyone from Pontius Pilate to Stalin was innocent. But we both know that's not the case. Fact is, almost all of your clients are guilty. Why should I believe this one is any different?"

"Because this one *is* innocent," Grace said.

"What's this innocent client's name?"

"Come on, Jack. Do you really have to ask? You're a hotshot detective. Put two and two together, you'll figure it out in three seconds."

It didn't take Dantzler that long to come up with the answer. It was all right there in front of him. An easy puzzle to solve.

Grace West, defense attorney, Chicago, a high-profile murder dominating the TV airwaves.

"You're defending the ex-soldier who murdered that U.S. senator."

"*Allegedly* murdered the senator," Grace quickly corrected.

"Allegedly, of course. You guys use that word like it had been sent down from heaven."

"Danny Kafka is innocent, Jack. And I need you to prove it."

"Why me, Grace? You must have a dozen investigators at your disposal."

"Two reasons. I can trust you, and I know you won't stop digging until you find the truth. You are the one person who can help get this kid out of trouble."

"I don't know, Grace. They have his fingerprints on the murder weapon, and he confessed on that tape the TV folks keep showing over and over. That's hard evidence to get around."

"Come to Chicago, Jack. Drive, fly . . . I don't care. Sit down and talk to Danny for one hour. Hear his side of the story. If you don't like what he has to say, if you don't buy his story from beginning to end, you walk away, no hard feelings. And I'll pay you well for your time."

"What is his story?"

"I would rather you hear it straight from him. If I try to tell it, there's a good chance I might mess up and say something that would influence you to say no. I don't want to risk that."

Grace was pleading her case but it wasn't her voice Dantzler was hearing:

*There is no fucking way Danny Kafka committed that murder. No way in hell.*

Jake's words.

The deciding factor.

"Okay, Grace, I'll leave for Chicago first thing Monday morning. E-mail me your office address and I'll meet you there. Then I'll go talk to Danny Kafka, listen to what he has to say."

"Thank you, Jack. I appreciate this more than you can imagine. And you won't be sorry."

"I have a couple of ground rules we need to clear up."

"Let me hear them."

"First, I speak to Danny alone. Is that a problem?"

"No."

"Second, if I don't buy into his story one-hundred percent, or if I get so much as get a whiff that he is lying to me or conning me, I'm out the door. Understood?"

"Absolutely."

"See you Monday."

*Okay,* Jake, Dantzler said to himself as he shut off his phone and headed for the bedroom. *Let's see if your blind faith in Danny Kafka's innocence is warranted or badly misplaced.*

# Chapter Six

D antzler left Lexington for Chicago around five on a warm
Monday morning. Knowing Chicago was in the Central
Time Zone, meaning he would gain an hour along the way, he
drove at a fairly leisurely pace, even stopping twice to stretch his legs
and to purchase a new bottle of water. Despite driving slower than
normal, he judged his arrival time to be sometime around noon.

To divert his thoughts away from the Danny Kafka situation, he
listened to music on his CD player. Leonard Cohen (his all-time
favorite), Neil Young, Peter Gabriel, Mark Knopfler, and Pink Floyd
accompanied him on this trip. Grizzled veterans, to be sure, but in
every regard their music still held up. Old doesn't necessarily have to
be sentenced to the scrap heap, just as excellence doesn't diminish
with time.

Or as Neil Young once put it: Rust never sleeps.

Despite the music—and the best efforts of those great
singer/songwriters—Dantzler's mind kept drifting back to the
Kafka-Shapiro case. Warring factions fought a vicious battle for
supremacy. One side said you're a fool for getting involved, while the
opposing side countered by arguing that you have no choice *but* to
get involved. Based on the fact that he was now heading to Chicago,

it was obvious that his you're-a-fool argument was being soundly defeated.

Inner conflict aside, deep down he wasn't disappointed knowing which side was proving to be victorious. In reality, he understood that he wasn't making the trip to help prove Danny Kafka's innocence, or to bolster a highly successful defense attorney's already healthy self-esteem. No, the reason why he was on his way to Chicago was crystal clear in his own mind.

He was doing it for Jake Thomas.

---

PRIOR TO LEAVING LEXINGTON, Dantzler plugged in the directions Grace had given him into his car's GPS and then let technology take it from there. With those directions proving to be on the money, he found the place without a hitch. Grace's office was located on Sheffield Avenue, which, Dantzler knew from watching many Cubs' games on TV, was close to Wrigley Field. That was his first surprise. He would have bet a huge sum of money that Grace worked in one of the large and expensive high-rise buildings in downtown Chicago. That wasn't the case. Not by a longshot. In fact, Grace's office was a two-story brick house located in the middle of a long row of expensive-looking homes. This was a pricey neighborhood, not a business district.

Outside in the front yard there was a small wooden sign that said, Grace West, Attorney at Law. Were it not for the presence of that sign, which also had a phone number below Grace's name, Dantzler might have driven right past the place.

Three vehicles were lined tightly together in the driveway, leaving Dantzler no choice but to park on the street. After locking the car, he made his way up the front steps and rang the doorbell. From inside the house he could hear Frank Sinatra singing "My Kind of Town." It didn't surprise him that a Chicago girl like Grace would utilize that particular song as her doorbell tune. Who better than the Chairman of the Board to welcome a visitor inside while hailing Chicago as his kind of town?

The door was opened by a young woman in her early twenties who immediately said, "You must be Mr. Dantzler."

"Jack."

"Pleased to meet you, Jack. We've been expecting you."

She was attractive, almost but not quite beautiful, with long brown hair, hazel eyes, and a warm smile that displayed a perfect set of white teeth. Introducing herself as Maggie, she shook Dantzler's hand, and then motioned for him to follow her through the house. Along the way, she introduced him to the rest of the staff, beginning with Angela, a tall, lithesome black woman who bore a close resemblance to Halle Berry. Next came Jenny, a tiny lady of Asian-American persuasion, Edward, a huge, massively built, completely bald guy who looked like he could bench press a mid-size car, and then Mary-Louise, who was easily the youngest member of Team West.

Along with making the introductions, Maggie also supplied job descriptions for each of her co-workers, all of whom were similarly dressed in Levis, sweatshirts, and sneakers. They reminded Dantzler of college kids rather than employees working for one of the most-successful defense attorneys in America. Maggie was the secretary/receptionist, Angela, Jenny, and Edward were paralegals, while Mary-Louise, a recent college graduate, was a researcher. This was Dantzler's second big surprise. Again, he would have bet a bundle that Grace's work place would be crowded with a legion of partners, paralegals, secretaries, and other personnel normally found in big-city law firms.

When Dantzler pointed this out to Maggie, she replied, "We are a small band of warriors, but with Grace as our leader, we tend to win most battles."

Spoken like a loyal soldier.

Dantzler expected to find Grace in her office but once again he was wrong. She was in the kitchen, standing next to the stove, stirring something in a large crock pot that sat on the counter. Seeing Dantzler, she turned down the crock pot temperature, laid the spoon on the counter, grinned, walked over, and gave him a chaste peck on the cheek.

"You hungry?" she said.

"Starved." Dantzler answered.

"Great. I've concocted a goulash that is to die for. My own recipe. Tasty, isn't it, Mags?"

Maggie looked at Dantzler, nodded, and said, "It really is delicious."

Precisely the answer he'd expect from a loyal soldier.

Grace went back to the stove, picked up the spoon, and continued to sir. "Maggie, show Jack into the dining room and get him comfortable," she said. "The food is almost ready. Want something to drink, Jack?"

"Water will do."

"Water it is, then."

A few minutes later, Grace rolled a three-tier silver tray into the room and skillfully maneuvered it next to the table. On top of the tray were two steaming bowls of something brownish and thick accompanied by spoons, a bottle of water, a chunk of bread, and some oyster crackers. Dantzler eyed what Grace tabbed as goulash with deep skepticism.

"Dive in, Jack," Grace said, smiling. "It won't kill you. Promise. And who knows? You might even like it."

Dantzler dipped out a spoonful, blew on it to knock some of the heat, and then gave it a try. Maggie wasn't exaggerating—it was delicious.

Grace said, "You haven't changed a bit, Jack. Still as handsome and sexy as ever."

That statement, especially the sexy reference, elicited a cough from Maggie.

"Same goes for you, Grace," Dantzler replied.

That was an honest assessment and not simply his way of repaying the complimentary remark she made about him. Grace West was a truly beautiful woman, standing a shade under six feet tall, with dark hair, green eyes, and a killer body. She could easily hold her own against the most gorgeous ladies Hollywood had to offer. Even now, dressed as casually as her young staff members, and with little or no make-up, she could only be described as stunning.

"Nice setup you have here," Dantzler pointed out. "It's certainly not what I expected."

"What did you expect?"

"I don't know. Downtown location, fancier office, bigger staff."

"I've had all those things in the past. Don't need any of it anymore."

"Is this your usual staff?"

"What you see is what you get."

"I'd say Edward enjoys it, being surrounded by beautiful young women."

Grace tossed a glance at Maggie, grinned, and said, "Edward has no interest in the girls. You, however, he might find interesting."

"Got it. Tell you one thing, Edward looks like one very strong individual."

"Don't let his muscles fool you, Jack. He is very intelligent. So are all the girls."

"Do you live here?" asked Dantzler.

"Nope. I have a nice condo downtown that overlooks Lake Michigan. You can stay there if you decide to take the case. Or you can stay here. There are three bedrooms upstairs."

"Let's hold off on my sleeping arrangement until I get a better handle on the situation."

"How do you plan to proceed with the case," Grace asked between bites.

"Don't get ahead of yourself, Grace. No plans until I speak with Danny Kafka."

"He's in deep shit, isn't he, Jack?"

"About as deep as you can get."

Grace shifted her eyes to Maggie and gave a slight nod, a silent signal for the young woman to leave. When Maggie was out of the room, Grace said, "I'm going to be honest with you, Jack. This case is different. *I'm* different. I have handled hundreds of cases, yet with this one I'm feeling something I've never felt before . . . fear. I'm terrified that I will lose this case, that I won't be able to save Danny. And that kid is innocent. I know it deep in my heart."

"If I take the case I'll do my best. You know that. But the tape, his fingerprints on the murder weapon . . . that's difficult evidence to get around. Plus, this is Federal, which translates into the other side having unlimited resources at their disposal."

"Believe it or not, the Feds have pretty much handed off the case to the locals."

"Why? The vic was a U.S. senator. Doesn't that make it a Federal case?"

"You'd think so. However, these days the Feds are all about homeland security. That's their top priority. They apparently have no interest in a lone homicide, not even one involving a member of Congress."

"Have you been in contact with anyone from the FBI?"

"An agent named Kate Flanagan. She's thorough, nice, professional, but not really engaged, if you catch my drift. Mostly, I've dealt with a local homicide detective named Sly Douglas. He strikes me as being a solid, fair-minded cop. I came away with the feeling that he hopes Danny is innocent."

"An ally is good to have on our side, but whether or not he can really help us is questionable."

"Finish your goulash, Jack," Grace ordered. "It's time you met Danny Kafka."

# Chapter Seven

Grace's silver Beemer was parked in front of two compact cars so they took Dantzler's Mercedes for the drive to the jail. After they were in the car, Grace opened her leather bag, removed her IPhone, punched in some numbers, put the call on speaker, and waited. When the call was answered, she asked to speak with someone named Frank. Almost instantly the call was transferred. She informed Frank that she was on the way to meet with Danny Kafka, and that she was being accompanied by her investigator, a former homicide detective. She then told Frank that her investigator would speak with Danny alone. Frank seemed to have no issues with her plan, said he would have Danny waiting in the usual place, told Grace he was looking forward to seeing her, said goodbye, and hung up. Grace replied with her own thank-you before ending the call.

"Seems like Frank is a fairly accommodating guy," Dantzler noted. "I take it you have dealt with him in the past."

"More times than I care to remember."

"Tell me, Grace. How can a young man like Danny Kafka, a struggling actor, possibly afford your services?"

"Pro bono."

"Of course," Dantzler said, laughing. "Let me flesh this out for you, then you tell me if I'm wrong. You defend the kid, maybe he gets off, maybe not, but either way, when it's all over, you get the big book deal, you write it, a movie company obtains the film rights, the movie gets made, and your bank account soars. You take a pass on the up-front money, then make a haul on the back end. Does that about sum it up?"

"God, Jack, when did you become so cynical? I'm doing this pro bono because I'm convinced Danny is innocent. My goal, my *only* goal, is to prove his innocence. Using Danny to make money is one thought that has never entered my mind."

Dantzler realized he'd touched a nerve with Grace. Her answer hadn't been typical defense attorney gospel. She meant what she said. Her words came from somewhere deep in her soul. He started to apologize but didn't, recalling from their past experience together that she detested apologies more than she loved to be praised. And Grace West lived for praise. With that in mind, Dantzler remained silent, choosing instead to concentrate on safely negotiating the Chicago traffic.

Sometimes silence is not only golden, it's the preferred method for avoiding all-out verbal warfare.

---

THE COOK COUNTY JAIL, or more accurately, the Cook County Department of Corrections, was located approximately ten miles from Grace's office, a thirty-minute drive, according to Grace. That turned out to be an ambitious prediction. Heavy traffic, combined with Dantzler having to drive cautiously while awaiting her directions, extended the trip to nearly fifty minutes. Many of the street names were familiar to Dantzler, though he had never before traveled on any of them. Clark, Halstead, Division, the Kennedy and Eisenhower Expressways, Homan . . . he kept going until they finally arrived at 2700 South California Avenue, site of the massive concrete structure that had once been home to some of this nation's most notorious criminals.

To call the Cook County Jail massive was doing it a great disservice. It was truly colossal, easily matching—and perhaps surpassing in both size and scope—the largest medieval castles and forts found in any country on the planet. Covering ninety-six acres, it had the distinction of being the largest single structure jail in the United States. As a pre-detention facility, it housed more than nine-thousand inmates, most of whom were pre-trial detainees. And until nineteen sixty-two, it was one of three Illinois locations that utilized the electric chair as a means of execution.

From the outside, Dantzler judged it to be a cold and depressing place. He doubted it would be any different inside. Being incarcerated here for any length of time couldn't be anything but a miserable experience.

Dantzler parked the Mercedes, then he and Grace entered the facility. After passing through security, Grace asked one of the guards to buzz Frank. The guard hastily made the call, and following a five-minute wait, Frank showed up. He was a big man with a thick chest, wide shoulders, and powerful Popeye-like forearms. Judging by his broad smile and the look in his eyes, it was obvious to Dantzler that the man had a thing for Grace. Dantzler suspected that she had that effect on most men.

"Good to see you again, Counselor," Frank said, moving close enough to give her a hug, which she artfully avoided by offering her hand instead. Frank shook it, disappointment registering on his face. "And this is your investigator? Must be a new one."

"Jack Dantzler," Grace said.

The two men shook hands.

"According to Grace, you're an ex-cop," Frank noted. "Where'd you work?"

"Lexington, Kentucky. Homicide for twenty-seven years."

"Well, there is no shortage of killers in this place," Frank said. "Some real nasty dudes, too. I probably shouldn't say this, but I have my fingers crossed that your client didn't do what he's being accused of. He's a legitimate war hero and a damn nice young fella."

Dantzler believed Frank was being honest while at the same time trying to impress Grace, a suspicion that Frank solidified with his next statement.

"If anyone can get the kid off the hook, it's you, Grace," Frank said. "He's lucky to have you in his corner."

Dantzler's thoughts: *Don't beg, Frank. You've got no shot.*

"Is Danny ready for us?" Grace asked, ignoring Frank's feeble attempt to score points.

"Yes, he's in the same interview room you saw him in yesterday." Frank moved closer to Dantzler. "Do you mind if I pat you down? It's nothing personal, and I know you've cleared security, but it's a habit of mine. Hope you're not offended."

"Not at all," Dantzler said, lifting his arms above his head. "If I were in your shoes I'd probably do the same thing."

Having patted down hundreds of individuals over the years, Dantzler judged Frank's efforts to be thorough and professional. When Frank was satisfied that Dantzler was in possession of neither a weapon nor drugs, he led them down a long corridor, made a left, and then followed another corridor that had interview rooms on either side. They stopped at the last one on the right.

"We have arrived," Frank said, taking out his keys. "Grace, if your investigator is going in alone, where are you planning to wait while they talk?"

"Well, if you would be kind enough to secure me a chair, I'll wait out here in the hall," Grace said, practically purring.

"For you, Grace, I'll go you one better." Frank tapped on the door next to the room where Danny Kafka was waiting. "This room is not occupied, and it has a comfortable chair. If you prefer to wait in there, I'll open it for you."

"You're a saint, Frank," Grace said. "I would very much appreciate that."

"No problem," Frank said while unlocking the steel door. To Dantzler: "You're in this one, sir."

Dantzler nodded but didn't respond as Frank inserted the proper key, turned it, and opened the door.

Time to finally meet Danny Kafka.

Medal of Honor recipient.
Accused murderer.

# Chapter Eight

Television distorts.

That was Dantzler's initial thought when he got his first up-close look at Danny Kafka. Based on what he'd seen on that incriminating tape, Dantzler figured Danny to be about six-one, one-eighty. His assessment was badly off the mark. Danny Kafka was much smaller in person, going maybe five-ten and one-sixty. Not skinny by any means, just lean and wiry, one of those guys who would likely never have an issue with weight. He had blond hair that brushed against his shoulders, strikingly blue eyes, tanned skin absent any visible tattoos or piercings, and the sensitive features one might associate with a movie star, not a Medal of Honor recipient. More like a surfer than a war hero.

Not at all what Dantzler expected.

Nor did he expect to see Danny still dressed in civilian clothes rather than a standard-issue jail outfit. Danny was wearing jeans, a white T-shirt with John Lennon's picture on it, and dusty military boots. They were, Dantzler guessed, the clothes Danny had on when he was taken into custody Friday afternoon.

When Dantzler entered the small room, Danny instinctively stood and attempted to offer his hand. He couldn't; his right arm was shackled to a thick iron ring protruding from the side of the table. Realizing there would be no handshake, he smiled, shrugged apologetically, waited until Dantzler was seated, and then sat back down in his chair.

"Pleased to meet you, Mr. Daniels," Danny said. "Miss West told me you were coming to see me."

"It's Dantzler, Danny. But just call me Jack."

"Sorry for the miscue. I'm usually pretty good at remembering names, but my thoughts are a little scrambled right now."

"Don't worry about it, Danny. I've been called a lot worse names than Daniels."

"Well, Mr. Dantzler—Jack—I appreciate the fact that you're here, that you are at least willing to hear my side of the story. Miss West says you were a great homicide investigator. She said if anyone can get me out of this jam I'm in, it would be you. I'd certainly like to have you in my corner. Right now, Miss West is about the only person alive who believes I'm innocent."

"She's not the only one. There is one other person who believes you."

"Who?"

"Jake Thomas."

"Jake? How do you know him?"

"He worked homicide with me in Lexington, Kentucky."

"Jake made homicide? Good for him. He always said that's where he eventually wanted to work. His goal was to hunt down and put away murderers. Now that I think about it, I recall him saying he wanted to work for someone named Jack. That had to be you."

"Probably was."

"I'd wager money he's good at the job."

"You would win that bet, Danny. Jake is a top-notch investigator."

"He was a helluva warrior too."

"According to Jake, he dominated you at chess."

Danny chuckled, said, "If he made that statement while taking a polygraph those needles would go haywire. We had some real battles, but I ended up holding a slight edge. Neither of us dominated the other. We were pretty evenly matched."

"Do you want something to drink, Danny? I can get you a bottle of water if you're thirsty."

"I'm okay." Danny briefly looked away, then turned back to face Dantzler. "I guess you're ready to hear my side of the story, right?"

"We'll get to that," Dantzler said. "But first, tell me a little about yourself."

"What do you want to know?"

"The basics. A quick biography."

"Born and raised in St. Louis, dad is executive vice president at an insurance agency, mom teaches in an elementary school, and my sister, who is two years older than me, and the smart one in the family, is a law professor at Yale. I was an average student in school, a pretty fair second baseman—a four-year letterman for the high school team—an avid reader, and a lover of movies. From the time I was a young kid I had my sights set on becoming an actor, much to the dismay of my father. I enrolled at the University of Missouri, studied theater and acting there for two years, decided to put my education on hiatus, so I enlisted in the Marines. Busted my ass to become a good soldier, served three tours in a part of the world I never want to see again, was wounded twice, came home, got discharged, then went to New York in hopes of realizing my dream of becoming a working actor. That just about sums it up."

"And along the way you were awarded the Medal of Honor. That's better than a Tony or an Academy Award, Danny. Better by miles."

"Yeah, right. Medal of *Dishonor* recipient is probably how I'm being referred to these days."

Dantzler took out a notepad and pen from his shirt pocket. "Okay, Danny," he said, "it's time for you to make your case for being innocent. Take me back to the beginning. How did this all get started?"

"I got a call from my agent. He . . ."

"What's your agent's name?"

"Abe Pearlstein. Lives in Brooklyn, has an office in Manhattan."

"Will he be willing to speak with me?"

"Oh, sure. Abe is a terrific guy. He'll be more than happy to help out."

"So, Abe calls, says what?"

"That a producer named Carson Welles specifically wanted me to test for a key role in a movie he was getting ready to film in and around Chicago. He said Nicole Kidman and Tom Hardy were starring in the movie."

"And his name didn't cause alarm bells to start ringing?"

"No. Why would it?"

"Carson Welles? *Orson* Welles. That's got phony written all over it."

"Damn, that never crossed my mind."

"Did he give you a business card? Something, anything, with his name or the name of his production company on it?"

"Not to me, he didn't. You should check with Abe. He probably got something from the Welles guy."

"Okay, you've been asked to audition. What happens next?"

"You know what happens. I read for the part. The speech I was given is what everyone is seeing on that tape the TV stations keep showing nonstop. Well, at least part of it."

"Where did this audition take place, Danny?"

"In my apartment."

"You're telling me that what I saw on TV was filmed in your apartment?"

"Yes."

"Didn't you think that was strange?"

"Mr. Dantzler—Jack—to be perfectly honest with you, I wasn't thinking anything beyond one single fact: here is this producer who wants me to be in his movie. You have to understand, this was my first shot at being in anything. Nothing else was on my mind at that time other than to just do the job and don't screw it up. Does that make any sense?"

"Makes perfect sense, Danny. And I'm not putting you down. I'm only seeking information." Dantzler thought for a few seconds, then said, "Okay, this Welles guy comes in alone to film. . ."

"He wasn't alone," Danny interrupted. "There was another man with him. He put up the lights, and then sat in the corner. Never spoke a word the entire time."

"Could you identify either of those men if you saw them again?"

"Carson Welles, definitely. I'm not so sure about the second man. He was mostly out of my line of vision."

"Describe Welles for me."

"Taller than me but not close to your height. He was maybe five-eleven, possibly six-foot. He had light brown hair almost as long as mine, a deep tan, and he looked like a guy who kept himself in good shape. To me, he fit the stereotype of a California playboy asshole."

"I'm assuming they came with the rifle seen on that tape?"

"They came with two rifles. An AKM, which is the one you saw on the tape, and an M107, a favorite weapon of snipers. It's what Jake used when he was in combat."

"Welles asked you to handle it, didn't he?"

Danny nodded, said, "He didn't ask, he insisted. Said he wanted to be certain that I was comfortable handling it. Like I had never been in the military, much less combat. What a joke. All he really wanted was my fingerprints on the damn thing."

"On the tape you specifically said the weapon you were holding, the AKM, was the one you would use to shoot Dana Shapiro. But that's not the one used by the real killer. Jake claims an accurate shot from that distance using the AKM was simply not possible. Is Jake right?"

"Absolutely. No sniper would use an AKM in that situation. And I wasn't a sniper."

"Why do you think they wanted you holding the AKM rather than the actual murder weapon while making your speech?"

"Because they didn't know shit about rifles."

"What about the script?" Dantzler asked. "Was it already written out for you when they arrived?"

"Yeah. I was to memorize it while they were setting up the camera and lights."

"You film the scene, then what happens?"

"Nothing. They packed up the camera and lights, put both rifles in a large metal case, and then left without uttering a single word. I had no idea if I had done well, or if I had bombed out. It wasn't what I expected. But hey, I really didn't know what to expect."

"How much time transpired between the audition and when you found out that the movie role was yours?"

"Abe called the next day and told me. That's also when he gave me the details given to him by Carson Welles."

"What were those details?"

"Catch an early morning Friday flight to Chicago, and then check into the suite that had been reserved for me in the Blackstone Renaissance Hotel. I had been given the number of a producer that I was to call, which I did. She instructed me to go down into the lobby and wait until an Uber driver showed up. That's what I did."

"How long before the Uber driver arrived?"

"I don't know. Ten or fifteen minutes, no more than that. The driver's name was Brian."

"What was the purpose of this trip?" Dantzler asked.

"The producer wanted me to check out the building where my first scene was to be filmed. According to Brian, the building was on South State Street. I asked him if I could go inside and get a closer look, but he said that wasn't part of the deal. After we drove by the place, he took me back to the hotel and dropped me off."

"What time was this?"

"I don't know. Noon, maybe a little later."

"What did you do next?"

"I was starving but I was also beat. More tired than hungry, I guess. Anyway, I lay down on the bed thinking I'd take a short catnap. Instead, I ended up sleeping for close to five hours. I woke up feeling groggy, so I slapped cold water on my face to revive myself, turned on the TV, and there I was, bigger than life, announcing to the world that I was going to assassinate a United State senator. Ten minutes later, I was on the floor being handcuffed by FBI agents."

"How did the FBI know where you were staying?"

"Good question."

Dantzler put down his pen, leaned back, and rubbed his eyes. After a few seconds of silence, he said, "I'm gonna have to be honest with you, Danny. There is one aspect of your story that troubles me. It's also the biggest hurdle you'll have to overcome if you expect me to take the case."

"What part of the story are you referring to?"

"Were you familiar with Dana Shapiro? Did you know she was a U.S. senator?"

Shaking his head, Danny said, "Never heard of her. Had no clue she was a senator."

"On the tape you mention her by name. Of all the women in this country, you single her out. That's extremely incriminating. What's your explanation for that?"

"I filmed the scene three times, each time using a different name. Carson Welles told me he wasn't sure which name would end up in the movie, so he had me use a different one each time. Dana Shapiro was number three."

"Do you recall the other two?"

"Sure. Jill Masterson and Tiffany Case."

"That's cute."

"What do you mean?"

"I'm assuming, Danny, that you aren't a big fan of Sean Connery as James Bond. If you were, you'd recognize those names as characters in a couple of Bond movies. Jill Masterson in *Goldfinger*, Tiffany Case in *Diamonds Are Forever*."

"Damn, I love Sean Connery's Bond. How could I have missed that?"

Dantzler turned his notepad around and handed Danny his pen. "Write down Abe's office address," he said. "If you also know his home address, give me that one as well."

Danny quickly scribbled the two addresses in the notepad, and then handed it back to Dantzler. "Does this mean you believe me?" he asked. "That you are going to take the case?"

"Yes to both questions, Danny," Dantzler said, putting the notepad and pen back into his shirt pocket. "You were, to quote Lee

Harvey Oswald, 'a patsy.' I'm not sure about Oswald, but I am sure about you. You were definitely set up. And this wasn't some slouch operation that was put together overnight. This was sophisticated and very elaborate. The folks who did this were professionals."

Dantzler stood, reached across the table, and gave Danny a pat on the shoulder. "You hang in as best you can, Danny," he said. "I'll get started on this as soon as I leave here. But be warned—this is not going to be a quick fix. This will take some time. While this is happening you're bound to get frustrated and angry. That's only natural. But you can't let it break your spirit. Just keep the faith, don't listen to all the bullshit coming from the TV echo chamber, and cling to the belief that the truth will win the day."

"Will the truth win?"

"It usually does, Danny. And in this case, it will. You have my word on it."

"Thanks, Jack," Danny whispered. "And tell Jake I said hello."

"You got it, Danny."

Danny's eyes were clouded with tears as Dantzler left him alone.

# Chapter Nine

Dantzler exited the small room just as a guard came strolling down the hall. The man was tall, thin, and most important of all, not Frank. Dantzler had no desire to watch Frank make a fool of himself while attempting to capture Grace's affections. That was never going to happen, which Frank, in his heart of hearts, had to know. His efforts were both futile and embarrassing.

"Perfect timing," the guard said, smiling. "I was on my way to see how much longer you were going to be. Looks like I got here at just the right time."

"You couldn't have timed it better, Tony," Dantzler answered, seeing the man's name on the front of his shirt. "Let me get Grace and we'll be on our way."

As Tony got on his walkie-talkie and asked for someone to come and escort Danny Kafka back to his cell, Dantzler tapped on the door to the room where Grace had been waiting. She was sitting at the table typing a text on her IPhone. When she saw Dantzler come into the room, she finished typing, put the phone into her bag, and stood. He could tell that she was about to ask him a question.

"Let's talk later," he said, "after we're out of here."

Grace didn't necessarily like his suggestion but she said nothing, responding only with a tight-lip smile and a slight nod of the head. Both were indications of her displeasure with having to take orders.

Tony led them on the twisted path back to the front of the building, a journey that took a few minutes. Before leaving, Grace thanked Tony for his help, and then asked him to let Frank know how much she appreciated all he did for her. Tony said he would deliver the message to Frank.

In the parking lot, Dantzler tossed his car keys to Grace, saying he wanted her to drive. They both got into the Mercedes, and after Grace adjusted her seat forward and fired up the engine, they took off for her office.

Dantzler leaned his head back and closed his eyes, sending her a clear signal that he still wasn't ready to talk. He needed the quiet, not a steady stream of questions from Grace. He wanted to pore over what he'd learned from Danny, to break his story down into the smallest detail, and to try and formulate a strategy that might lead to a positive outcome.

If indeed a positive outcome was even a remote possibility.

Grace remaining silent wasn't possible. Ten minutes into the trip, she said, "What are you thinking, Jack?"

"That I need a drink. What time is it?"

"Almost four-thirty."

"Then take us to the bar of your choice."

"That would be my office. I don't have either of your favorites, Guinness or Jameson, but I do have a broad selection of high-quality alcohol. I'm sure you can find something that will meet with your approval."

"That's fine with me. But why your office?"

"Because I want my staff to be there when you do finally tell me what you learned from Danny. I wasn't speaking hyperbole when I told you those kids are very intelligent and very insightful. They might ask questions that I overlook."

Although late-afternoon traffic was heavy, Grace got them back to her office in twenty-five minutes. All three cars were still lined up in the driveway, so she parked his Mercedes on the street. After adjusting the driver's seat back to its previous position, she got out of the car, saw that Dantzler was almost at the porch, and practically had to sprint in order to catch up with him.

Once they were inside, Grace went straight to a cabinet, opened it, and pointed. "Like I told you, Jack," she said. "We have a full bar. Pick your poison."

"Have any good Scotch?"

"The Famous Grouse. It's superb. In fact, that's what I'm having."

"Never heard of The Famous Grouse, but I'll give it a try. With soda, please."

By the time Grace finished her bartending duties the rest of her team had assembled in the big room. Handing Dantzler his drink, she said, "Okay, children, thanks to Jack, Happy Hour has arrived early this afternoon. Get something to drink, and then join Jack and me at the table."

The gang didn't need to be told twice. They scurried to the bar, made plenty of noise dumping ice into glasses, chose their drink of choice, and then took a seat. Angela and Jenny each had a screwdriver, Maggie a vodka and cranberry juice, Mary-Louise a bottle of Coors Light, and Edward a club soda with a twist of lime.

Once everyone was settled in, all eyes shifted to Dantzler, who sat at the head of the table. Angela and Jenny pulled out notepads and pens, and Edward turned on a tape recorder. A feeling of expectation filled the room.

Unable to contain her curiosity any longer, Grace broke the silence by asking the big question she had been eager to ask since the moment Dantzler knocked on the interview room door.

"Tell us, Jack," she said. "What do you make of Danny's story?"

"I believe him one-hundred percent. He's been framed for this murder."

"Does Danny have any idea who might be behind it?" Angela asked.

"No, he doesn't. But like I told Danny, this plan was thought out and executed by professionals. This was a crime that took serious planning. You don't just decide one day to pick up a rifle and gun down a U.S. senator. Something like that takes hours of thought and detailed preparation."

Dantzler took a sip of Scotch, then said, "You're looking at an expensive investigation, Grace. You prepared to handle the cost?"

"Money is not an issue," Grace responded. "If I have to, I'll mortgage the condo, this house, and lay off my entire staff." She waited the appropriate few seconds before adding, "Just kidding, kids. I would keep one or two of you."

"You couldn't survive without us, Grace," Edward said.

"You're probably right, Edward." Grace shifted her attention to Dantzler, said, "Where do you start, Jack?"

"Fly to New York and meet with Abe Pearlstein, Danny's agent. Hopefully, he can provide some information about the two men who showed up to film the audition. After I talk to him, what happens next is anybody's guess. Depends on what Abe tells me."

"When do you want to go?"

"Tomorrow, if possible. I packed a suitcase, so I have enough clothes for a trip to Manhattan. After that, who knows? I may have to swing through Lexington and pick up more clothes."

"Going to Lexington isn't necessary, Jack," Grace pointed out. "If you need clothes, get them here in Chicago. I'll buy them for you."

"I'll take care of my wardrobe, Grace. You'll have more than enough expenses as it is."

Edward said, "What do you want us to do? How can we help?"

"There is plenty you guys can do," Dantzler said. To Grace: "First, you need to get back in touch with that lady FBI agent and see if you can persuade her to get involved in the case. Do everything possible to convince her that Danny was framed for this. The FBI has unlimited resources; we need to tap into some of them."

"I don't think that's going to happen, Jack. She made it clear that Chicago PD was taking over the case."

"Okay, do this. If we can't have access to FBI resources, then let's do what we can to cultivate . . . what's her name?"

"Kate Flanagan."

"Let's try to cultivate Kate as a source for us. Tell her you understand that the FBI is handing off the case to the locals, but ask her to provide us with any pertinent information relating to the case that comes across her desk. Plead with her to keep us in the loop. If she agrees to do that, it will be a big help to us."

"I'll see what I can do, but I'm not holding my breath," Grace said. "What else?"

"You said this local detective, Sly Douglas, indicated his belief that Danny might be innocent. We definitely need to get close to him. In fact, I'll want to speak with him at some point along the way."

Dantzler looked around the table, said, "Those are Grace's immediate tasks. What I need from you guys is a complete and thorough investigation into the life of Dana Shapiro. Consider this: There are one-hundred U.S. senators, yet she was the only one gunned down. What reason would anyone have to murder her? Clearly, someone did have a reason. If we can figure out the why that will go a long way toward helping us uncover the who. To do that, you have to rip into her past. Family, finances, close friends, enemies, political or otherwise, lovers, financial donors . . . you get the picture. Nothing is off limits. Leave no stone unturned. Somewhere under one of those stones we'll find the answer we're looking for."

"I will take care of that," Angela said.

Dantzler took another drink before continuing. "I find it very curious that the building where the shot came from just happened to be empty at that time. Supposedly, it was due to a gas leak. We need to make sure that's true. Someone from building maintenance should be able to answer that for us. While you're at it, find out who owns the building.

"You guys do this any way you see fit," he added. "But I want one of you to zero in on finding the person who was closest to Dana Shapiro. Start with someone on her staff. People in positions of power almost always have one individual they confide their deepest secrets to. I need to talk with that person."

"I can do that," Jenny said, writing furiously in her notepad.

"Something else to consider," Dantzler pointed out. "Shapiro is typically a Jewish name. Could be we need to look into the anti-Semitic angle. That's . . ."

"Dana wasn't Jewish," Grace said. "Her maiden name was Dana Lynn O'Connor. Father was Boston Irish, her mother a Moscow-born Russian. Dana's husband, Benjamin, was Jewish."

"*Was?*"

"He died three years ago from Lou Gehrig's disease."

"The Jewish angle may not be a top priority, but information relating to her husband is. Find out all you can about him."

Dantzler finished his drink, leaned back, and looked around the table. "Any thoughts, observations, or insights?" he asked. His question was met with silence. "Come on, Grace bragged about you guys. Let me hear what you have to say."

Mary-Louise started to raise her hand but quickly brought it down.

Grace said, "Speak up, Mary-Louise. Don't behave like a second-class citizen. If you're at this table, your thoughts are as important as mine. Say what's on your mind."

"Well, I was thinking that we ought to take a close look at the movie angle."

Dantzler nodded, and said, "That's a good call, Mary-Louise. I was thinking the same thing. Just because Danny's movie was a sham doesn't mean the folks who filmed the audition aren't in show business. I'm betting the people behind this murder work in or around the movie industry."

"That might mean a trip to Hollywood," Grace noted.

"New York City first. Tomorrow morning, if I can get a flight."

"I'll take care of it," Maggie said, standing. "How early is too early?"

"You book it, I'll be there."

"You can stay in my condo tonight, Jack," Grace said. "I promise to get you to the airport on time."

"Think I'll stay here tonight."

"Suit yourself. Like I said, there are three bedrooms upstairs. Pick the one you like best." Grace stood, said, "Care for another drink? I'm having one."

"No thanks. I'm good."

After Grace made her second drink and returned to her chair, Maggie came rushing into the room waving a piece of paper. "I have you booked on an eight-thirty Delta flight from O'Hare to LaGuardia," she said. "That's the earliest one I could get."

"That's perfect," Dantzler said to her. "It'll give me time to sleep in. Will one of you be here to drive me to the airport?"

"We'll all be here, Jack," Grace said. "Will you take him, Mary-Louise?"

"Be more than happy to."

Grace said, "Okay, kids, it's almost six. I'm sure you are all tired and hungry. I know I am. Go home, get some rest, and be back here bright and early tomorrow morning. We have a lot of work staring us in the face. We need to get it done sooner rather than later. Danny is counting on us."

"That reminds me of something I meant to bring up earlier," Dantzler said. "I'm sure the Cook County Jail has a regular schedule for visiting hours. Find out what those times are. I think one of you should go see Danny whenever visitors are allowed. Maybe a different person should go each time. Just to sit and talk, you know? We have to make an effort to keep his spirits from sagging. I don't want him feeling like a forgotten ghost lost in the machine."

"We can do that," Grace said.

After the troops had left, Grace asked Dantzler what his dinner plans were. She was stunned when he inquired if any of the goulash had survived the lunch rush.

"You like it enough to have it a second time?" she said.

"I liked it, Grace. But to be honest with you, even if I hated it, I would happily partake of it again. I'm too damn weary to go out and eat."

"Let me warm it up for you. Then you can eat and head straight to bed."

"That's the best plan I've heard all day."

# Chapter Ten

Dantzler awoke with the feeling one often has after having slept in unfamiliar surroundings. Disoriented, like he was on the moon, or in a foreign land. His mind initially registered him as a stranger, some exiled refugee waking up on a distant shore. He glanced at the clock—it was a little past six—felt like it was too early to get up, and then remembered that he had to catch a morning flight to New York City. He hopped out of bed, went into the bathroom, brushed his teeth, and took a quick shower. While toweling off he heard someone knocking on the door to his room.

After slipping on his underwear and a pair of slacks, he said, "Yeah, come on in."

Edward.

"You're quite the eager beaver, Edward," Dantzler said. "I didn't think anyone would be here at such an early hour."

"We're all here," Edward replied. "This is most unusual, I'll admit, but we all have a lot of work to do. Along with the Danny Kafka case, Grace is also defending a young woman who is accused of murdering her boyfriend. In fact, Grace is due in court at ten."

"Do you think the woman is innocent?"

Edward offered a devilish grin, said, "The reason I'm here is to let you know that I'm making omelets downstairs, and I wanted to see if you'd like to have one. I make a mean omelet, Jack. There's also link sausage, bacon, toast, and hash browns. If you're not up for an omelet, I can cook the eggs any way you like."

"Sounds tempting, Edward. But I'll settle for a large glass of orange juice."

"Let me know if you change your mind. I'll be more than happy to make your breakfast."

"You look like you might have played some football in your time," Dantzler said as Edward opened the door. "Am I right?"

"Lettered four years at the University of Illinois," Edward answered.

"Let me guess. Defensive guard?"

"Linebacker."

"Ah, one of the really tough guys. Did you have any interest in going pro?"

"I was interested, the pros weren't. Turns out, I caught a lucky break when they passed on me. Too many of those NFL guys are screwed up for life. They hit fifty, and they either can't walk, or all those concussions have caused irreparable brain damage. That's a heavy price to pay for playing a damn game. Nope, I'm perfectly happy being a paralegal."

When Edward was gone, Dantzler finished dressing, stuffed his dirty clothes into his bag, and headed downstairs. Maggie and Mary-Louise were sitting side by side at the desk in the front room. Both women smiled and nodded.

Dantzler went into the kitchen and poured a glass of orange juice. Rather than sit at the table and drink it, he decided to check out the downstairs area. He was curious to see how the house had been transformed into an office.

The large room where the table was located also served as the library. Bookcases crammed with law books, journals, and periodicals—along with occasional true crime books or mystery novels—covered three walls. A hallway on the right ran parallel to the big room. At the top of that hallway was a small room that had Edward's nameplate on the door. Next, there was a bathroom, then a larger room that was shared by Angela and Jenny. At the end of the hallway was Grace's office. Her room was smaller than Angela's and Jenny's, but slightly more spacious than Edward's.

Grace was sitting at her desk when Dantzler knocked. She looked up as he walked in. "Did you sample one of Edward's famous omelets?" she asked.

Dantzler shook his head, said, "Nah, too early to eat."

"You are missing out on heaven, my good friend. They are scrumptious."

"So this is a restaurant masquerading as a law office? Is that what you're running here?"

"It's unusual for us to be here this early, so breakfast is a rarity," Grace noted. "When it comes to lunch, that's a different matter. Edward or one of the girls will ask if anyone is interested in eating here, and if the answer is yes, they whip something up. Other times, we may order a pizza or Chinese and have it delivered. I run a tight ship, Jack, but I'm not Captain Bligh."

"Edward said you have court this morning."

"I'm not due in court until ten, but I'm leaving in a few minutes. I need to confer with my client. The D.A. has made an offer, and I want to run it by my client, see if she's interested in accepting it."

"How will you advise her?"

"This is a tough one, Jack. We might get a hung jury but we'll never get an acquittal. If the jury is deadlocked, that means a second trial. And in my experience second trials rarely favor the defendant."

"Better you than me when it comes to making that decision. Compared to what you have to do, I've got it easy. The only thing on my agenda today is to speak with an eighty-eight-year-old New York agent. Which reminds me . . . I neglected to get Abe Pearlstein's phone number when I spoke with Danny. Do you happen to have it?"

"Have it here somewhere," Grace said, thumbing through papers on her desk. "Yeah, here it is."

She copied the number on the back of a business card and handed it to Dantzler. Standing, she picked up her leather bag and her briefcase, gave Dantzler a second chaste kiss on the cheek, and said, "I'm out of here. Just let Mary-Louise know when you want to leave for the airport."

"You got it, Captain Bligh."

---

"MARY-LOUISE, you're gripping that steering wheel like you want to strangle it to death," Dantzler said. "Is something bothering you?"

"Just a little on edge, is all. I've never driven a Mercedes, and I'm terrified that I'm going to wreck it."

Dantzler chuckled, said, "Don't worry about it. The car is well-insured. Unless we both get killed in this wreck you are concerned with, everything will be okay."

"I'll do my best to keep us alive," Mary-Louise replied, although her grip on the steering wheel remained unchanged. "What did you think of our little band of legal warriors?"

"Bright, talented, dedicated . . . just the way Grace described you guys. My question is, do you always get along that well, or was it false comradeship because a stranger was in the house?"

"No, there was nothing phony or false about it. We're a very tight-knit group. We all get along well with each other."

"In your opinion, which one of your colleagues do you rate as the most-talented, the most-intelligent?"

"I wouldn't dare answer that question. If you want to know the truth, I couldn't answer it. They are all equally talented and intelligent, all really, really bright."

"That's a very diplomatic answer, Mary-Louise. But what about you? I have a sneaking suspicion that you're every bit as intelligent as any of your co-workers. Maybe not as educated, but certainly as smart."

"Well, I'm fresh out of college, so I'm definitely not as educated as Angela, Jenny, or Edward. Maggie isn't a paralegal but she does have her master's. All I have is a bachelor's in Comparative Religion."

"I took a couple of Comparative Religion courses when I was in college. I really enjoyed them."

"Grace said you have a doctorate in Philosophy."

"Not quite. I never got around to writing a dissertation."

"Seems like you did all right without adding that final touch."

"How did you get hooked up with Grace?" Dantzler asked, eager to change the subject.

"She and my mom have been friends since they were kids. They even went to law school together. Grace hired me part-time while I was still in high school. This was back when she had an office downtown. I continued to work for her during summers throughout my college years. When I graduated she hired me as her full-time researcher."

"Do you plan on staying with her?"

"I love it there, so, yes, I'll stay," Mary-Louise stated. "Grace keeps encouraging me to go back to school and get a law degree, but that doesn't interest me at all."

"Good for you," Dantzler said. "The world already has more than enough lawyers."

"Be honest with me, Jack. What are the chances that you can prove Danny Kafka didn't murder Dana Shapiro?"

"Mary-Louise, I can't allow myself to think in those terms. Worrying about what my chances are will only serve to keep me from my real goal, and that is to strictly focus on finding facts, on locating evidence that will exonerate Danny. Nothing else matters."

"Do you mind if I toss in another observation?"

"Any observation at this point is more than welcome."

"You know, I said you should look into the movie industry, which you agreed with. But I was thinking that maybe you should also take a look at someone in our government."

"Anyone in particular come to mind?"

"No."

"What's your reason for thinking this crime has anything to do with the government?"

"Because of how soon Danny was arrested. How did the FBI know where Danny was staying? How could they have been absolutely certain that Danny was the shooter? Sure, they had him confessing on that tape, but at the time he was arrested they didn't have the weapon or his fingerprints. I may be way out of line, but I think it's worth looking into."

"Those are excellent questions, Mary-Louise. Really good observations."

"You don't think they're too bizarre?"

"Not at all. But in your scenario the FBI is behind this. That part I'm not sure about."

"No, I didn't mean the entire FBI," Mary-Louise corrected. "Maybe it's just a few agents. Or it could be a single agent. Maybe it's one of the higher-ups. Maybe it's one of the other branches of government. Maybe it's . . . maybe I'm just talking out my ass."

"Be forewarned, Mary-Louise. I'll take help anywhere I can get it. So you keep those thoughts and observations coming, no matter where they come from. Is that a deal?"

"It's a deal."

---

THE PLANE RIDE to LaGuardia gave Dantzler plenty of time to chew over Mary-Louise's list of possibilities. As he filtered through her words, he realized that some of what she said could be dismissed outright. For starters, there was no way an entire judiciary agency like the FBI would ever be part of a plot that involved the assassination of a United States senator. Mary-Louise was dead wrong about that. True, the FBI has a somewhat unsavory history of doing some shitty things, but outright murder isn't included on that list

However, one of her secondary possibilities couldn't be cast aside or dismissed so quickly.

What if a lone individual, high up in our government, for any number of reasons, set things in motion? Not an entire agency, but a leader and a small group of zealous disciples.

That scenario wasn't outside the zone of possibility.

But did such a plan pass the smell test? Was it plausible to believe that one person could concoct what amounted to a major conspiracy? Yes, anything was possible; history has proved that any number of times. But how probable was it? That was the real question. Not very was Dantzler's answer. And yet this was a conspiracy, which by its very nature involved more than a single individual, regardless of which agency, if any, those people worked for. Thinking about it now, Dantzler hoped that a small outside group was responsible for the crime, because if Mary-Louise's hunch was right, that an employee from *any* of our government agencies was behind it, then getting to the bottom of this case may be next to impossible.

Right or wrong, Dantzler had to give Mary-Louise her due for planting seeds that had the potential to bear fruit.

But she wasn't a seasoned investigator; Dantzler was. Unlike him, she didn't think outside the box. She zeroed in on one thing and one thing only. That normally means death to any investigation. You don't solve cases unless you broaden your scope and cast a wide net. Dantzler saw what Mary-Louise overlooked, that there were scenarios that made far more sense. To him, they stood out like lights in the northern sky.

Mary-Louise's big question concerning the speed in which Danny was located and apprehended was a good one. The response of the FBI was indeed lightning fast. She was also correct to wonder how the FBI knew for certain that Danny was the shooter. After all, as she pointed out, they didn't have his fingerprints at that time. It was easy to see why she had issues with the way certain events unfolded.

However, Dantzler felt that Mary-Louise had her sights set too high in the sky, that she had overlooked more earth-bound possibilities. The way the crime played out definitely involved a conspiracy; more than one individual was behind it. That wasn't in question. But Mary-Louise targeted a government agency when it just as likely might have been a low-level deal pulled off by a small group who simply wanted Dana Shapiro out of the way.

Mary-Louise asked how the FBI knew where Danny was staying. Good question, but one that could be answered in several ways, the most obvious being that the person who set the plan in motion knew where Danny was. He informed the FBI. So did Carson Welles, who, Dantzler had already decided, was a gofer and not the crime's architect. Brian, the Uber driver, knew. Perhaps he recognized Danny on the tape, said, "Whoa, I gave that guy a ride today," picked up the phone and called the authorities, hoping for either a cash reward, or to be interviewed on TV. Probably both. And, of course, someone from the hotel may have given up Danny's location.

Any one of those explanations was far easier to believe than the one proposed by Mary-Louise. Plenty of people knew where Danny was staying, any of whom could have alerted the FBI.

But her fingerprint question wasn't so easy to explain away. That one, Dantzler had to admit, lingered like a vulture hovering over a dead carcass.

That question deserved a closer look.

*How could the FBI be absolutely sure Danny Kafka was the shooter if they didn't have his fingerprints?*

That was Dantzler's last thought as the plane began its descent into LaGuardia.

## Chapter Eleven

The flight into LaGuardia was like floating on a heavenly cloud compared to the earth-bound terror Dantzler felt on the taxi ride from Queens into Manhattan. He had been to The Big Apple numerous times, had taken many taxi rides, and each one turned out to be nothing short of a blood-curdling experience. They say there are no atheists in a foxhole; Dantzler was dead certain there were no atheists in New York City taxis.

After arriving at the airport Dantzler phoned Abe Pearlstein, identified himself, and asked if they could meet and talk about the Danny Kafka situation. Abe agreed, adding that he "would do anything possible to help get that boychik out of trouble."

"Where do you want to meet?" asked Dantzler.

"Are you in the City?"

"At LaGuardia, getting ready to grab a taxi."

"Come to the corner of Forty-Seventh Street and Fifth Avenue. There, you'll see a tall building that says Pearlstein Diamonds. My office is on the second floor. You get all that?"

"I did. I'll be there as soon as possible."

"You hungry? If you are, I'll bring you a corned beef and

pastrami sandwich from Katz's Deli. Best in the five boroughs. You can repay me when I get to the office."

Smiling, Dantzler said, "I'm good, Abe. I'll take a raincheck on lunch."

"Then I will see you in my office."

A half-hour later, when the taxi pulled to a stop in front of the Pearlstein Building, Dantzler realized that he was in the heart of Manhattan's Diamond District. This marked the first time he had ever been in this section of Manhattan. It was a beautiful area of town, very crowded and very busy. Looking up at the name on the building, Dantzler couldn't help but wonder how Abe was connected to the diamond trade.

Pearlstein Diamonds, where business was conducted, was located on the ground floor at street level. To the right of the front entrance was a narrow hall that separated the Pearlstein Building from its next-door neighbor. Dantzler wandered down the hall until he came to a glass door, through which marble stairs could be seen. He tugged at the door but it was locked. Looking to his right, he saw an intercom with a small buzzer beneath it. He pressed the buzzer and waited. No one answered but the door clicked open. He stepped inside and went to the bottom of the stairs.

"You Dantzler?"

Dantzler heard the question but couldn't see the one who asked it.

"Yeah, I'm Dantzler."

"Come on up."

There were three offices and a bathroom on the second floor. Abe's office, identified by the ***Abe Pearlstein, Theatrical Agent*** written on the glass door, was the one in the middle. The door was halfway open. Dantzler opened it fully, entered the office, and let his gaze drift around the large, cluttered room. There wasn't much to it, and what there was looked to be ancient. A wooden desk balanced by an old telephone book under one of the front legs, two wooden chairs, a metal bookcase, and a dilapidated couch that appeared to be old enough to have once been used by Freud when he analyzed his patients.

Abe Pearlstein looked like he might have been around when Sigmund was doing his thing. Danny Kafka said Abe was eighty-eight but Dantzler felt that was off by about fifty years. Abe was old, really old. And yet, strangely enough, there was something about him that projected a youthful quality. Maybe it was his dark, alert eyes, his soft smile, or a kindness that radiated like an outer garment. He looked, Dantzler thought, like he might have been one of God's gentle angels.

Abe was standing in front of his desk, an unlit cigar in the corner of his mouth. He had on a dark blue suit, white shirt, red suspenders, and brown leather shoes. The suit and shirt were old and badly in need of a good pressing. His well-worn shoes had clearly traveled many miles. He had probably been close to six-feet in his prime, but the passage of time had shaved off two or three inches. His hair was thin, but for an eighty-eight-year-old man there was still plenty left for him to deal with. All in all, Abe was a fine specimen for a senior citizen.

As Abe struck a match and lit his cigar, Dantzler turned his attention to what he found to be the most interesting aspect of the office—the collection of photos showing Abe with a legion of celebrities. There were dozens of them, more than enough to cover every inch of three walls. Looking at them, Dantzler had to wonder if there was a famous person Abe Pearlstein *didn't* know. From what Dantzler was seeing on those walls, he had his doubts.

There was Abe standing between Joe DiMaggio and Ted Williams. One with Jackie Gleason and Toots Shore, Marlon Brando and Montgomery Clift. Abe with Norman Mailer and Philip Roth, Barbra Streisand and Bette Midler, Al Pacino and Robert De Niro, George H.W. Bush and Bill Clinton, Muhammad Ali and Jim Brown . . . the famous faces extended all the way around the office. Dantzler recognized most of those faces, but there were a few he wasn't familiar with.

"That's my favorite," Abe said, pushing away from the desk and pointing to a slightly larger photo behind Dantzler. It was a picture of Abe sitting in the dugout with Sandy Koufax and Jackie Robinson. "That was taken when they were still playing for the Brooklyn

Dodgers. Back in fifty-six. That's a few years before Sandy became the greatest hurler to ever step on a pitcher's mound."

Dantzler, however, was more interested in the photo next to Abe's favorite. In that one, Abe was standing between Pancho Gonzales and Lew Hoad. "What about this one?" he asked. "When was it taken?"

"Madison Square Garden, nineteen fifty-eight," Abe replied without hesitation. "I promoted that match. Hauled in a bundle of cash with that one. Why does that picture interest you so much."

"I once hit with Pancho."

"What do you mean you once 'hit' with Pancho?"

"Pancho saw me win a match in a junior's tournament out in Vegas. The next day he spotted me walking around, and asked if I would like to hit with him. Naturally, I jumped at the opportunity. We ended up hitting for about an hour. It was one of the great moments in my life."

"He was a damn fine tennis player, one of the greatest-ever, but one mean, hot-headed son of a gun. He didn't take crap from anybody. Hoad was also a terrific player. That bad back of his slowed him down."

Abe lit the cigar a second time, moved behind his desk, sat down, and motioned for Dantzler to do the same. Dantzler chose one of the wooden chairs rather than the couch.

"Pancho Gonzales taking the time to play tennis with you tells me you must've been pretty good," Abe acknowledged. "That's fine and dandy. But why should I believe that you can prove Danny's innocence? What are your credentials?"

"I worked homicide for twenty-seven years."

"Any good at it?"

"I did all right, yeah."

"Do you really think there's a chance that you can get Danny out of this jam he's in?"

"I won't lie to you, Abe. It's gonna be tough. They have him confessing on tape, and they have his fingerprints on the murder weapon. That's an awful lot to overcome."

"Have you spoken with Danny?"

"Yes."

"What did he say about the tape, the fingerprints?"

"Danny says it's all bullshit, that he didn't murder Dana Shapiro. I believe him," Dantzler said. "But Danny's words don't carry much weight at this point. Those words need to be replaced by facts if we have any hope of clearing his name. What I need now is to hear your words. Tell me everything you know."

Abe flicked ashes off the cigar onto the floor, said, "That's a problem, because there's not much I can tell you."

"You may know more than you think."

"What's your first question?"

Taking out his notepad and pen, Dantzler said, "Was Carson Welles the person who contacted you about Danny being in the movie?"

"Yes. He phoned sometime around noon, said he knew Danny was looking for work, and wanted to know if Danny was available. Said he had a big movie in pre-production, one with a lead role that Danny was perfectly suited to play. I took that to mean he was aware of Danny's military record."

"Did he specifically say Danny's character was a sniper?"

"I don't recall him mentioning sniper," Abe said, lighting his cigar for the third time. "What he told me was that Danny would play the part of an assassin. I took that to mean sniper."

"Then what happened?"

"I asked him what the next step was. He wanted to know how soon Danny could be available for an audition. I told him to set the time and place, that Danny would be there. He said let's do it tomorrow afternoon in Danny's apartment. I said fine, and that's how we left it."

"Did he ask you for Danny's address?"

"No. Come to think of it, he didn't."

"Two questions, Abe. Didn't you think it odd to schedule an audition in Danny's apartment, and how did Carson Welles know where Danny lived?"

"Getting the address of an actor isn't all that difficult. Danny is a member of Actors' Equity and the Screen Actors Guild. Both of those organizations would have Danny's address. As for your other question, yes, I thought it peculiar to have the audition in Danny's apartment. However, Carson Welles didn't think it would be a problem."

"Danny told me that he, Welles, and a third man were the only ones present during the filming of that scene where he announces his intention to kill Dana Shapiro. Why weren't you there?"

"Since Danny's apartment is quite small, and because he had no idea how many people might accompany Welles, he thought it best that I not be present. Considering what happened, I would give anything to have been there."

"So you never met Carson Welles? Or anyone from a movie studio?"

"No. My only communication was those two phone calls."

"When did that second call take place?" Dantzler asked.

"Around three-thirty the next afternoon. That's when I was told that the film was being shot in Chicago, that Danny was to fly into O'Hare the following Friday morning, and that a suite had been booked for him in the Blackstone Renaissance Hotel. That's also when he informed me that Danny's salary was a million-four. I immediately phoned Danny and gave him the good news."

"Did Welles say what studio was backing the movie?"

"That was the first question I asked him. He said it was an independent production that he was actively pitching to the big studios. According to him, several executives had expressed an interest in releasing the film through their studio. They liked the fact that Nicole Kidman and Tom Hardy were attached to the project. He also told me the bigshots felt the presence of a Medal of Honor winner in the cast was another strong selling point. Of course, everything the man said to me was a lie."

Dantzler leaned back in his chair, thought for a few moments, then said, "I'm assuming that over the years you have dealt with movie studio executives on a few occasion, right?"

"Many more than a few. Why do you ask that?"

"Based on your past experience, would you say Welles sounded like someone familiar with the movie business? In other words, did he sound legit?"

"Yes. He came across as a man who had a deep knowledge of the film industry and the movie-making process. Why? Do you suspect someone from the movie business is behind this?"

"That's my working hypothesis at the moment."

"What reason would someone from Hollywood have for murdering a United States senator, and then framing a war hero for the crime?"

"I don't know, Abe. But unless I can come up with an answer, Danny is doomed to spend the rest of his life behind bars." Dantzler stood, took out a business card from his shirt pocket, and handed it to Abe. "If you think of anything that might be helpful, give me a call."

"That boy is no murderer," Abe said, forcefully. "Sure, I know he killed people in the war, but that's different." He pointed to a photo on the wall behind Dantzler. "Know who that man is?"

Dantzler shook his head.

"'Crazy' Joe Gallo. *He* was a murderer. Danny's not cut from the same cloth as that ruthless bastard."

"It was good meeting you, Abe," Dantzler said as he headed for the door. "I can tell that you think the world of Danny. And I know he feels the same about you."

Dantzler had just opened the door when Abe called out to him.

"Wait. I just remembered something I neglected to tell you," Abe said.

"What's that?" Dantzler asked, moving back toward the desk.

"Carson Welles didn't make that second phone call, the one that came the day after Danny's audition. It was made by a different man."

"How can you be sure of that if you never met anyone from the movie studio?"

"Because that caller's voice was very deep, and he spoke with a foreign accent. He sounded Russian, or Polish, or German . . . one of those Baltic countries."

Damn, Abe. Hollywood is bad enough. Throw in Russia, and we're tossing a rotten salad."

---

DANTZLER THOUGHT about spending the night in New York City but decided instead to catch a late flight back to Chicago. There was no good reason for him to stick around; he wasn't going to learn anything beyond what Abe had already told him. Also, staying would only be an unnecessary expense for Grace. He was already feeling a twinge of guilt for spending Grace's money on the New York trip. What little Abe had shared with him could just as easily have been elicited in a phone call. By heading back he would save her a few bucks.

His taxi ride to LaGuardia was yet another chilling and terrifying experience. He marveled that no pedestrians were killed along the way. How any of those drivers avoided vehicular homicide charges was nothing short of a miracle.

At LaGuardia he booked a flight, and then to ward off his hunger he picked an eating place that charged a small fortune for a burger and fries. That came as no great shock; airport restaurants are ridiculously overpriced. The food was good, but not *that* good.

Finished eating, he took out his cell phone, called Grace, and told her he was waiting to catch a Delta flight to Chicago. He said his flight was scheduled to land at O'Hare around eleven p.m.

"I will pick you up at the airport," Grace said. "You can spend the night at the condo."

"Don't bother. I'll take a taxi to the house on Sheffield and stay there. What I need from you is a key to get in."

"I will leave one on the ledge above the door."

"Thanks. I'll see you tomorrow morning."

"Why do I have this feeling that you're avoiding me, Jack? You know, we could be spending some quality time together. There is such a thing as life beyond business."

"How about we concentrate on getting Danny Kafka out of that jail cell he's sitting in? If we do that, then we can have our quality time."

"Fair enough, Jack."

"See you tomorrow, Grace. And, hey, don't forget to leave that key."

# Chapter Twelve

D antzler found the key where Grace said it would be. He inserted it, opened the door, went inside, and locked the door behind him. After turning on some lights, he went into the big room, laid his travel bag on the table, and made his way to the liquor cabinet. Grabbing a clear glass, he filled it with ice, then added the key ingredients, Scotch and soda. He took a sip, judged it to be a perfect drink, flipped on the hallway light, and headed for Grace's office.

It was nearly one a.m., but there was information he wanted to gather, if possible. Sitting at Grace's desk, he fired up the computer. It was time to let Google do some detective work, namely to help him figure out if Carson Welles actually existed.

First, Dantzler typed in the name. Nothing. There was one Carson Wells, but it turned out that he couldn't possibly be the man who spoke with Abe Pearlstein. Next, he typed in *Carson Welles, Hollywood*. Again, he came up with nothing. Then he tried *Carson Welles, Actor, Carson Welles, Producer*, and finally, *Carson Welles, Director*. He came up empty with each of those searches.

His next move was to give Facebook a shot. That route also turned up nothing helpful. There were a couple of Facebook users with that name, but both were in their teens. On this night Google proved to be as void of information as Dantzler was.

It was now almost three-thirty in the morning. His Scotch was long gone, and he had no real desire for a second drink, so he decided to get some sleep. With any luck he could get maybe four hours of shuteye before Grace's gang began arriving. Not much but better than nothing.

―――――

DANTZLER WAS AWAKENED by a soft knock on his door. Rolling over, his initial thought was that those four hours flew by in a hurry. But he was badly mistaken. When he sat up and looked at the clock next to his bed, he saw that it was almost noon. He'd been asleep for close to eight hours.

"Jack, are you awake?"

Mary-Louise.

"Yeah, give me a second to slip on some pants," Dantzler said. After getting them on, he opened the door. "What's up, Mary-Louise?"

"You left your cell phone downstairs," she said, offering him his phone. "You got a call from a detective. He says it's urgent."

"Thanks," he said, taking the phone from her. When she was gone, he said, "This is Jack Dantzler."

"I know who the hell you are. Why else would I ask for you by name?"

All it took was that one wiseass response to know who the caller was. Bobby Brennan, a New York City homicide detective who worked with Dantzler on the Victor Sammael case more than a decade ago. Brennan was a classic New Yorker—brash, cocky, streetwise, and unflappable. He was also a superb detective.

"Ah, it's the less-intelligent of the two Brennan brothers," Dantzler chided. "The way I remember it, Mike is the smart one."

"He went from being a cop to working in the D.A.'s office. That should put to rest any notion that he's the smart one. Better dressed? Yes. More intelligent? No way."

"Been a long time, Bobby. How the hell have you been doing?"

"I float like a butterfly and sting like a bee."

"Just like Ali once did, right?"

"Absolutely. Hang on, Dantzler, I need to refill my coffee cup." A few seconds later, he said, "I see that you are no longer a homicide investigator, that you're now a P.I."

"It was time for a change, Bobby."

"Tell me, Dantzler. What business did a novice private investigator have in my fair city?"

"How did you know I had been to Manhattan?"

"Found one of your business cards in the coat pocket of a murder victim. An elderly gentleman named Abraham Pearlstein."

"Abe is dead?"

"Yeah. Being badly tortured, and then taking a bullet to the back of the head will do it every time."

Dantzler sat on the edge of the bed, shocked and saddened by the news he'd just heard. Although he really didn't know Abe at all, he'd taken an instant liking to the man. "Damn, Bobby," he said, "I was with the guy yesterday afternoon."

"Where?"

"His office."

"The Pearlstein Building on the corner of Forty-Seventh Street and Fifth Avenue?"

"Yeah."

"What time did you get there, and how long did the meeting last?"

"I got there a little past noon, stayed maybe two hours. When was he killed?"

"Not long after you left. Coroner says between four and six. What did you do after you left him?"

"Took a taxi back to LaGuardia, caught a late flight to Chicago."

"Why Chicago?"

"I'm working for Grace West, the defense attorney. She's representing Danny Kafka. He's . . ."

"The war hero accused of murdering that U.S senator," Bobby

interrupted. "What's Abe Pearlstein's connection to the Kafka kid?"

"Danny's an actor, Abe was his agent. I was hoping Abe might provide me with some information. Turns out, he couldn't."

"Well, it's for certain he won't be sharing any information with anyone in the future, nor will he be representing any actors. Someone made sure of that." Bobby paused, then said, "As you were leaving did you notice anyone hanging around, anyone suspicious looking, anyone who seemed out of place?"

"I didn't see anyone, Bobby. Just flagged down a taxi, hopped in, and we took off."

"Did Abe seem edgy or out of sorts in any way?"

"Not at all. He was obviously upset about what's going on with Danny Kafka, but otherwise he was fine."

"Did he indicate that he had someone else to see later in the day?"

"He didn't say. But you should be able to find that on his computer."

"Did you see a computer when you were with him?"

"Actually, I didn't."

"Old guy like Abe probably didn't own one."

"Listen, Bobby, do you need me back in New York to answer any questions you might have? I'll hop the first plane if you want me to."

"No reason for you to do that at this time. Maybe down the road if something breaks, although I can't imagine what might happen that involves you."

"Just let me know if you do need me."

"I've gotta be honest with you, Jack. I'm having a difficult time accepting the fact that you are now working to keep people out of jail rather than put them in jail. That goes against the laws of nature."

"In or out doesn't matter, Bobby. Only the truth does. In that way, it's no different from being a detective."

"And you believe Danny Kafka is innocent?"

"I'd stake my life on it."

"And you intend to prove it?"

"Yes."

"Good luck with that, Jack. Confessing on tape, fingerprint evidence . . . virtually impossible shit to get around."

"I didn't say proving it was going to be easy."

"Like I said, good luck."

"Hey, Bobby, will you do me a favor?"

"If I can, sure."

"When you dump Abe's phone calls, would . . ."

"Already done."

"Check calls Abe received on May ten around noon, and May eleven sometime around three-thirty. I would be interested to know those numbers, and who made those calls."

"Same answer, Jack. Already done. Two suspicious calls, both obviously made on burner phones, both probably tossed seconds after the call ended, no way to know who made them. That one is a dead end. Sorry."

"It was a longshot at best. What about his calendar or his schedule book? Anything of interest on them?"

"Thus far, I have found nothing that will help either of us. Wish I had better news for you, but I don't," Bobby said. "Don't be a stranger, Jack. And if there is anything I can do to help with the Kafka case, you know I will."

"Stay close to your phone, Bobby. I just might take you up on that offer."

———

IT WAS all hands on deck when Dantzler came downstairs. Maggie was at her desk talking on the phone, Mary-Louise stood at the copier collecting printed pages, Angela, Jenny, and Edward were sitting at the big table. Grace could be heard rattling glasses in the kitchen. Two large pizza boxes, paper plates, plastic cups, napkins, and soft drinks were in the middle of the table.

Dantzler sat down and poured Diet Coke into a cup. Maggie and Mary-Louise soon joined them, followed seconds later by Grace. No one spoke, and all eyes shifted to Dantzler.

"The call I just received was from a Manhattan homicide detective informing me that Abe Pearlstein is dead," he announced. "Murdered . . . a single bullet to the head after he'd been tortured. He was killed two or three hours after I spoke with him."

"What does that mean, Jack?" asked Grace.

"That someone is silencing potential witnesses."

Angela said, "But how could anyone know you were there, or that your conversation with Abe Pearlstein had anything to do with Danny?"

"Maybe they didn't know. Maybe they simply weren't going to take any chances. They had to suspect that sooner or later someone in law enforcement was going to talk to Abe about what happened with Danny. Rather than risk him saying something that could possibly be incriminating, they killed him. Dead men don't give up critical details."

"This news will devastate Danny," Grace said. "Should we hold off telling him?"

"No. You should tell him, Grace," Dantzler advised. "It is better he hears it from one of us than to hear it from a stranger. See if you can set a meeting with him later this afternoon."

"Did Abe say anything that might be helpful?" Edward inquired.

"Abe wasn't able to give me much, but he did tell me that the second call he received was from someone other than our mysterious Carson Welles," Dantzler pointed out. "He said the caller was a male with a deep voice, and what sounded to Abe like a Russian accent. The presence of a second person eliminates any doubt that we are dealing with a conspiracy."

Dantzler took a drink of Diet Coke, then said, "Last night I spent a couple of hours on the computer trying to find out if Carson Welles is real. I came up empty. Same with Facebook. I found two individuals with that name, both of whom were teenagers."

"Carson Welles is a phony name, right?" Jenny said.

Dantzler nodded.

"What about those two phone calls to Abe?" Edward asked.

"Did the New York cops trace them?"

"Both were made on burner phones," Dantzler answered. "And they were discarded soon after the calls were made. There is no way to know who made those two calls."

"So . . . what? We're spinning around going nowhere?" Jenny said, sounding thoroughly dejected.

"Don't get discouraged, Jenny. If you spin long enough you'll eventually go somewhere," Dantzler said. "Okay, enough with my bad news. You guys tell me what you've learned."

Silence ensued until Angela said, "Here's what I learned about the senator. Born Dana Lynn O'Connor on March the third, nineteen sixty-three, the only child of Glenn and Katerina O'Connor in Brookline, Massachusetts. Her father, Glenn, born in Boston, was a high school history teacher and basketball coach. He passed away in nineteen ninety-eight. Katerina—Kate—Petrovich was born in Moscow and came to America when she was three, settling also in Brookline with her mother. She had some talent as an artist, and for many years she was curator of a high-end Boston Arts Gallery. She died five years ago. Dana earned her undergraduate degree in Russian History from the University of Chicago, then went on to get her law degree from Harvard. After spending the next decade working in the State Department, she decided to run for the United States Senate. Although not well known, she easily defeated her more-established Republican opponent. Six years later, she ran for re-election, this time winning by an even greater margin. She had less than two years remaining on this term at the time of her death."

Angela took a drink of water before continuing, "Dana was single until ten years ago when she married Benjamin Solomon Shapiro, a prominent Washington D.C. attorney. It was his second marriage, the first ending in divorce four years prior to marrying Dana. He was twelve years Dana's senior. As we know, he died from Lou Gehrig's disease. Benjamin had no children from his first marriage, nor did he have any with Dana. She was a member of the Subcommittee on Emerging Threats and Capabilities, which is under the Senate Armed Services Committee. They have jurisdiction over Department of Defense policies, and programs geared to assess threats from WMDs, terrorism, illegal drugs, and a whole range of other things. As I'm sure you can discern, that's an important committee."

"She certainly wasn't one to sit on the sidelines," Maggie said.

Grace asked, "What about Dana's personal life? Find anything there that might be of interest?"

Angela shook her head, said, "I didn't find any dark secrets."

"I can't believe she was Miss Perfect," Grace noted. "No one lives as long as she did, or climbs a career ladder to those heights without having a few skeletons hiding in their closet. Take a closer look, Angela."

"Any particular areas you want me to check out?" Angela asked.

"Boyfriends, past or current lovers, the state of her marriage prior to Benjamin's death—those are good places to start. Also, find out all you can about her finances. Was she well off moneywise? Did she have any big debts? If so, who did she owe the money to? Who were her big campaign contributors? While you're digging, find out what you can about her husband. Could be Dana's death is connected to Benjamin in some way."

Dantzler turned to Jenny, and said, "Did you come up with the name of the person closest to Dana?"

"That would be Emily Rosburg," Jenny answered quickly. "She was Dana's personal assistant. I haven't been able to get in touch with her yet, but I'll keep trying."

"Don't bother," Dantzler said, shaking his head. "Just give me her contact information. I'll speak with her."

As Jenny began writing down Emily's address and phone number, Grace's cell phone buzzed. She listened for a few seconds, a perplexed look on her face, and then said, "No need for me to give you that information. He's sitting right here." Standing, she handed the phone to Dantzler. "It's for you, Jack."

Reaching for the phone, Dantzler said, "The way my luck has been running with recent calls, do I really want to take this one?"

"Yes, Jack, you do."

Grace was right.

It was the call that changed everything.

# Chapter Thirteen

W hen the caller identified himself Dantzler was more perplexed than Grace had been when she answered the call. There was an obvious reason for this. Grace was perplexed because she recognized the caller, Dantzler because he didn't. It took several seconds before the caller's name finally registered with Dantzler.

Sly Douglas. The Chicago homicide detective who spoke with Grace regarding the murder of Dana Shapiro.

"What can I do for you, Detective Douglas?" Dantzler asked.

"For starters, you can call me Sly. And if you have no objection, I'll call you Detective."

"I am no longer a detective, Sly. I'm now a private investigator."

"I'm aware of that. However, until recently you were a homicide detective, and my research indicates that you were a damn good one. In fact, rumor has it that you never failed to solve a case. That's more than a little impressive."

"Had some luck and good fortune along the way. Also, worked with terrific people."

"Hell, man, if I had a perfect solve rate I wouldn't be so damn modest."

"Why are you calling, Sly?"

"Grace West indicated that you might be coming aboard to help with the Danny Kafka case. Based on the fact that you are in her office, I take it that you agreed to help. Is that accurate? Am I even close to hitting a home run?"

"You're rounding third, Sly, but I'm still baffled as to why we're talking."

"Because I'm currently involved in an investigation that I suspect is in some way connected to the Danny Kafka case."

"Sly, do you object to me putting this call on speaker? I would really like Grace and her crew to hear what you have to say. I won't, if you think our conversation should stay between the two of us."

"Not a problem."

Dantzler handed the phone to Maggie, who made the adjustment.

"Okay, what have you got for us?" prompted Dantzler.

"Late yesterday afternoon I caught a double homicide. A young couple was found in an abandoned former apartment building by a group of pot-smoking teens. The man was identified as Robert Lee Conrad. He'd been shot once in the face at close range. The female was Molly Ann Jackson. Her throat had been slashed. According to the medical examiner, Robert died a few hours before Molly. Both had been deceased for several days. Turns out, they died this past Friday, same day Dana Shapiro was killed."

"Body lies around for three, four days, with all that decomp, TOD can be difficult to pinpoint."

"That's true."

"Why are you so sure they died on Friday?"

"I'll get to that in a minute," Sly said. "But first, a little background on Robert Conrad—Bobby to his friends. Until two years ago he was in the army. Served with distinction during a couple of tours in Afghanistan. Brought home a shitload of medals. Take a guess what his job was in that war?"

"Sniper."

"Damn, they were correct—you are sharp. Yes, that's exactly what he was. But lest you think he might've been a run-of-the-mill sniper, let me lay that thought to rest. I contacted one of his former commanders, a captain stationed at Fort Bragg, and he said Bobby Conrad was, and I quote, 'One of the three or four best shooters this country has ever produced,' unquote. Don't know how you size all this up, but I find it very intriguing."

"Intriguing isn't evidence," countered Dantzler. "He was a sniper, okay. But what connects his death to Danny Kafka's situation?"

"Have you had an opportunity to meet with Danny yet?"

"I have."

"Then I'm sure he told you the story about coming to Chicago to be in a big movie, right?"

"Yes, that's what he said."

"Here's where things get really interesting. Molly Jackson's cell phone was under her body when we found her. In a brief period, fifty-three minutes to be exact, she made thirteen phone calls to Bobby. He had yet to return home, she was becoming increasingly concerned, so she tried to contact him a bunch of times. She left messages with the first half-dozen calls, and then on the others she hung up without saying anything. Those early messages were the usual 'where are you, Bobby, you're running late.' Or variations of that theme. But it's the fifth message that is important. Here, you listen to it, then tell me what you think."

Following a brief pause and a single click, a female voice could be heard.

"Bobby, honey, I'm really starting to get worried. You're already about three hours late. What's taking so long, and why aren't you answering my calls? Did the shoot take longer than expected? If it did, that's all right. Just call, let me hear from you. Please. You know, if I wasn't so sure that you love me, I might begin to worry that you met Nicole Kidman, and the two of you ran off together. Just kidding . . . I know that didn't happen. Did it? Please call me. I love you, Bobby."

Everyone was silent as Sly punched the button to end the message.

Sly said, "When you spoke with Danny, did he happen to

mention that Nicole Kidman was going to be the big star in that movie?"

"Nicole Kidman and Tom Hardy," Dantzler said.

"About an hour ago I contacted a lady at Illinois Film Commission who assured me that no major movie is currently being filmed in or around Chicago. And according to everyone I've spoken with, there have been no recent sightings of the lovely Nicole Kidman." Sly waited a second or two before continuing, "As you stated earlier, intrigue is not evidence. But what I just heard on that tape is more than enough to make me think our war hero might be telling the truth."

"I knew that before hearing the tape."

"Well, Detective, that's why you're special," Sly said, adding, "Wouldn't you agree that we should put our heads together, see what we can come up with? We just might end up solving three homicides."

*Four*, Dantzler could have said but refrained from doing so. He didn't see the need to inform Sly about the murder of Abe Pearlstein at this time. Maybe later, after he met Sly and developed a certain level of trust with the man. Right now, Sly Douglas was a total stranger, and Dantzler was never comfortable sharing important information with someone he didn't know.

"Sure, Sly, I do think we should meet. When and where?"

"You are in Grace West's office, right? That's on Sheffield?"

"That's correct."

"I can meet you there in an hour. Will that work for you?"

"An hour is perfect."

"All right, Detective. I will see you then."

Dantzler handed the phone to Grace, said, "Call your wannabe boyfriend at the Cook County Jail and tell him you want Danny on the phone in fifteen minutes. If Frank gives you any grief, just coo. He'll cave."

"You know, kids, more often than not Jack isn't nearly as funny or clever as he thinks he is," Grace said, glancing around the table.

"Just get Danny on the phone, Grace. It's a simple request. You can handle it."

Grace glared at Dantzler, then began punching in the Cook County Jail number. "Yes, connect me to Frank, please," she said when her call was answered. While she was waiting to hear from Frank, she asked Dantzler, "Are you going to tell Danny about Abe Pearlstein?"

But Dantzler didn't respond. Instead, he bolted out of his chair and raced up the stairs.

"Well, that was just plain rude," Jenny said.

"No, Jenny, that was just Jack Dantzler being Jack Dantzler."

Upstairs, Dantzler went into his room, grabbed his cell phone, scrolled through his contacts until he found the name he was looking for, and then punched in the number. Jake Thomas answered on the third ring.

"Hey, Boss, I was just thinking about you," Jake said. "How is the case going? Is Danny holding it together?"

"Danny is doing okay, given the shitty circumstances. As for the case, I'm still in the process of collecting information. But I will say that things look a little brighter today than they did yesterday."

"Is there anything I can do to help?"

"You can answer this question for me, Jake. When you were in Afghanistan did you know a guy named Bobby Conrad?"

"Only by reputation . . . I never met him in person. I'm fairly sure I was gone by the time he got there. If our time in-country did overlap, it was only for a month or so. Plus, he was in the army, I was a Marine. Why the interest in Bobby Conrad?"

"What do you mean, you knew him by his reputation?" Dantzler asked, deflecting Jake's question. "What was his reputation?"

"If Bobby wasn't the best sniper in Afghanistan, he ranked among the top two or three. He was right up there with Chris Kyle. I consider myself to be a superb shooter, definitely in the top five or six. That's not bragging . . . my record will back me up. But Bobby was better than me." Jake went quiet, then said, "Wait. Are you saying Bobby shot that senator?"

"I think that's a very real possibility. But it's going to be difficult to prove."

"Why would Bobby assassinate an innocent civilian? Makes no sense."

"I don't believe Bobby *knew* he was killing anyone. He was set up, just like Danny was."

"It would take serious planning by some diabolical people to pull off something that complicated."

"Gotta go, Jake. I'm getting ready to speak with Danny. I'll tell him you were asking about him."

Dantzler closed his phone and headed back downstairs.

Grace's team was sitting at the table, no one speaking or moving, tired, glazed-over eyes staring straight forward. It was almost as if the group was quietly posing while Da Vinci was painting another masterpiece. Grace held the phone to her ear, saw Dantzler enter the room, switched it to speaker, and placed it on the table.

"Frank is getting with Danny," she said to Dantzler. "Shouldn't be much longer."

It wasn't. Within a matter of seconds Danny was on the phone.

"Hey, Grace," he said. "How are things going?"

"We're doing everything we can, Danny," Grace said, adding, "Jack is here with me. He has some questions for you."

"Sure. What do you want to ask?"

Dantzler said, "Danny, when you were overseas did you know Bobby Conrad?"

"Bobby? Yeah, I knew him. We went on a couple of missions together."

"Good shooter?"

"*Great* shooter. The best one around when I was over there. Why are you asking about Bobby?"

"His name came up during my investigation. Not sure what it means at this point. Nothing. most likely."

"Bobby was a sniper," Danny said. "Are you saying he might have been the one who pulled the trigger and killed that senator?"

"No, that's not what I'm saying," Dantzler lied. "Right now, I'm simply gathering facts."

"Well, here's a fact for you: Bobby would never do something like that. Everyone will tell you he's a solid stand-up guy."

"You're probably right." Dantzler took a deep breath, let it out, and then said, "Danny, I have some really bad news to give you. Abe Pearlstein is dead. I hate having to hit you with this on the phone, but I thought you needed to know."

"Abe is dead? When? How?"

"He was murdered yesterday afternoon, not long after I met with him."

"He was murdered because of me, wasn't he?"

"Don't even think that, Danny. You had nothing to do with his death. Bad people killed Abe, and I intend to find out who those bastards are."

"I revered that old guy."

"And he felt the same way about you, Danny."

"Now he's gone."

"Yes, he's gone. Now I need to find the ones who took his life."

"God, I don't even know how to describe this. It's like a nightmare that is never going to end."

"It will end, Danny. You just have to keep believing that, okay?"

"I'm willing myself to think positive thoughts, but it's damn hard to do."

When the call ended, Maggie and Mary-Louise were both wiping tears from their eyes. Angela and Jenny were holding their emotions together, but not without great effort. Edward had his head bowed, eyes closed, like he was praying.

"You didn't tell Danny about Bobby Conrad and Molly Jackson," Grace noted.

"Hearing about Abe was bad enough. Telling him about those other two deaths would be piling on. I saw no need to do that."

"You're absolutely right, of course."

"Danny said he didn't know how to describe what's happening to him," Dantzler stated. "Well, I have the perfect word to describe it."

"What word?" asked Edward, without looking up.

"Kafkaesque."

# Chapter Fourteen

Detective Sly Douglas arrived a few minutes after Dantzler concluded his talk with Danny. Douglas parked on the street behind Dantzler's Mercedes, exited his car, moved quickly toward the house, and entered without knocking. Spying Grace, he hurried over and shook her hand. Grace then introduced him to her team, saving Dantzler for last.

"It's an honor to meet someone who is perfect," Sly said, grinning. "Perfection is in short supply these days."

Before Dantzler could respond Grace ordered her troops back to work. They scattered, reluctantly, clearly not pleased with having been dismissed from where the main action would be taking place. But being loyal soldiers they left without complaining.

Dantzler and Sly shook hands, then sat across from each other at the table. Grace, still standing, asked Sly if he wanted something to drink. "I realize it's too early for the hard stuff," she told him, "but I can get you Diet Coke, coffee, water."

When Sly turned down her offer she took the seat at the head of the table. As Grace settled in, Dantzler observed his new-found partner.

Sly Douglas was a heavy-set man in his early forties, thick but in no way could he be described as fat. Beefy, yes, but not overweight. As a young man, before age began to make its presence felt, he had probably been muscular and strong. Even now, Dantzler concluded, the man would be a formidable challenge for anyone looking to cause him grief. He had dark hair that had begun to go gray at the temples, hazel eyes. and a prominent nose. He also had a scar that curled from beneath his left eye down to the corner of his mouth.

"Do you object to me getting this little pow-wow started?" Sly asked Dantzler.

"Not at all."

"Earlier, you indicated that you've spoken to Danny Kafka. How long did your conversation last?"

"I spoke with him for a little over an hour."

"Thanks to the good Counselor here," Sly nodded at Grace, "I only had about ten minutes with him before she sent me packing. Therefore, I think it's safe to say that you know more about what's happening with Danny Kafka's case than I do. Truth is, I'm standing alone in my world. Because of that, why don't you fill me in on what you know? Then I'll share what I have, and we can hopefully begin to put two and two together. That way, maybe we will unravel what I see as a well-orchestrated and complex conspiracy."

"I'll give you well-orchestrated, Sly, but not complex. Pulling it off took serious planning, yes, but once the pieces were in place, the execution of the plan was relatively simple."

"Tell me how you see it unfolding."

"For reasons unknown to us, Dana Shapiro had to be elimi-nated. Those who wanted her gone needed a plan. An assassination was their choice. Having made that decision, their first task was to find an assassin. At the same time, they had to come up with a phony shooter. A fall guy. Someone, somehow, knew that a Medal of Honor recipient was a struggling actor in New York. That made Danny the perfect choice for the role. They contacted Danny's agent, saying they wanted to schedule a screen test. The next day two guys showed up at Danny's apartment, where they filmed the speech we've all seen on TV. They made Danny handle two rifles, one we see in that tape, a second one we don't see. Next day, Danny gets word that the movie role is his. He's also told that he'll be flying to Chicago, and that a suite will be reserved for him in the Blackstone Renaissance Hotel. He follows the instructions, gets to Chicago, checks in, and waits. We know what happened next—Dana is murdered, and the FBI shows up to arrest Danny."

"Okay, I'm with you so far. But that brings us to my two murder victims. How do you tie their deaths into this plan?" Sly asked.

"Bobby Conrad was recruited in much the same way Danny was," answered Dantzler. "The people behind this now needed an actual sniper, which, of course, Bobby was. He was contacted and told there was a movie role that fit him like a glove. He would play the part of a sniper. Bobby jumped at the chance. On Friday, he's told where to go and what time to be there. He shows up, is handed the rifle, scopes out Dana Shapiro, thinking all the time that it's a stand-in actress he's assassinating. He fires the shot, Dana goes down, blood flies everywhere—all part of what Bobby assumes is a make-believe scene. He leaves the rifle behind, exits the building, and at some point later in the afternoon he goes to an address where his handler had told him he was to be paid. He gets there, they kill him. Molly begins to grow concerned, she goes looking for him, and they kill her. Those two are silenced forever, Danny takes the rap. Nothing complex about that."

"So . . . you don't think Bobby was involved in this plot?" Sly said.

"No. He actually thought he was working on a movie. Molly confirmed that for us when she said, 'Did the shoot take longer than expected?' She's telling us that Bobby went to film his scene, and that he should have already returned home. He hadn't, and she was wondering why he was running late. Bobby Conrad was a fall guy just like Danny was."

"Complex or not, that's one cunning, evil plan," Grace said.

"But not a perfect one," Dantzler replied. "They made a few mistakes along the way, beginning with what Danny did in the war. My hunch is they assumed that if a guy receives the Medal of Honor he had to be a sniper. They got that wrong; Danny was never a sniper. The next mistake involved the rifles. Danny was asked to handle two rifles, but he was only asked to hold up one during the filming of his speech. It was the wrong one. On the film, he says he will use the AKM to kill Dana Shapiro. But he didn't; she was killed by an M107, presumably from a shot fired by Bobby Conrad. As a trained sniper, Bobby would be comfortable and very familiar with the M107. It's a sniper's weapon; the AKM is not."

"Danny Kafka's fingerprints were found on the murder weapon, Bobby's weren't," Sly said. "If Bobby was the shooter, shouldn't his prints be on the weapon?"

"Where did you find Danny's prints on the M107?"

"The stock and the barrel."

"But none on the trigger or anywhere close to the trigger, right?"

"Right."

"That's because they were wiped clean by the people handling Bobby."

Sly said, "Earlier, you stated that two men came to see Danny in his apartment. When I spoke with him he only mentioned one, but he didn't give me a name."

"Carson Welles. But don't bother looking him up; I've already tried. That name is phonier than a three-dollar bill. The second man is even more of a mystery. According to Danny, the guy never said a word the entire time he was in the apartment."

"Another question I didn't have time to ask Danny was how the bogus movie people knew where he lived. Manhattan's a big place."

"They got his address either from the Screen Actors Guild or Actors' Equity."

"How do you know that?"

"His agent, Abe Pearlstein, told me."

"You've spoken with him?" Sly asked.

"I have. He wasn't able to give me anything that was helpful." Dantzler rubbed his eyes with the back of his hands, then said, "Abe Pearlstein was murdered yesterday afternoon, an hour or two after I left him. A single gunshot to the back of his head. An execution-style hit."

"Who knew you were going to New York?"

"Only the people in this office."

"A coincidence, then?"

"I'm not a big believer in coincidences, Sly. Abe was murdered *because* he spoke with me. That means one of two things: either I was followed to New York, or Abe's office was under surveillance. I show up, they see me going into his office, and that causes concern. When I'm gone, they go in, get Abe to give them my name, if they didn't already have it, and then blow him away."

"If you were followed, that means the folks working here aren't the only ones who know about you," Sly noted.

*Or someone working here leaked my name.* "I have to consider that possibility," Dantzler said.

Grace asked, "Jack, do you still have a permit to carry a weapon?"

"Of course."

"Maybe you should start carrying it."

"I'd say that's sage advice," echoed Sly. "Four innocent people are already dead. You don't want to be number five."

"No, being dead is never a good option," Dantzler admitted.

Sly poured Diet Coke into a cup, took a drink, and said, "Despite what you've told me, Detective, I doubt that my superiors can be convinced to fold the senator's death in with my investigation into the murders of Bobby Conrad and Molly Jackson. I will give it a shot, but . . . they've all seen that tape of Danny's rant about killing her. Plus, his prints are on the murder weapon. To them, that translates into this being a closed case. Any attempt I make to connect the cases will be dismissed outright. They'll order me to focus solely on the Conrad-Jackson homicides. If any connection is to be made, I'm afraid you'll have to do it."

"There is one thing that has puzzled me from the beginning," Dantzler said. "Why was the FBI in such a hurry to hand the Shapiro murder off to Chicago PD? She was a United States senator. I can't believe the Feds wouldn't take charge of the case."

"No one was more shocked than I was. In fact, we were all stunned. All I can tell you is they turned it over to us less than three hours after the senator was killed. They were out the door before beginning a serious investigation. I can assure you that not everyone was pleased with that early exit. The agent in charge was pissed when she was informed that we were taking over."

"Kate Flanagan?" asked Grace.

"Yes. I was standing a few feet away from her when she got the order to stand down. That was one angry lady. She had fire in her eyes."

"Who gave her the order?" Dantzler said.

"Don't know. It was a phone call."

"Are you familiar with her?"

"Not really. But one of the FBI agents is a buddy of mine, and she says Kate Flanagan is a damn good law enforcement officer. Says Kate's a bulldog who won't quit until she gets what she's after."

Dantzler turned to Grace, said, "Will you contact Kate and see if she will meet with me? I would really love to know who told her to stand down."

"I don't see that as a problem," Grace answered. "I'll call her first thing tomorrow morning."

"One more thing," Sly said. "When Kate was on the phone, I got the feeling that she knew Dana Shapiro. Maybe I'm way off base, but she came across as someone who was taking this murder very personally. I'd be curious to know if I'm right about that."

Dantzler said, "There's something really hinky about all this, Sly. Especially the FBI punting to you guys. That makes absolutely no sense. Nothing against Chicago PD, but the FBI has more resources than any law enforcement agency in the world. Why not utilize them in this situation?"

"They promised to make them available to us if we need them."

"Not the same. This should be their case, not Chicago PD's."

"Well, like it or not, it's in our hands."

"Who's in charge of the investigation?"

"Brooke Mason."

"What's the scouting report on her?"

"From everything I've seen or heard she's a good cop. But . . . she's awfully young. Late twenties, early thirties—somewhere in that neighborhood. Most of us were surprised when she was assigned to head up the investigation. That's high profile for a detective with so little experience on the job."

"She was given the job because someone high on the food chain wants her to move up fast," Dantzler pointed out. "If Danny gets convicted, Brooke's star rises, even though she really didn't do much. That tape and Danny's fingerprints essentially did the work for her. But she will forever be recognized as the detective whose dedicated efforts led to the conviction of Danny Kafka for the brutal murder of Dana Shapiro. That will always look good on her resume."

"Do you plan on speaking with Brooke? Share with her what you've told me?"

Dantzler thought for a few seconds before answering. "That's a good question, Sly. My inclination is to say no, I'm going to hold off for the time being. I mean, what's the point, right? They're a hundred-percent certain that Danny is the killer. I'm not going to waste precious time trying to convince her otherwise. Speaking with Brooke Mason is not on my immediate to-do list."

Sly stood, stretched, said, "Detective Dantzler, I may be the only cop in Chicago PD who believes Danny Kafka is innocent. I'm in his corner. I'll help any way I can, even if I have to fly under the radar."

"I appreciate that," Dantzler said as he and Grace walked Sly to the door. "For the time being I think it best if we keep our conversation private. Sharing it could put someone else in harm's way. Whoever is behind these crimes has already eliminated four people. I don't want to provide them with more targets."

"Makes sense," Sly said, shaking Dantzler's hand.

After he was gone, Grace closed the door, and said, "Seems like a decent man. But was he helpful at all?"

"What did you expect, Grace? That Sly was going to waltz in here and hand us answers to our two basic questions: Who is behind the plot to murder Dana Shapiro, and why was she singled out for elimination? That was never going to happen. But yes, he is a decent guy, and he might be helpful to us in the future."

"Would you care for a drink, Jack? I'm having one."

"No, I'm going upstairs to pack."

"Are you leaving?"

"I'm heading back to Lexington first thing tomorrow morning. I need to get some things."

"Your Glock?"

"That's at the top of my list."

# Chapter Fifteen

Being keenly aware of what was happening around him had always been part of Dantzler's DNA. His acuity for being alert and forever cautious was as highly developed as his five natural senses. Vigilance was a requirement. For a cop, how could it be otherwise? For nearly three decades he had tracked down and arrested dozens of cold-blooded killers, some of whom had been released from prison during the intervening years. Those were the ones he had to be on the lookout for. Any one of them might get it in his head to seek revenge. Same goes for the families and loved ones of those still incarcerated. Although a jury rendered the verdict and a judge handed down the sentence, it was usually the high-profile detective who was the target for vengeance. He was that guy.

Being wary could mean the difference between staying alive or getting killed.

However, not once in all his years as a cop had he experienced a feeling of paranoia. Wary, yes, constantly believing someone was out to get him, no. Feelings of paranoia were *not* part of his DNA. But after today he could no longer make that claim. On the drive back to Lexington he had the feeling that a white Toyota Avalon was following him. His suspicion grew even stronger when the Avalon continued on after he pulled into a rest area, only to then glide in behind him once he was back on the interstate. For the remainder of the trip the Avalon was in and out of sight. By the time he arrived in Lexington it was nowhere to be seen.

When he got home, he unpacked, fixed a Pernod and orange juice, and went out onto the deck. Thinking about it now, he concluded that the whole thing had been imagined. He hadn't been followed by a white Avalon, or by any other car. What he'd experienced wasn't paranoia; his mind had simply played tricks on him. Four murders, unknown killers on the loose, the sudden need to carry a weapon . . . add all that up and it was no shock that his imagination got the best of him.

Shrugging it off as a weird experience, he picked up his cell phone and checked for messages. He had several, including three that had to do with upcoming tennis lessons he was scheduled to give. Those were out of the question at this point. He called the three students to let them know that he would not be available for the next few weeks, and then asked if they had a problem working with David Bloom. They didn't. Next, he had to call Bloom and inform him of the scheduled time for each lesson. He knew Bloom would bitch and complain, saying this necessitated his having to reschedule sessions with his patients, but that was a false front. In truth, Bloom enjoyed giving tennis lessons more than Dantzler did.

Dantzler punched in Sean's number and waited, fully expecting to be ordered to leave a message. But he was surprised when Sean answered after four rings, sounding chipper than usual for a late afternoon.

"Ready for a drink?" Dantzler asked.

"McCarthy's?" Sean said.

"Nah, come to my place. I have Guinness and Jameson here."

"Be there in thirty."

Dantzler responded to the remaining messages, then put in a call to Grace West. He wanted to know if she had made contact with Kate Flanagan, the FBI agent. Grace said she'd made the call and left a message informing Kate who Dantzler was, and then asked her to get in touch with him at her earliest convenience.

Sean breezed in twenty minutes later, made a stop in the kitchen, filled a glass with Jameson, and then joined Dantzler on the deck. Having been in court earlier in the day, he was dressed in a suit and tie, and he wore a tired look on his face that defied his upbeat demeanor.

"You know, Sean, in the past couple of days I've been to Chicago, New York City, back to Chicago and then to Lexington, and I look better than you do," Dantzler quipped. "Don't you ever sleep?"

"Oh, I grab a few hours here and there. You know how it is."

"You really need to start taking better care of yourself. You're not that young anymore."

"I'll take that under advisement," Sean said after taking a drink. "Now that my inadequate sleep habits have been discussed, why don't you tell me how the Danny Kafka case is progressing?"

For the next twenty minutes, Dantzler laid it all out for Sean, stopping only briefly to make them both a second drink. Dantzler's recitation went straight from his first meeting with Danny, to his talk with Abe Pearlstein, Abe's subsequent death, the FBI handing the case to Chicago PD, and, finally, his conversation with detective Sly Douglas about the murders of Bobby Conrad and Molly Jackson. When Dantzler's spiel concluded, both men remained silent for almost two minutes. It was Sean who spoke first.

"Hate to tell you this, pal, but you ain't got nothing," Sean said.

"Other than four murder victims and an innocent man facing life in prison, I'd judge your statement to be one-hundred percent on the money," Dantzler responded.

"What's your plan?"

"Truthfully, Sean, I don't have one. But unless I catch a lucky break it's going to be virtually impossible to save Danny. Trouble is, I can't see where that break might come from."

"And you have no idea who this Carson Welles really is?"

Dantzler nodded, said, "All I do know is that his name isn't Carson Welles."

"Locating him is the key," Sean said.

"I agree. But where do you start looking for a phantom?"

"You have to find a way to bring the FBI back on board."

"I have a call in to an agent; hopefully, I can convince her to take a closer look. If she turns me down I'm royally screwed."

"Here's something else you need to consider, Jack. Let's say you do get lucky and find the guilty folks. What do you do then? You're no longer a cop, which means you don't have the authority to start arresting people. You would need someone in law enforcement to handle that for you."

"Sean, if I get that far I'm not gonna concern myself with who puts the cuffs on the bastards. But if it should play out that way, Sly Douglas will be more than ready to help out. He's on our side."

"On a lesser note," Sean said, standing, "How are things working out between you and Grace? Is she still busting your balls?"

"Both Grace and my balls are just fine, Sean. Thanks for inquiring."

"Hey, what are friends for, right?"

---

BY TWO A.M., Dantzler had been in bed three hours yet sleep eluded him. His earlier feeling of paranoia had returned, wormed their way into his thoughts, and kept him tossing, turning and fighting his pillow like a madman. The feeling was like an ache that creeps into an old man's bones on a rainy afternoon. No matter how hard he tried to put those thoughts out of his mind, he couldn't. Getting any sleep tonight, he finally acknowledged, wasn't in the cards.

That white Toyota Avalon had not only followed him to Lexington, it was now parked next to him in his bed. But had he truly been followed by that car? he repeatedly asked himself. Or was his imagination playing cruel tricks on his mind? Yes, he had seen a white Avalon, and yes, it had trailed him for many miles during his trip back to Lexington. Then somewhere along the way it disappeared. Gone, out of sight, as if it had never been there in the first place. Why, then, did he suspect that it had been tailing him? He had no reason to believe it had been. For all he knew more than one white

Avalon kept drifting in and out of his rear-view mirror. Goodness knows there are thousands of them on the highways.

After a lengthy inner struggle he finally managed to convince himself that a white Toyota Avalon had not followed him to Lexington. That simply did not happen. There was, however, a second wave of paranoia, and this one wasn't so easily dismissed. It was triggered by a single question from Sly Douglas:

*Who knew you were going to New York?* Then: *If you were followed, that means the folks working here aren't the only ones who knew about you.*

The implication was clear: There might be a traitor on Grace's team.

Dantzler doubted that anyone in Grace's office had leaked his itinerary to someone on the outside, either intentionally or accidentally. They all appeared to be extremely loyal to Grace and deeply involved in helping get Danny Kafka out from under this murder rap. Ticking off the names of each employee, he couldn't land on one that he envisioned as likely being a traitor. And yet, unreasonable as it seemed, he had no choice but to consider the possibility.

The alternative option was the one he thought most likely. That someone, while watching Abe Pearlstein's office, witnessed Dantzler going inside. After Dantzler was gone, that person—or persons—went into the office, questioned Abe, forced him to give up Dantzler's name, and then put a bullet in the old guy's brain. Their mission was a two-way success: a potential witness was silenced forever, and they learned the name of an outside investigator.

But if that second scenario was accurate, didn't it lend credence to his having been tailed by the Toyota Avalon? Were Abe's killers in that car? Had they followed him to Lexington? Was Dantzler their next target?

Or was his paranoia getting out of control?

He didn't have answers for any of those questions, but there was one thing he did know for certain—beginning tomorrow, his trusty Glock would be glued to his hip.

RENEE HAD BUT ONE GOAL–TO be in the movies. Seeing herself up on that big screen, being more famous than a Kardashian, had been her dream since she was barely old enough to walk. Stardom hadn't happened for her yet, but the man she was now with could change all that in a nanosecond. All he had to do was pick up his phone and make the call. He was in the film business, highly respected, powerful, and judging by the size of his house, very successful. His place in Bel-Air was ten times bigger than the one she grew up in back in Lake Charles, Louisiana. While the house might not rank as a classic Hollywood mansion, it was damn close.

He was seventy-one, overweight, and bald. Renee was twenty-nine, thin, tan, and thanks to a nip here and a tuck there, she was a looker. She called him "Mr. K" and he called her "Kitten." When they were together she had but a single chore, and that was to keep him sexually satisfied. She didn't view that as a particularly pleasant task, but she desperately longed to be a movie star, so she acted the part of a willing—and enthusiastic—lover. She also played on his ego by constantly bragging about the size of his penis, which, among the many she had seen in the past, was on the small side. But no man wants to hear that, so she described it with words like massive or huge. A desperate girl has to say desperate things if she hopes to break into the movies.

They were sitting naked on the sofa. He was nursing a gin and tonic, she was running her fingers through the hair on his chest, occasionally letting her hand wander down between his legs. Nothing much happening there, nor was there likely to be for the foreseeable future. He had popped a Viagra a few hours ago, she got him off twice, once by hand, once orally, and now "Tiny," (her secret pet name for his cock) was down for the count. Her chores for the day were finished.

When the phone rang, Mr. K grumbled about a call coming at midnight, put down his glass, and punched the Speaker button on his phone. He stopped grumbling and sat up straight when he heard the caller's gruff voice and Russian accent. His heart pounded, and his blood pressure shot up through the roof.

"It appears as though we raised idiot sons," the Russian said before Mr. K could say hello.

"Are you just now finding that out?" Mr. K laughed. "Hell, man, I've known it for years."

"This is not the time to be clever. Our idiot sons have left us with a potential problem."

"Problems can be solved."

"Not always."

"What problem are you referring to?"

"The rifle our war hero had with him on that tape."

"What about it?"

"It was the wrong one," the Russian announced. "Our idiot sons should've had him holding up the other one. The one that was actually used."

"You're worrying over nothing."

"Maybe, maybe not. But until this matter is resolved to my satisfaction, I'll worry."

"Everything has gone exactly as planned, hasn't it?" Mr. K asked. "The senator is dead, our war hero is behind bars, they have him confessing to the murder, his prints are on the weapon, the FBI is off the case, and anyone who could pose a threat to us has been eliminated. It couldn't have gone any better. My advice: Open a bottle of vodka and chill out."

"Your advice is not worth one single ruble. Because of our two idiots, because of their blunder, we now have a private investigator looking into the case. He's been hired by the war hero's defense attorney. His name is Jack Dantzler. Look him up on the Internet. What you'll learn is that until very recently he was a homicide detective in Kentucky. Look even closer and you'll see that he was a damn good one. He never failed to solve a case. Guy with a record like that doesn't strike me as the kind of investigator who walks away until he finds what he's looking for."

"We've already killed four people," Mr. K reminded. "If he becomes too much of a problem, we'll make him number five."

"We do not live in Stalin's Russia. In this country, bodies can't be kept buried forever. They have a way of popping up. Taking out Dantzler would be a huge risk."

"We'll keep an eye on him, and . . ."

"That's already being done."

"If he gets too close, we eliminate him. If not, we leave him alone. Any problems with that and . . ."

The Russian slammed down his phone before Mr. K completed his last sentence. He was pissed, Mr. K knew, and that wasn't a good thing. He didn't ever want to be on that crazy Russian's bad side. We might not live in Stalin's Russia, but a bullet to the back of the head gets the job done anywhere, in any era.

After turning off the phone, Mr. K picked up his glass and drained its contents dry. He set the empty glass back on the table, shifted his body slightly to the left, leaned down, and gave his young mistress a kiss on the lips.

"Kitten, you heard things tonight that were not meant for your lovely ears," he whispered. "That's a bad break for you."

"I didn't hear a word," she said. "I was sound asleep."

"Oh, I don't think that's true," he responded, taking hold of her head and giving it a savage twist. Bones cracked as her neck snapped, killing her instantly, a surprised look on her face. He closed her eyes, leaned over, and gave her a gentle kiss on the lips.

Standing, he carefully laid her body on the sofa and walked over to the liquor cabinet. "You never would have hit the bigtime, Kitten," he said after filling his glass with gin and tonic. "I didn't have the heart to tell you this, but you lacked that mysterious 'it' factor all the great ones have. Stardom was never in the cards for you."

# Chapter Sixteen

Dantzler felt surprisingly good for a man who didn't get any sleep at all last night. A long, hot shower woke him up, and a glass of orange juice and a bowl of cereal were enough to kick up his energy level several notches and put some pep in his step. Failure to get adequate rest wasn't a winning formula; it would catch up with him in the long run. As an ex-athlete, he understood this better than most. The human body can take only so much abuse before breaking down. Perhaps he should follow the advice he'd given to Sean and try to get more sleep.

After putting his bowl and glass in the sink he went out onto the deck. The morning was clear and cool, thick mist floated above the lake like a ghostly cloud, and the crickets and frogs seemed to be battling for vocal supremacy. It was one of those mornings that made you appreciate being alive. Unless, of course, you were Danny Kafka sitting in a jail cell. There, in that hell hole, every day was dark and depressing.

Dantzler was reaching for his cell phone when it buzzed. Checking the Caller ID, he saw that the call was from Bobby Brennan, the NYC homicide detective.

"Bobby, tell me you have good news for me," Dantzler said, side-stepping their usual good-natured banter.

"Well, I have good news and bad news for you," Bobby replied. "The good news is that you are no longer a suspect in the murder investigation of Abraham Pearlstein."

"That's a relief. What cleared me?"

"Security cameras, of course. At twelve-eighteen, you were observed entering the hallway separating the Pearlstein Building from the one next to it. You were seen leaving at two twenty-eight. Abe made three phone calls after you left. You never re-entered the premises, so we ruled you out as Abe's killer. I'm kidding, of course. You were never a suspect."

"If the cameras caught sight of me, that means they should have caught the killer."

"Killers, plural . . . there were two. They went into the hallway at three forty-six and came out at four fifty-one," Bobby said. "Now for the bad news. There are no cameras in that hallway or anywhere on the second floor where Abe had his office. There are plenty out on the streets, which our killers were keenly aware of. These dudes aren't criminal virgins—they've danced this dance before. One kept his head down and away from the camera while his partner had one hand up to his face. We never got a look at either of their faces. One was tall and thin, his partner was shorter and stockier. Before they turned the corner and came into view of other cameras, they both had put on baseball caps and most likely separated. The area was very crowded at that time, making it easy for them to blend in. In short, we have *bubkes*."

"And Abe? How much damage did they inflict on him?"

"You mean, other than a twenty-two slug to the back of his head? Plenty. The autopsy revealed serious bruising on virtually his entire upper torso. His jaw was fractured, he had two cracked ribs, both knees had been badly beaten, and they broke all five fingers on his right hand. There were burns on his left arm. They covered his mouth with duct tape to keep him quiet while he was being tortured."

"Jesus."

"Clearly, the killers were after information."

"Yeah, they wanted to know the name of the guy who just spent two hours in Abe's office," Dantzler said, adding, "and that would be me."

"You can bet they got what they were after."

"I'm sure they did. No one could withstand torture like that for very long. But I'll give Abe credit. He made the bastards work hard for the information they were seeking. He had to be a tough hombre."

"One more item I'll share with you, Dantzler, although given the current set of circumstances I'm not sure how much relevance it really has. Abe left a will, one he made revisions to last week. In the new one he left fifty percent of his entire worth to Danny Kafka, which makes Danny a rich boy. But as we both know, unless Danny can somehow escape this murder charge, it only means he'll be a very wealthy prisoner."

"How much money are we talking about?"

"Ole Abe may have dressed like a pauper, but he wasn't. According to his attorney, who is also Abe's cousin, the old guy was worth somewhere in the neighborhood of twenty million bucks. Seems Abe hit the stock market jackpot back in the fifties and sixties, when certain companies were just beginning to take off, thus making Abe a guy with an impressive portfolio. Half of Abe's fortune goes to Danny."

"Do you know if Abe's attorney has informed Danny about this?" asked Dantzler.

"No, he hasn't. I instructed him to hold off until I spoke with you."

"Thanks, Bobby. I don't see how telling this to Danny could do anything but add to his feelings of depression and frustration. To know he has ten million dollars in the bank, yet he might spend the rest of his life behind bars, that couldn't do anything but send him spiraling downward. No, tell the attorney to keep this under wraps, at least for the time being."

"What about you, Dantzler? If Abe did give up your name, you know what that means don't you?"

"Yeah, I'd better watch my back."

---

DANTZLER'S ENERGY level was sky high after ending his conversation with Bobby Brennan. He wasn't quite sure what caused the sudden spike, whether it was the news that Danny Kafka was now a wealthy young man, or the almost-certain realization that a pair of deadly killers might have him in their crosshairs. Perhaps it was a combination of the two. Either way, he was jacked up. His question now: What to do with all this energy?

His answer came almost instantly: Call Emily Rosburg, Dana Shapiro's personal assistant and closest confidant, and see what, if any, information she can provide. He dug through his briefcase until he found the paper Jenny had given him with Emily's contact information on it. Picking up his cell phone he started to punch in Emily's number. But then he hesitated, remembering something he saw on TV late last night. Dana Shapiro's memorial service had been held yesterday afternoon. Perhaps now wasn't the best time to give Emily a call. Maybe waiting a few days would be more considerate. Holding off would give her more time for some of the grief to wear off.

But waiting was no longer an option, Dantzler decided. He had to begin digging for the truth, and if being inconsiderate to a grieving Emily Rosburg was the shovel, then so be it. Time for her would move on very quickly. Time for Danny Kafka would hardly seem to move at all. Given that set of parameters he had no choice but to make the call.

Emily answered on the second ring, her voice soft and low. She listened quietly as Dantzler identified himself, let her know who he was working for, and told her the purpose of his call. When she responded, her voice was barely above a whisper.

"Grace West is defending the man who shot Dana, isn't she?" Emily asked.

"She's defending Danny Kafka, yes. But Danny isn't guilty."

"According to what's on that tape, his guilt seems clear-cut to me. And didn't I hear that his fingerprints were on the murder weapon? That seems fairly conclusive."

"Emily, he was set up by some very bad people."

"Naturally, I would expect you to say something like that. After all, his attorney is signing your paycheck. But can you prove it?"

"Not yet, but I'm working on it."

"Why do you believe he's innocent?"

"Think about this, Emily: Why would Danny Kafka, a war hero and a struggling actor, a guy who has zero interest in American politics, assassinate a United States senator, one he knew absolutely nothing about? And how is it that the FBI, even before they had Danny's prints on that rifle, zeroed in on him as the shooter? And finally, how did they know Danny was even in Chicago, much less where he was staying? Ask yourself those questions. If you do, and if you're the least bit objective, you have to entertain the possibility that Danny was framed. And if that's true, it means the senator's real killer—or killers—is still out there."

"Right now, all I can think about is that my friend is gone and I'll never see her again," Emily said, her voice choked with emotion. "You'll probably think this is a horrible thing to say, but I really don't care who did it. Find the killer, don't find the killer . . . neither one brings Dana back to life."

"Emily, I was a homicide cop for a long time. Believe me, I know exactly how you feel. You're angry and you're hurt. That's understandable. But Dana was a senator and an attorney. Those jobs are all about uncovering the truth. Do you really believe Dana would rest easy if she thought for a second that an innocent man might be convicted of a crime he didn't commit? I don't think so, and I'll wager you don't either."

"I don't see how I can be of any help in a murder investigation."

"Maybe you can't. But we won't know until we give it a try."

"What exactly do you want from me?"

"Answers to a few basic questions regarding Dana's personal life. I was told you knew her better than anyone. I'm sure she shared things with you that she didn't share with anyone else. Private stuff that no one knew about but you and Dana. That's why I've come to you."

"Okay, what's your first question?" Emily asked.

"Was Dana involved with anyone?"

"You mean, like, dating?"

"Yes."

"Are you aware that Dana only recently became a widow?"

"Yes, I am aware of that."

"So why would you ask me that question?"

"Her husband died more than three years ago. Life goes on, people move forward, even those who have suffered the loss of a spouse. New relationships can happen."

"Dana didn't move on. She was still grieving for Ben. Next question."

"What about her financial situation? By that I mean, did she have any outstanding or sizable debts that you know about?"

"No, Dana knew how to take care of a dollar."

"Was Ben a gambler?"

"How would I know that?" Emily said, frustration rising in her voice. "All I can tell you is that Dana never said anything about it to me."

"Did Dana have any enemies that you're aware of?"

"She was a United States senator, so, yeah, she had enemies. Her office received hundreds of phone calls, letters, and e-mails from unhappy constituents and ideological opponents. Dana was a liberal, a progressive, so she caught hell from conservatives who felt she was doing too much. Liberals complained that she wasn't doing enough. She caught flak from both sides."

"Did any correspondence threaten her life?"

"Sure, there were a few crackpots who made threats. Those were turned over to the authorities. After that, I can't tell you what happened."

"Emily, I'm facing a desperate situation here. Danny Kafka is facing an even more desperation situation. I can't help him unless you help me. Is there one thing Dana told you, a piece of information no one else knows, a deep secret between the two of you that you can share with me?"

"Well, there is . . ." a pause, then, "no, nothing like that comes to mind. Sorry."

"Emily, I was a detective for a very long time," Dantzler said, softly. "Over the years I've interviewed thousands of honest and dishonest individuals. I could usually tell rather quickly which ones were telling the truth and which ones were lying. I also developed a keen sense of when a person had something important to say but felt constrained to let it out. Right now, I have that feeling about you. That you have something you want to tell me, but probably because of a promise you made to Dana, you are reluctant to share it with me. If I'm right, if you do know something that might be important, please tell me. I need to hear it."

"It's just that . . . like you said, I promised Dana to keep it to myself. If I tell you, I'm betraying my oath to her. I can't do that and look at myself in the mirror ever again."

"Will you be able to look in that mirror if an innocent man gets life in prison for a crime he didn't commit? Can you live with that outcome, knowing you might have been the difference between him being found guilty, or his being set free? Ask yourself those questions, Emily. Then ask yourself what Dana would want you to do."

"If I do tell you, will you promise to keep it between the two of us?"

"I can't make that promise, Emily, because I haven't a clue where your information will lead me. What I can do is promise you that it will stay between us until circumstances demand that I share it with law enforcement, should that situation ever arise. You have my word on that."

"Dana was going to be named Ambassador to Russia," Emily stated after several seconds of silence. "She was offered the position two weeks ago, and she accepted. Only about a half-dozen people know at this point."

"Why is that such a big secret?"

"Because the current ambassador has been diagnosed with cancer and will soon be retiring. Until he returns home and officially resigns from the position, the announcement that Dana will be his replacement was on hold."

"Who offered her the position?"

"The president."

"She has to be confirmed, right?"

"That won't be a problem. Dana was a well-respected senator, her mother was from Russia, she was fluent in the language, and she had a degree in Russian History. She would have sailed through those confirmation hearings with no problems whatsoever."

Dantzler said, "Was she willing to vacate her senate seat? It's my understanding that she still had a couple of years remaining on her term."

"She couldn't wait to leave the senate, which she regarded as having become broken and totally ineffective. She detested the lack of bipartisanship, the unwillingness of the two parties to work together for the greater good. Today's politicians focus on getting re-elected rather than doing what is best for the country. Dana was appalled by their lack of moral courage. Most of all, though, she hated having to constantly beg for money; that was an endless process. She once told me that with every penny she asked for, every deal she made, and every promise she gave, she lost a little part of her soul. No, she couldn't get out of the senate fast enough."

Dantzler let this bit of news settle in. Was it important, or was it extraneous and insignificant? He had no way of knowing at this time. What he did know was that it merited a deeper look.

Emily broke the silence, saying, "Since I've already broken my word to Dana, I might as well share something else with you. When you ask if Dana was seeing anyone I told you she wasn't. That wasn't entirely truthful."

"So Dana was involved with someone?"

"I hesitate to use the word involved because I don't think Dana was ready for a serious relationship. But . . . there was a guy she went out with a couple of times. His name was Todd, and according to Dana, he was several years younger than she was. She described him as being very handsome, polite, and a war veteran. I got the feeling that she found him to be very attractive."

"Why do you think the relationship failed to go anywhere?"

"I don't think it was a relationship. I believe she just thought he was an interesting guy."

"Well, relationship or not, it ended rather quickly. Any idea why?"

"Dana said he had some real problems that needed to be addressed."

"Drugs?"

"Yes, drugs, and possibly PTSD. Dana offered to get him into a rehab center, but I never heard if he actually entered the facility. Dana didn't say."

"When did they first get together?"

"Six weeks ago."

"Did Dana say where they went?"

"No, she never told me that."

"Todd, huh? Did you happen to catch his last name?"

"Nope, just Todd. All Dana said about him was that he came from Los Angeles, and his father was a movie producer."

That little nugget of information caused Dantzler's heart to skip a beat.

"Have you given this information to the FBI?" he inquired.

"Not the FBI, no. I did talk to a female detective from Chicago PD."

"Brooke Mason?"

"Yes, that's the one."

"What did you tell her?"

"Everything I just told you, except for the stuff about the Russian ambassadorship and the Todd guy."

"Thanks for speaking with me, Emily," Dantzler said. "I really appreciate it. The information you've given me could be very helpful. As for the promise I made to you, I'll do everything in my power to keep it. Good luck in the future, and I am sorry for the loss of your friend."

Dantzler closed his phone, tossed it on the table, and leaned back, knowing at least one issue had become crystal clear: at some point in the future he might be going to Hollywood.

# Chapter Seventeen

Mr. K stood next to the fireplace as two men wrapped Kitten's body in a blanket and then bound it with three strips of duct tape. Once that was done, they picked up her body, hauled it out to their van, and placed it in the back. After getting the nod to leave from Mr. K, they climbed in the van and drove away. Their destination was a funeral home in West Hollywood, where a small man named Henry would be waiting to meet them. Henry, the owner of the place, wasn't normally on the job at two a.m. Dealing with the dead at such a late hour wasn't in his job description. But when Mr. K called, Henry went to work, asking no questions and offering no complaints. As he saw it, losing sleep was a small price to pay for earning ten grand in cash just to torch another body.

This wasn't the first time Mr. K sent a corpse Henry's way, and it likely wouldn't be the last. Mr. K didn't bury the dead; he had their ashes dumped into the Pacific. That's what would happen on this night. When this poor woman—Henry didn't know her name, nor did he care to know—had been cremated, he would put her ashes in a cheap box, which the two men who brought her body to the funeral home would then drive up Pacific Coast Highway until they found a secluded spot, one they had used on past occasions. Then one of the two men would wade several yards out into the surf, flip the box upside down, and return Renee Lynn Munroe, aka "Kitten," back to the waters from which our oldest ancestors first emerged.

When the sun rose tomorrow it would be as though Kitten never existed.

Mr. K, having watched the van drive away, decided to go for a midnight swim. But after removing his robe he had a change of heart, deciding instead to sit in the hot tub. Spending time in the pool without Kitten held no interest for him. Her sexual exploits, particularly those underwater, were nothing short of spectacular. How she could give head without drowning was something of an aquatic miracle. Mr. K was certain of one thing: if giving under-water blow jobs was an Olympic event, Kitten would have claimed the gold medal.

Sitting in the hot tub, his face and upper body dripping sweat, Mr. K shifted his thoughts from Kitten to the Russian. Despite having worked with the Russian for more than a decade, he did not trust the man. He doubted that he ever would. Russians, he had long ago concluded, were strange, unhappy people who came out of the womb already completely paranoid. They simply trusted no one, especially Americans. Well, to Mr. K's way of thinking, that worked both ways. No rational American could possibly trust a Russian. And Mr. K considered himself to be a rational man.

What existed between him and the Russian was a kind of one-on-one Cold War détente. A partnership based on self-serving ambitions. Despite their mutual distrust, the interests of the two men were best served by standing together rather than tugging in separate directions. Were that to occur, mutual distrust could lead to mutual annihilation. Neither man wanted that. So they worked hand in hand with one another, while each man secretly held a knife in the other hand.

The two men met purely by chance. The Russian had a young mistress who longed to be in the movies. He sent her to an agent, who politely informed her that he wasn't interested in taking her on as a client. Two days later, the Russian and his son paid a visit to the agent. Within a matter of minutes the agent agreed to represent her. Knowing Mr. K was producing a horror movie and in need of several young female actors, the agent sent her to meet with him. Mr. K liked what he saw. She was young, beautiful, and exotic. Perfect not only for a part in his movie, but also as his mistress. His dream was short-lived. On the first day of filming, the Russian showed up on the set and began pawing at the young actress. She seemed to not only welcome his advances, she also enjoyed them. This made it painfully clear to Mr. K that she was the Russian's property, and his alone. Making a play for her might be a dangerous and unhealthy undertaking. Staying away was the wise thing to do. So he kept his distance.

But the two men did talk—size each other up would be the more appropriate assessment—and within a couple of hours and a few drinks, they agreed that an alliance could be financially beneficial to both parties. Neither man trusted the other, but greed has a way of breaking down or eliminating barriers, especially those standing in the way of making money. And the two men did lust for money.

Since that fateful meeting more than a decade ago they had worked together on many occasions. Normally, the Russian had something that needed to be taken care of or handled in a specific way, and Mr. K saw that it got done, performing the required tasks without asking too many questions. Where the Russian made his money, or who paid him, Mr. K didn't know, nor did he care to know. All that mattered was that he got what was coming his way. Money, not answers to questions, was what he wanted.

Those previous jobs varied in size, scope, and degree of difficulty, but none came anywhere close to matching this most-recent job. Not even remotely similar. Killing a United States senator was serious business with extreme consequences if they got caught. This meant there was no room for screw-ups. Execute the job perfectly, or spend the rest of your life locked away in a cold prison cell. There was no neutral ground.

The Russian informed him about the job six weeks ago, saying the senator had to be taken out on a certain day in Chicago. When

Mr. K asked the Russian how he knew of the senator's travel plans, the Russian smiled, and said, "Don't worry about that. She'll be there."

Mr. K took this to mean, don't ask too many questions.

One thing Mr. K did know—whoever was pulling the strings had to be big. And whoever that individual was, he had to be extremely wealthy. Money for this job was flying all over the place. For his part on this job, Mr. K's cut was thirty million, three times more than he'd made on any previous job. If he was getting paid that much, he had to believe the Russian was getting an even bigger cut. This much money being shelled out for a single assassination could only mean one thing—someone had a genuine fear of Dana Shapiro.

The Russian pressed Mr. K on the timing issue, inquiring if the plan could be implemented and executed on such short notice. Three weeks wasn't much time, but Mr. K assured the Russian that although it wouldn't be easy, it could be done. He'd never share this with the Russian, but for what he had in mind three weeks was more than ample time to put the plan together.

When Mr. K offered the Russian a brief preview of his plan, he was met with deep skepticism.

"Where will you find two shooters?" the Russian wanted to know. "Finding one will be difficult enough. It cannot be done. This plan will not work."

"Don't worry about the shooters," replied Mr. K. "I already have two in mind."

"How can you be positive that you can arrange it?"

"Hell, man, don't you know that everyone wants to be in the movies? That dream is the carrot I'll dangle to bring them into our movie. Trust me, they'll both be eager to show up."

Mr. K climbed out of the hot tub, his body pink from mid-chest down. After drying himself off with a large beach towel, he slipped on his robe, went back into the den, mixed a gin and tonic, and sat down on the sofa. His thoughts kept drifting back to what the Russian had told him . . . the news that a private investigator was now looking into the case.

This was disturbing, no question about it. True, higher-up law enforcement, namely the FBI, had taken itself out of the picture— again proving that whoever was pulling the strings had serious power—and handed off the investigation to Chicago PD. Thanks to evidence that had been planted—the tape, the fingerprints— Chicago detectives were no longer looking into the Shapiro murder. To them, it was a closed case. They were continuing to investigate the murders of Bobby Conrad and Molly Jackson, but that was also destined to hit a dead end. With no solid evidence at their disposal, Chicago PD would soon be forced to acknowledge that those two homicide cases were headed straight for the unsolved file.

The plan had worked to perfection.

Except . . .

Now a lone wolf asshole had come out of nowhere and was sniffing around talking to people and asking questions. That could be dangerous for everyone concerned, especially if he didn't get discouraged and walk away. Based on what the Russian said, the guy didn't sound like someone who stopped running until he crossed the finish line. A man with that mentality could cause problems. Having no bureaucracy to tangle him up or restrict his movements, he was free to go off in any direction he chose. That made him even more dangerous.

Already, his actions forced a move that had not been planned— the murder of Abe Pearlstein in Manhattan. The old Jew didn't know anything, nor had he met anyone, so he wasn't deemed to be a threat. Not initially, anyway. However, that changed when a stranger was seen going into the old man's office, where the two men spent several hours talking. After the man departed, and the old man coughed up the information that his visitor was a private investigator working to help free Danny Kafka, the two 'idiot sons' (as the Russian referred to them) had no choice but to silence the old guy permanently.

That same fate might befall this investigator if he becomes a serious threat.

Mr. K had long ago come to realize that Russians, like the Chinese, are inscrutable and virtually impossible to read. They seldom give much away, either by look or sound. It's difficult to know what a Russian or a Chinaman is thinking at any given time. They usually give you nothing but a blank stare.

But Mr. K could tell that the Russian was genuinely concerned about the presence of this private investigator. The Russian wasn't a fearful or reckless man but he was cautious. If the Russian was worried, Mr. K thought, perhaps I should be as well. After all, if he goes down, I go down with him.

And thirty-million bucks does you no good if you are dead or in prison.

---

FOR THE RUSSIAN, the presence of a lone wolf investigator represented only half of his concerns, and it was one that could easily be taken care of. If a United States senator could be eliminated, then making a nosey private investigator disappear presented next to no challenge whatsoever. That could be handled at a moment's notice. And maybe it would be. Only time and circumstances would determine the interloper's ultimate fate.

The Russian's other concern, the more pressing of the two, had to do with the "idiot sons," his, Sergei, and Mr. K's, Brad. Both were in their late twenties, strong and trustworthy, but not particularly intelligent. Not dumb, exactly, but lacking common sense. Too often they acted without thinking. They were—what was the precise term he was looking for?—impetuous. Yes, that's the word. They were impetuous, rash, impulsive. Those were not ideal characteristics for anyone choosing to work on the wrong side of the law. Cemeteries and prison cells are filled with men who behaved in a reckless, thoughtless manner.

The Russian couldn't decide which of the two, Sergei or Brad, was the one who needed to be more closely monitored. Probably, it was Brad; he typically came across as behaving like a buffoon. But was the Russian making this judgment because he truly believed it to be true, or because he was reluctant to cast blame toward his own flesh and blood? In matters of such importance, and with big consequences at stake, one was required to be objective. Personal prejudice had no place when assessing potential liabilities.

Sergei was the more dominant of the two, and the one who tended to be more serious. But he wasn't without his own shortcomings. He loved sex and gambling, and he wasn't shy about spending huge amounts of cash to satisfy those urges. The Russian had once been outraged when he learned that Sergei had unloaded more than twenty-thousand dollars on gambling and prostitutes during a two-day stay in Las Vegas. A lack of discipline such as that simply could not be tolerated. He had laid down the law to Sergei, telling him in no uncertain terms that the next outrageous episode would lead to dire consequences. This was ambiguous enough to get Sergei's full attention, and from everything the Russian had seen in recent months, his youngest son had taken the warning seriously.

The Russian never had to worry about his oldest son Mikhail. Never had to be stressed over decisions and actions taken by his first-born child, the light of his life. No, Mikhail, "Misha" to family and friends, possessed a level of maturity and responsibility that far exceeded those found in his younger brother. His two sons, the Russian acknowledged, were more different than Old Testament siblings Jacob and Esau. He often wondered how two humans, born of the same parents and raised under the same roof, could have turned out to be so vastly different as adults. His only conclusion was that it had to be the eight-year age difference separating them, though deep in his heart he suspected the answer to that conundrum was much more complex.

Misha was also far more intelligent than Sergei. He was guided by his intellect, while Sergei ruled with muscle and strength and force. Despite having brainpower that could be useful in the family business, Misha had no desire to work for his father, whom he loved with all his heart. Instead, he chose to attend college at New York University. His dream was to become a writer. Or, as he often said, "a magnificent wordsmith." Misha's dream was snuffed out before it had a chance to become reality. A brain tumor ended his life a week before his twenty-third birthday.

The Russian was left with an ache that never went away, along with the belief that his beloved Misha would have been a great writer like Tolstoy and Dostoyevsky. Resenting such underserved cruelty laid upon one so innocent, cursing the pain and suffering Misha had to endure, the Russian carried within him a palpable anger aimed directly at God. How could he not feel such anger? How could any parent give God a free pass after burying a child? Didn't handing down a death sentence to one so young and gifted make God something of a hanging judge? How could a supposedly loving God sanction such a cruel fate?

The Russian had cried only once as an adult—at Misha's funeral. He vowed to never shed another tear for the rest of his life. And thus far, he hadn't.

In truth, he wasn't sure there were any tears remaining.

# Chapter Eighteen

D antzler put in a call to Jake Thomas before beginning the
drive back to Chicago. He wanted to know if Jake knew a
former soldier named Todd. It was a longshot, Dantzler knew, but
the call didn't cost anything, so why not take the chance? Sometimes
a longshot pays off.

As it turned out, Jake was familiar with a GI named Todd, a
black warrant officer from Conway, South Carolina. Jake remembered this Todd as being a good soldier and a "stand-up dude."
Although Jake couldn't be positive, he did have grave reservations
about Todd's father being in the movie business. Dantzler concurred
with Jake on that issue.

Dantzler would have to travel other avenues if he hoped to
locate Todd or Todd's father, the alleged movie producer. As he realized earlier, one of those avenues might take him to Los Angeles. If
so, where to start once he arrived? That was the big question. Dantzler didn't know a single soul in Hollywood, or in the film world. He
had no connections there at all. The notion of undertaking a
journey to California, unfamiliar with everyone and unsure who he
was looking for had the ring of a hopeless undertaking. But time
wasn't standing still, and the days Danny Kafka spent in jail weren't

getting any shorter. Dantzler needed answers; he just was certain they could be found in California.

There were other stumbling blocks standing in his way as well, beginning with the fact that he had no way of knowing for certain that there was a movie producer. Perhaps that was only a wild assumption, a reach on his part. Even if the producer did exist, there was no guarantee that he lived in California, or that he was Todd's father. There were probably hundreds of guys who call themselves movie producers, most of whom claim the title even as they wait tables for local Southern California restaurants, or pump gas at the nearest Arco station. And if this man was a legitimate producer, it's not a certainty that he worked in Hollywood. He might work in New York or Montreal or London. Hollywood isn't home to all movie producers.

During the drive to Chicago, Dantzler tried to push the Kafka case out of his thoughts by listening to some music. The music was great, but the thoughts persisted. It was impossible to enjoy music knowing an innocent man was sitting in a jail cell losing hope by the minute. As a cop, Dantzler had long ago realized that he would rather see a guilty person go free than see an innocent person locked up. It was a lousy formula either way, but one side of the equation was much worse than the other.

He had to get Danny Kafka out of jail.

---

WHEN DANTZLER ARRIVED at the house on Sheffield, he parked, went inside, and was met by no one. Maggie and Mary-Louise were not at the front desk, nor were any of the other team members milling around. It wasn't until Dantzler went into the big dining room/library that he finally encountered someone. Two people, in fact, one he was familiar with—Sly Douglas—and one he'd never seen before, although he had a pretty good idea who she was. His money was on Brooke Mason, the Chicago homicide detective.

They were sitting across from each other at the table, the only two people in the room. Seconds later, Grace walked in carrying two bottles of water. Seeing Dantzler, she smiled, nodded, and motioned for him to take a seat, which he did. She asked if he wanted some water, he declined.

"Sly, why don't you introduce Jack to your friend?" Grace prompted.

"I'm guessing she's Brooke Mason," Dantzler said, beating Sly to the punch. "The homicide detective in charge of the Dana Shapiro investigation."

"What'd I tell you, Brooke?" Sly said. "The guy's really smart. By the way, his name is Jack Dantzler."

Brooke Mason started to smile but couldn't quite finish the job. She was like someone who wanted to laugh at a joke but caught herself when she realized that to do so would be inappropriate. Instead, she stared at Dantzler with a deadpan look on her face that seemed to say, you don't look all that smart to me.

Sly had previously said Brooke was in her late twenties or early thirties, which may have been accurate, although she certainly didn't look to be that old. In fact, Dantzler was positive that if you stood her next to Maggie and Mary-Louise most people would say she was the youngest of the trio, when, in truth, Brooke was older than the others by at least five years. She was small, maybe five-two, and she couldn't weigh more than one-ten. Her eyes were blue, her hair was light brown and cut very short, and she wore wire-rim glasses. She had, Dantzler felt, a pixie-like quality about her. There was, however, a steely hardness in those blue eyes that indicated she might be a lot tougher than she looked.

It was Brooke who broke the silence.

"Sly has informed me that you are working with Miss West on the Danny Kafka case," Brooke said to Dantzler. "And he has also made you aware that I'm heading up the Dana Shapiro investigation. Is that accurate?'

"Accurate and concise."

"Sly tells me—and Miss West has confirmed it—that you are convinced Danny Kafka is innocent. Is that also accurate?"

Dantzler couldn't decide whether he was being interrogated or lectured to. Either way, he wasn't thrilled with the way this conversation was going. It was, he felt, time to flip the conversation upside-down. Time for him to take charge.

"Detective Mason, why don't we start all over again," Dantzler said. "And the best place to start is for you to tell me where the Shapiro investigation currently stands."

If Brooke was thrown off by Dantzler's abrupt conversation coup she didn't show it. No smile, no frown, nothing. The only thing that changed was the look in her eyes. The steel somehow seemed even harder than before.

"The investigation is on-going," she replied, "but as of now we have found no evidence anywhere that comes close to exonerating Danny Kafka. I am eagerly looking forward to hearing the evidence you have that proves he didn't assassinate Dana Shapiro, or that the Kafka case is linked in some way to the murders of Bobby Conrad and Molly Jackson. That there was some kind of conspiracy at work here."

Brooke paused, somewhat dramatically, and put her hands up to her ears. "Oh, what's that I hear?" she inquired. "You don't have any evidence? I suppose that means your guy really is guilty."

She was being snippy and bitchy but Dantzler took an instant liking to her. He could tell she was a cagey, smart interrogator. He also knew his early assessment was correct—Brooke Mason was definitely tougher than she looked.

But Dantzler also knew he was smarter and far more experienced than she was. He would use that to his advantage.

"Detective Mason, I'm not impressed with your speed reading version of three homicides," Dantzler said, forcefully. "I find flippancy to be repugnant when talking about the death of three human beings, or when an innocent man is sitting in a cold jail cell. And Danny Kafka is as innocent as we are. You can help me prove his innocence, or you can go back to your office, sit around, and twiddle your thumbs. In short, you can either shit or get off the pot."

The room suddenly became very quiet. Grace and Sly Douglas, appearing somewhat stunned by Dantzler's outburst, quickly glanced at each other before shifting their gaze toward Brooke

Mason. Sly didn't know Brooke very well, and Grace wasn't familiar with her at all, so neither one had a clue how she was going to respond.

Neither did Dantzler, but unlike Grace or Sly he didn't really care how she responded. What mattered now was that he had control of the conversation.

Brooke's response came as surprise to Grace and Sly but not to Dantzler. They expected Brooke to go ballistic, to fly off the handle, and rip into Dantzler for being everything from a bully to a misogynist pig. However, Grace and Sly had badly misjudged the young detective.

Dantzler knew she wasn't going to come apart at the seams. And she didn't. Her eyes softened, and for the first time she managed a slight smile. Then she nodded at Dantzler, her way of showing respect to a fellow detective.

"Point taken, lesson learned, Detective Dantzler," Brooke said. "Suppose we start fresh, just as you suggested. Where do you want to begin?"

"With you answering several questions that continue to gnaw at me," Dantzler answered, "beginning with how the FBI knew where Danny was staying? Better yet, how did they even know he was in Chicago? And then they find the murder weapon one block from where the shooting took place? That's awfully convenient, don't you think? The release of that tape also troubles me, especially the timing. Funny that it hits CNN just minutes after Dana Shapiro was gunned down. Who released the damn thing in the first place? And do you really believe Danny Kafka, a bright, intelligent young man, a war hero, would be stupid enough to send out a tape that shows him admitting to a cold-blooded assassination?"

"Why are you asking me? Those questions are for the FBI."

"Okay, why is the FBI sitting on this information? Why haven't they shared it with you? What are they hiding?"

"Wait, slow down a second," Brooke said, holding up her hand. "Are you inferring that the FBI was somehow involved in the murder of Dana Shapiro?"

"I'll get to the FBI in a couple of minutes," Dantzler answered.

"But there are a few more things I need to point out before I get to the Feds. Did Detective Douglas brief you on the weapons' issue?"

"He said something about two different weapons," Brooke responded. "I'm not sure I was clear about what he was saying."

"On the tape, Danny says he's going to use an AKM to kill Dana Shapiro. But that's not the weapon used by the actual shooter. That person used an M107."

"You see that as a big difference?"

"It's a *huge* difference. It gives us two critical facts. First, the people who set Danny up didn't know much about weapons, and second, it tells us that Danny wasn't the shooter. He couldn't have been the shooter."

"How can you be so sure?" Brooke asked. "The guy was a legitimate war hero."

"Yes, but he wasn't a sniper. Which brings us to Bobby Conrad. He was not only a sniper, he was one of the best this country has ever produced."

"So . . . Bobby Conrad murdered Dana Shapiro? Is that what you're telling me?"

"That's precisely what I'm telling you."

Brooke shook her head, said, "Why? What reason would he have to kill a United States senator?"

"He had no reason to kill her. Like Danny, Bobby probably didn't know who the hell Dana Shapiro was."

"Yet, you maintain that Bobby Conrad was the shooter."

"Yes, Bobby fired the shot that killed Dana Shapiro."

"Where are you heading with this, Detective Dantzler?"

"Bobby Conrad killed Dana Shapiro without knowing that he was really killing her."

"How is that even remotely possible?" Brooke inquired.

"Bobby thought he was filming a scene for a movie. Same goes for Danny Kafka, except he was under the impression that he was auditioning for a movie role. Both of those guys were used by some very clever individuals."

"Surely, you don't believe that malarkey, do you?" Brooke said, looking at Grace and Sly, "because I certainly don't."

"Well, unless you change your way of thinking, the clever guys will win. Look what's happened thus far, Detective Mason. A United States senator is dead, Bobby Conrad is dead, and Danny Kafka is facing what you believe to be an air-tight case against him. The phony shooter and the actual shooter have both been taken out of the picture while the ones who pulled this off are walking around scot free. If that doesn't trouble you, then you're in the wrong line of work."

"Evidence, Detective Dantzler, where is your evidence that proves Danny Kafka is innocent? Or the evidence that ties the Kafka case to the Conrad-Jackson investigation? I just don't see it."

"Consider this, Detective Mason. In Danny's case, you have perfect evidence. In the Conrad case, there is absolutely no evidence. What does that tell you?"

"It doesn't tell me the two cases are linked."

"Then you are failing to see the big picture. As for a link, it's Bobby Conrad. He connects phony with real. Bobby was a sniper, one good enough to easily make that killing shot. Once he'd done that, he and his girlfriend were murdered, their silence ensured forever. Like I said, we're dealing with some very clever people. And unless I'm way off-base, one of those involved is very high up in our government."

"Now you're telling me this conspiracy has tentacles that reach into our government. Is that what you want me to believe?"

"Yes."

Brooke again looked at Grace and Sly before turning her attention back to Dantzler. Shaking her head, she said, "I hate to keep beating you with the same hammer, Detective Dantzler, but where is your evidence for any of this? You can't build a case based on a bunch of allegations, or some lame theory. First, you tell me Danny Kafka and Bobby Conrad were filming a movie, and . . ."

"No, what I said was they *thought* they were filming a movie."

"And now you're saying our government was involved."

"No, I said *someone* in our government was involved."

"A distinction without much of a difference, if you want my

opinion," Brooke Mason said. Then: "Did this mysterious government someone also set up the fake movie part of your plot?"

"No. My hunch is that part was actually handled by people in the movie business," Dantzler said.

"First, allegations, then conspiracy, and now hunches. Not exactly strong building blocks for solving homicide investigations, wouldn't you agree?"

"Maybe so, but oftentimes a hunch is all you have. And not to brag, but my hunches usually turn out to be right."

"This movie person—you have a lead on him yet?" Brooke asked.

"Only a first name."

"Care to share it with me?"

"Not yet."

"So much for us working together."

"When I know more I'll certainly share it with you. You have my word on that."

"Does this mean our little chat is finished?"

"Not quite," answered Dantzler. "I still haven't asked the most important question of all. Why do you think the FBI was so quick to hand off the Shapiro case to you guys? This was the murder of a United States senator we're talking about. There is no way that's not the FBI's case. And yet, they pitch it to Chicago PD without even giving it a serious look. Makes no sense."

"How the hell am I expected to answer that question?" Brooke replied. "I don't work for the FBI, and I'm no mind reader. What I can tell you is that the murder happened on my day off. I got a call from my lieutenant instructing me to go directly to a certain address, which, as it turned out, was the building where the shot was fired. When I arrived, he pulled me aside and immediately introduced me to FBI agent Kate Flanagan, who informed me that Chicago PD was taking over the investigation. Then she walked away, clearly very unhappy with the message she just delivered. After she was gone, my boss, Lieutenant Morris, said I was now in charge of the investigation."

"I repeat . . . that makes absolutely no sense," Dantzler stated.

"Then you'd better take it up with the FBI, Detective Dantzler. I can't speak for them."

"I plan to do just that." Dantzler cut his eyes toward Grace, said, "Have you spoken to Kate Flanagan?"

"Left several messages, but she hasn't returned my calls," Grace noted.

By this time, the rest of Grace's team had found their way into the room. Angela, Jenny, and Edward were sitting at the table, while Maggie and Mary-Louise were leaning against the liquor cabinet. All five were intently listening to every word being spoken.

"To hell with it," Dantzler said. "I'll contact her myself. She's a key to solving this case."

"Is Kate Flanagan your mysterious government someone?" Brooke Mason asked.

"No, she's not. But her answer to one important question might lead me to that someone."

"Care to share that question with me?"

"Not yet."

"Of course not. Why be on the same team, right?" Brooke said, sarcastically. Standing, she asked, "Are we are done here? Or do you have more information you refuse to share?"

Dantzler grinned, said, "We're done. It's been a joy meeting you, Detective Mason. Believe it or not, you get high marks from me. You have all the makings of a superb homicide investigator."

"Thanks. And feel free to share your evaluation with my boss," Brooke said, extending her hand. "As for any future information you come up with, feel free to share that with me as well."

When Brooke and Sly were gone, and the rest of the gang had dispersed, Grace said, "You like that young lady, don't you, Jack?"

"She may look like a weak blade of grass, but I have the feeling she's a tough little turd. I'm not sure I'd want to get on her bad side."

"Don't get any big ideas concerning the young detective, Jack. You have enough to worry about here."

"What are you talking about?"

"Maggie and Mary-Louise both have a big crush on you."

"Just proves they have good taste in men."

"Whatever, lover boy. Just don't encourage them, is all I'm asking. I need that pair to be friends, not rivals for your affection."

"I will fight them off with all my strength."

"As for the investigation, what's your next step?" Grace asked.

"Track down and speak with Kate Flanagan. After that, try to get a last name for this Todd guy who had a couple of dates with Dana Shapiro. Then, who knows? I'll probably have to make a trip out to California."

"Meanwhile, Danny Kafka sits in a jail cell."

"I'll get him out, Grace."

"Promise?"

"Promise."

# Chapter Nineteen

Dantzler awoke the next morning with a dark dream still shaking around in his head. In the dream, a man (him? Danny Kafka? a stranger?) watched from his jail cell as a black bird soared up above freely writing its own poem against the sky. At some point the bird came to rest on the ledge just outside the steel bars. It sat there for a while, his shiny eyes staring intently at the prisoner, as if to say, "I'm free, you're not." Then, suddenly, the bird let out a loud squawk, perhaps as a way of announcing his freedom, and flew away, leaving the prisoner standing alone in his cell.

Dantzler wiped perspiration from his face as he slowly climbed out of bed, the dream lingering like the ultimate nightmare. He knew it didn't take Freud to figure out that the prisoner represented him *and* Danny Kafka. Both men were carrying a heavy weight— Danny was looking at life behind bars, Dantzler was burdened with the task of trying to prevent that from happening. In Dantzler's view, real life, not that damn dream was the darker nightmare.

Both men were, in their own way, a prisoner.

A shower and fresh clothes did little to improve Dantzler's mood. Maybe getting some food on his empty stomach might do the trick. Still feeling groggy, he plodded down the stairs in search of sustenance, which turned out to be a chocolate doughnut and a bottle of water. Not nutritious but greasy and filling.

"Who brought the pastries?" Dantzler asked Edward, who sat at the big table scribbling notes on a legal pad. He was the only team member on site at seven-fifteen in the morning.

"Angela," Edward replied. "She's going to visit Danny later this morning. She'll take some to him."

"Have you been to see Danny?"

"Yeah, two days ago."

"How is he holding up?"

"In my opinion, surprisingly well. Helluva lot better than I'd be, that's for sure. He's a pretty damn tough kid."

"They don't pin the Medal of Honor on you unless you're plenty damn tough."

"He really has faith in you, Detective Dantzler," Edward said. "I think it's his belief in you that is keeping him strong."

Dantzler bit into the doughnut rather than acknowledge that his own belief might not be a match for Danny's. With that in mind, he didn't respond to Edward. Maybe, Dantzler reasoned, it was in everyone's best interest to continue having faith in him. If they wavered, sooner or later their despair would reach Danny, thus eroding his hope for a positive outcome. But Dantzler was keenly aware that belief can oftentimes be little more than an illusion. Of course, the same holds true for faith. Either one is more fragile than glass, forever under assault by doubt and uncertainty, always in danger of being broken and shattered.

Dantzler had never been a man burdened by self-doubt; he'd always held a strong conviction that he was up to whatever challenge he was faced with. Now was not the time to let self-doubt enter into his thinking. His belief that he could solve this puzzle had to match Danny's.

Easier said than done, considering the circumstances.

When Dantzler's phone buzzed, Edward said, "Little early for a phone call. Must be important."

Dantzler shrugged, looked at the number—he didn't recognize it—and then said, "Jack Dantzler."

"Yes sir, this is Emily Rosburg, Dana Shapiro's personal assistant. Do you remember speaking with me?"

"Of course. What's on your mind, Emily?"

"Well, you asked me to contact you if I came across something you might find interesting or helpful. I think maybe I have."

"Okay, what do you have?" Dantzler asked, grabbing the pen and legal pad Edward was using.

"You probably aren't aware that Dana had no immediate family," Emily said. "Those of us who worked closely with Dana were really all the family she had. Because of that, virtually everything family members normally do in these circumstances has been left for us to take care of. One of our tasks was to write Thank-You notes to everyone who attended the memorial service in Washington and the funeral service in Boston. That amounts to almost two-thousand people. As you can imagine, writing and sending out that many cards is a time-consuming chore."

"I have no doubt that it has kept you busy," Dantzler replied, unsure where this conversation was heading. "What did you find that might be interesting or helpful?"

"When I was going down the list of those paying respects at the Washington service, one name caught my attention . . . Todd. Unfortunately, he didn't write down his last name, nor did he give an address. Just Todd."

"Same name as the guy who Dana went out with a couple of times, isn't it?"

"Yes. That's why I thought you would find it of interest."

"No last name, no address . . . that's not much to go on."

"I know, but there's something else. The name on the next line."

"What name?

"Jon—J-o-n—Crofford, spelled C-r-o-f-f-o-r-d. He didn't give a street address, but he lists Arlington, Virginia, as his place of residence."

"Okay, why is that so interesting?" asked Dantzler, writing down Crofford's name and the city he'd listed.

"Well, because it's obvious that both lines were written by the same person. The handwriting is unmistakable. Plus, the writer used a different pen than the one that came with the guest registry. The ink in his pen was a totally different shade of blue."

"It's your opinion, then, that Jon filled out both lines? Is that what you're saying?"

"It looks that way to me."

"Can you make a copy of that page and e-mail it to me?"

"Sure. Just give me your e-mail address."

Dantzler gave her his address, then said, "This is good news, Emily. You may have helped me more than you know."

"Wonder why Jon didn't write down Todd's last name?" Emily said.

"Todd didn't want him to. No way to know why, but I'm sure he had his reasons."

"Are you going to look for Todd?"

"I'm going to start looking the moment I hang up with you."

"I'd better let you go."

"You did great, Emily. When true justice comes to Dana Shapiro and to Danny Kafka, we'll all have you to thank."

———

DANTZLER NOW HAD two individuals he desperately needed to speak with—Dana's friend, Todd, and the illusive FBI agent Kate Flanagan. He was certain one of them—perhaps both—could provide the information he was seeking. This was especially true for Todd, if, indeed, he was the son of a Hollywood producer. If it turns out that he's not, then finding answers hinges on what Kate Flanagan has to say.

Kate, Dantzler suspected, held the string that could unravel a big part of the mystery.

Pushing the legal pad back to Edward, Dantzler said, "Can you get me a phone number for this guy?"

"Jon Crofford? Shouldn't be too difficult," Edward said. "I'll use the computer in my office. If you need anything else, let me know."

"Thanks, Edward."

Dantzler stood, left the table, went into the front room, and sat on the sofa next to Maggie's desk. Taking out his phone, he punched in Sly Douglas's number. The Chicago detective answered after the second ring.

"A call this early tells me you are in need of my assistance," Sly said.

"And they say I'm smart," Dantzler replied. "Yes, I do need your help."

"Name it."

"Are you close with anyone in the FBI office who has access to Kate Flanagan?"

"Agent Flanagan still hasn't answered your calls?"

"She's a female Claude Rains."

"*The Invisible Man*, I get it. A terrific old movie."

"I don't need a movie review, Sly. I need to talk with Kate Flanagan."

"Not a problem. Laura Cunningham is a good pal of mine, and she's tight as hell with Kate. I'll contact her and see what I can work out for you."

"When can you do that?"

"Two seconds after this conversation comes to its conclusion?"

"Consider it concluded," Dantzler said, ending the call.

---

THE RUSSIAN, whose name was Yuri Lazarov, picked up his phone and typed out a text message to Sergei. Although he would prefer to speak or write to Sergei in Russian, his youngest son, having lived virtually his entire life in the United States, was a stranger to his own native language. It was a failure on his part, Yuri conceded, that his son was able to read and rattle off endless, mindless Hip-Hop lyrics, yet wasn't conversant in his mother tongue. As a Russian to his core, Yuri felt shame for allowing such a thing to occur.

The message to Sergei was brief: *Separate and give me a call.*

Yuri had a direct order he needed to give his son, and he didn't want Brad to know about it, or to be involved in what was soon to take place. Sergei was foolish and irresponsible, but he was at the very least reliable. The same could not be said of Brad. With him, everything tended to be hit or miss. There was no consistency in his actions or his behavior. Worse, he was a talker, especially when he got a few drinks in him. A drunk could never be counted on to keep secrets. And this job required extreme secrecy.

Less than an hour ago, Yuri had received a call from a man he had not expected to ever hear from again. Their last conversation, which took place four weeks ago, concerned a United States senator who had to be eliminated—Dana Shapiro. Her name, of course, meant nothing to Yuri at the time. Therefore, he had no way of knowing why she had to be killed. Nor did he really care. All that mattered to him was the money to be received when the job was successfully accomplished. It was an astronomical sum, a figure far surpassing anything he'd ever made in the past. It was a dangerous undertaking, to be sure, but for such a huge financial windfall there was no way he would turn down the offer.

Yuri said he would make it happen, and he did. He'd contacted Mr. K, told him the senator had to be eliminated, then ordered Mr. K to put a plan in place. Initially, Mr. K was reluctant to join what he termed "an impossible and suicidal mission," but he quickly changed his tune when Yuri informed him what his cut of the money pie would be. Within three days, Mr. K contacted Yuri to let him know that plans for the operation had been finalized and were soon to be set in motion.

That plan, as everyone now realized, had worked to perfection.

The phone call that came an hour ago, surprising though it was, wasn't all that different from the previous call four weeks ago. The man making the call wanted someone else eliminated. This time, however, there were a couple of rather noteworthy variances. For this job, the intended target wasn't high-profile, and the paycheck wouldn't be nearly so substantial.

Yuri's initial reaction was to turn down the offer, which he knew wasn't possible. Refusal was simply not an option. Although he might get away with saying no to the man who made the call, Yuri

knew someone higher up on the food chain was behind both opera-
tions. And that individual was not only handing out the big
paychecks, he was also pulling the strings. Yuri wasn't sure who that
man was, but he did have his suspicions. If he was right, the man
was not someone who took no for an answer.

Yuri's ringing phone jarred him back to the present. Picking it
up, he immediately said, "Are you alone, Sergei?"

"Yes. Brad is in the restaurant, eating. I came outside to smoke.
What do you need?"

"We have a job that I want you to handle alone. Brad is not to
be made aware of what you are going to do."

"What am I going to do?"

"Eliminate a problem."

"Where?"

"Arlington, Virginia. I will text you the target's name and the
address where he can be found."

"What about keeping an eye on the investigator?" Sergei asked.
"Is that off?"

"For you, yes. Brad can continue following him."

"What am I supposed to tell Brad? He'll flip out when he hears
we're splitting up."

"I don't know, Sergei. You figure it out. Try using that brain of
yours for something other than women and gambling. It would be a
refreshing change if you were to do that."

"Brad will be upset and angry if I run off and leave him alone.
He'll insist on going with me."

"Goddammit, Sergei, do you really think I give a damn how
upset or angry Brad will be?" Yuri practically screamed. "I have
given you a direct order—a job—and you will perform it without
Brad. If he complains too much, tell him to contact me. I'll handle
him if you can't."

"Okay, I will tell Brad that you are ill, and that I need to be with
you for the next few days. That should work."

"Tell him they found life on Mars . . . I don't care. Just make
certain you go to the address I'm about to send you, and that you
take care of business there. Do it quick and clean, and leave no

evidence behind. And do not whisper a word of this to Brad. Understand?"

"Yes, I got it."

Closing his phone, Yuri muttered, "Такой идиот," in Russian, and then repeated it in English, "Such an idiot."

# Chapter Twenty

When Dantzler ended his call with Sly and went back into the big room, Edward handed him a piece of paper with Jon Crofford's street address and phone number on it. Dantzler studied the information for a few seconds, then said, "Any idea if that phone number is for his home or his cell?"

"Can't say for sure, but my guess is it's his cell phone," Edward replied. "Do you want me to give him a call?"

"I'll do it later. But thanks again for your help, Edward."

"Anything for Danny. That's kind of become our motto around here."

Dantzler spied the box of pastries, gave thought to grabbing another doughnut, but decided against it. He didn't need the sugar rush, or the calories. Instead, he opted for a glass of water.

Grace arrived a few minutes later, set her briefcase on the floor, opened a bottle of water, and sat down at the table across from Dantzler. She was dressed in a blue pants suit, white blouse, and low-cut, comfortable shoes. She had on just enough make-up to accentuate the positive while hiding the negative, a silver earring dangled from each ear, and a gold cross rested on her chest. If you looked up professional in the dictionary, this image of Grace is what you might see.

"You're heading to court," Dantzler announced.

"How can you tell?" Grace asked.

"You're dressed for combat. I've seen you in that battle gear before, remember?"

"Sure, when I eviscerated you on the witness stand."

"You didn't eviscerate me, Grace. But keep dreaming if it makes you feel better about yourself."

Grace nodded toward Edward, who was now sitting next to Dantzler, and said, "I destroyed that man, Edward, regardless of how much he argues to the contrary. It was a slaughter."

Throwing up his hands, Edward said, "Call me Switzerland, call me a coward, I don't care. I'm not getting in the middle of this skirmish."

Dantzler sipped some water, said, "If you're going to court, that must mean your client turned down the plea offer."

"She wants to roll the dice, which I feel is a mistake," Grace pointed out. "But, hey, I'm only her attorney. If she wants to go to trial, then we go to trial. I don't like our chances; like I told you, a hung jury is about the best we can hope for. An outright acquittal is never going to happen."

"Don't be so negative, Grace. If you can eviscerate me, surely you can work your special brand of magic and get a not guilty verdict for her."

"You were easy, Jack," Grace said, standing and picking up her briefcase. "This is next to impossible."

When Grace was gone, Edward tapped Dantzler on the arm, and said, "She likes you, Detective Dantzler. She likes you a lot."

"Why do you say that, Edward?"

"It's plain as day. You can see it in her eyes."

"I'm thinking you are seeing something I'm not seeing, Edward."

"You're not looking hard enough, Detective Dantzler."

SERGEI ALMOST FELL over when he read the text message sent to him by his father. He was stunned, couldn't believe what he was looking at, certain a mistake had been made. It took multiple readings before he convinced himself that his eyes were not playing tricks on him. They weren't; the message was there, the man's name glowing green on the phone Sergei held in his shaking hands.

But why? Why would his father want this particular man eliminated? Sergei kept repeating that question again and again in his mind. Killing this man made no sense, at least not to Sergei. It hit too close to home.

*No wonder his father forbade him from sharing the message with Brad.*

True, Sergei only met the man on one occasion, so he had no great trepidation about killing the guy. But there were other considerations to be factored in, such as what other individuals might think if they found out that his father ordered the hit. Blood was sure to flow if that information ever saw the light of day.

This order simply made no sense to Sergei.

Should he call his father and verify that no mistake had been made? Better to be positive than to commit a blunder that in all probability would lead to devastating results. But Sergei understood that to make the call would cause his father's notorious volcanic rage to erupt. Sergei definitely didn't want any part of that. He'd seen it too many times in his life, borne the brunt of his old man's fiery temper more often than he cared to remember. Also, he had no desire to hear his father once again refer to him as an imbecile like he'd done so many times in the past.

No, Sergei concluded, if the old man wants this guy taken out, then I will see that it gets done. I will follow orders and ask no questions. That was the smart thing to do, he mumbled to himself, the only thing to do. Anything less would cause his father's anger to explode.

That's the last thing Sergei wanted.

# Chapter Twenty-One

"How much longer?" Dantzler asked.

"Five minutes, tops," Mary-Louise replied.

They were in Dantzler's Mercedes on the way to St. Peter's Church on West Madison Street. Mary-Louise was driving, intently focused on her task, her hands once again clenched tightly on the steering wheel. Traffic was thick, but she maneuvered through the rush like a pro.

"What if she's already gone?" Mary-Louise said.

"Let's keep our fingers crossed that she has a lot of sins to atone for."

"That's a terrible thing to say, Detective Dantzler. You should atone for that while you're in there."

"Not a Catholic, Mary-Louise."

"If she is still inside, what do you want me to do?"

"Find a place to park, if you can. If not, drive around. Either way, come back to get me in thirty minutes."

Dantzler had been on Grace's computer when Laura Cunningham, the FBI agent, phoned to let him know that she was following up on Sly Douglas's request that she give him a call concerning the possibility of getting in touch with Kate Flanagan. According to

Laura, Kate went to St. Peter's Church around ten each morning, and normally spent close to thirty minutes there. Laura said she knew for certain that's where Kate was at the moment. Dantzler thanked Laura, went into the front room, tossed his car keys to Mary-Louise, asked her if she knew where St. Peter's Church was located—she did; "It's my church"—and together they raced toward his vehicle.

"You've never met Kate Flanagan," Mary-Louise correctly pointed out when they were a few blocks away from the church. "How will you know if she's even in there?"

"Mary-Louise, I can spot an FBI agent, male or female, from a mile away. Trust me, they all look the same. If Kate is in there, I'll recognize her."

Kate was still there, and Dantzler did instantly recognize her. She was sitting about a dozen rows from the back, head bowed, hands clasped, obviously praying. Dantzler took a seat on the opposite side, several rows behind her, and studied her closely. Although he was only viewing her profile, he could see that she had strong features, soft skin and brown hair, most of which was covered by a silk scarf. He would also venture a guess that she was tall and well-proportioned.

Finished praying, Kate wiped her eyes and stood, proving that Dantzler's tall, well-proportioned guess was accurate. She stepped out into the aisle, knelt, crossed herself, stood, and began walking toward the exit. She was almost even with Dantzler when he spoke.

"Agent Flanagan?" Dantzler whispered.

"And you are?"

"Jack Dantzler."

"Ah, yes, Grace West's investigator. I've been meaning to call you, but you were about number twenty on my to-do list, so I never got around to it."

"Now you don't have to," Dantzler said, ignoring the dig. "We can chat now and save the Bureau the cost of a phone call."

"I don't have time to chat now. I have a meeting in half an hour."

"Come on, Kate. Five minutes is all I'm asking. You can spare that."

"Now we're on a first-name basis?"

"Sure, let's be pals. I'm Jack."

Kate glanced at her watch, said, "You have five minutes, starting now," as she scooted in next to Dantzler.

"You guys need to jump back into the Dana Shapiro investigation," Dantzler said.

"If that's what you are here to talk about, *Jack*, then we don't need five minutes. We don't need one minute. Talk to Detective Brooke Mason about that investigation. I have nothing to do with it."

"The FBI walking away from the murder of a United States senator makes no sense," Dantzler said. "That's exactly the kind of case you guys work."

"Not this time."

"Why not?"

"Look, I understand you're fighting on behalf of Danny Kafka. I get that. But the man is guilty. It doesn't require Bureau resources to prove it. Danny admitted killing Dana."

"You knew Dana Shapiro, didn't you?"

Kate nodded.

Dantzler said, "Were you close friends?"

"Yes, very close."

"Is that why you were so pissed when given the order to stand down and hand off the case to Chicago PD?"

"How do you know I was pissed?"

"I spoke with someone who saw you take the call."

"You have two minutes remaining," Kate said, after looking at her watch. "Anything else you want to know?"

"Danny Kafka is innocent, Kate. And deep down in your gut, you know it."

"No, you're dead wrong. I don't know it. But I'm a good sport, so out of curiosity I'll play along. If you're so sure Danny didn't murder Dana, then who did?"

"Bobby Conrad."

Kate sneered, shook her head, and said, "Then why did Danny Kafka admit to killing Dana?"

"He didn't actually *admit* to it, he only said he *intended* to do it."

"Boy, talk about parsing language. Bill Clinton has nothing on you. Okay, I'll play along for a second time. What reason would Bobby Conrad have for killing Dana Shapiro?"

"This was all part of an elaborate plan, Kate. When Danny made that statement, he thought he was auditioning for a movie role. When Bobby Conrad fired the killing shot, he thought he was filming a scene for the movie. They both got played by some real professionals."

"In all my years with the Bureau that's the most preposterous story I've ever heard."

"Which is exactly why it's succeeding. Because it's so out there no one is willing to believe it."

"Except you, right?"

"It's the only scenario that makes sense."

"Maybe there is no scenario. Maybe it's just another insane act by an angry individual hell-bent on making a statement. Did you ever consider that possibility?"

"It's all too neat, too tied up with a big red ribbon," Dantzler argued. "Tell me this, Kate. How did the FBI know Danny Kafka was in town? That he was staying in that hotel? You guys had him in cuffs less than thirty minutes after that tape went on CNN. That's what I call a rapid response. How did you find out where Danny was?"

"An anonymous call from someone in the hotel."

"Did you speak with the caller?"

"No, we never located him. What I do know is the call came from a phone in the lobby."

"And that doesn't trouble you? Come on, Kate, you're a seasoned pro. You know that's part of a set-up."

"Plead all you want, Jack, but the FBI is not taking the case," Kate said, standing. "Now, if you don't mind, I really do need to get moving."

"One last question, Kate."

"Make it quick."

"Who gave the order for you to stand down?"

Kate hesitated momentarily, then said, "James Weatherford."

"The attorney general?"

"Yes. And you didn't hear that from me."

"Why would the attorney general, the highest law enforcement individual in our country, tell you to abandon a case involving the death of a United States senator?"

"You would have to ask him that question. Jim Weatherford is the highest rung on my chain of command ladder, so when he gives an order, I follow it without hesitation. This conversation is finished. I have a meeting to attend, and I'm already running late."

Dantzler remained seated for several minutes after Kate left St. Peter's. He was trying his best to digest and understand that last bit of information she had revealed. He couldn't; it didn't compute. Jim Weatherford, the country's AG, should've been all over the Shapiro investigation, making certain it got resolved to everyone's satisfaction. This wasn't typical; Weatherford was known as a serious law-and-order Republican, a reputation he earned when he was a senator from Virginia. Yet, in this instance he was backing off the case. Dantzler was baffled as to why.

Dantzler had met Weatherford several years ago at a law enforcement conference in Miami. While at the meeting, Dantzler came across the attorney general's bio. Reading it, he learned that prior to his years in the senate, and before becoming attorney general, Weatherford served in the army, had risen to the rank of captain, and spent a year in Vietnam. Having worn the uniform and been in combat, he, more than anyone else, should have harbored doubts that a Medal of Honor recipient would be capable of committing such a horrible act. Even if there was only a hint that Danny might be innocent, Jim Weatherford should have led the charge to uncover the truth.

Yet . . . he didn't.

And Dantzler aimed to find out why.

# Chapter Twenty-Two

D antzler didn't say a word on the ride from downtown Chicago back to the house on Sheffield. His thoughts were squarely on what he'd been told by Kate Flanagan, that James Weatherford was the person who ordered the FBI to walk away from the Dana Shapiro investigation. What was the AG's reason for making that call? Surely, there had to be a legitimate reason for him to make such a bizarre decision. But try as he might, Dantzler couldn't come up with one that answered his questions.

Sensing that Dantzler was lost in thought while offering no inclination or desire for conversation, Mary-Louise also remained quiet during the nearly thirty-minute return trip. It wasn't until they pulled to a stop in front of the house and she had cut the engine that she finally broke the silence. And what she said, a question, snapped Dantzler back to the present.

"Did you ever have the feeling that you were being followed?" she asked.

"Why? Do you think you were followed?"

"I don't know for sure. It's just that, well, there was this one car that . . ."

"A white Toyota Avalon?" Dantzler interrupted.

"No, it was a black Audi. It stayed a couple of cars behind me while I was searching for a parking space. When I did find one, the Audi drove on past, went down the street until it was out of sight, then came back and parked several cars behind me. I'm probably being paranoid, I know, but it just felt kinda weird. Gave me the creeps, to be honest with you."

"Were there two men in the vehicle?"

"No, just the driver."

Dantzler got out of the Mercedes, closed the door, and looked up and down Sheffield. He saw plenty of cars, a few that were black, but no Audi. After Mary-Louise was at his side, he pressed the fob locking the car, and they went into the house.

Grace and Maggie were standing in the front room flanked on both sides by Angela and Jenny. The three older women were trying to console Maggie, who was clearly very distraught. Her red, swollen eyes indicated that she had been crying.

Dantzler nodded at Grace and gave her a "what's going on?" shrug.

"Maggie visited Danny this morning," Grace said. "He's extremely depressed, and has all but abandoned any hope that he will be exonerated. She said he has resigned himself to spending the rest of his life in prison."

"Call Danny, Grace," Dantzler said, "and give him the message that I'm getting closer to uncovering the truth. Tell him to hang tough, that it's only a matter of time until he walks out of that jail cell and has his old life and reputation back the way it was before all this happened. Make him believe that."

"Do you believe it, Jack?"

"I'm trying to."

———

DANTZLER WENT upstairs to his room, found the crumpled piece of yellow paper in his pants pocket, took it out, smoothed it, and began punching in Jon Crofford's phone number. He was expecting to hear a voice telling him to leave a message, but to his great surprise, Jon answered after a single ring.

"Talk, it's your quarter," Jon snapped.

"Jon Crofford?" Dantzler inquired

"Who's asking?"

"Jack Dantzler."

"And you are?"

"An investigator who would like to ask you a couple of questions."

"About?"

"A murder case I'm looking into."

"Whose murder?"

"Dana Shapiro."

"I thought they already caught her killer," Jon said. "That war hero guy. He confessed, didn't he?"

"He's innocent, Jon. And I think you can help me prove it."

"How?"

"Did you attend Dana's memorial service in Washington with someone named Todd?"

"Todd Holland, yeah."

"I desperately need to speak with him. Is he with you now?"

"No, he left late yesterday afternoon. He's on his way to visit an army buddy of his."

"Do you have a phone number where I can reach him?"

"Sure. But I'm not giving it to a total stranger. How the hell do I even know who you really are?"

"Google me, Jon. Jack Dantzler, Lexington, Kentucky, police. You'll see that I was a homicide cop for twenty-seven years."

"Why is a Kentucky cop working this particular case?"

"I'm no longer a cop. I'm now working for Grace West, Danny Kafka's defense attorney."

"Okay, I've found you on the website. You look legit. Still, I won't give you Todd's number. What I will do is contact Todd, let him know that we spoke, and that you need him to give you a call. That's my best offer. Take it or leave it."

"I'll take it," Dantzler said. "But first, would you tell me a few things about Todd. I've heard some stuff that I'd like you to confirm or deny."

"Okay, what have you heard?"

"That he and Dana Shapiro went out a couple of times, they appeared to hit it off in a positive way, then she ended the relationship because he had some problems or issues that she wasn't prepared to deal with."

"What problems or issues are you referring to?"

"That he was on drugs and possibly suffered from PTSD."

"Who was your source for that load of crap?" Jon asked.

"Dana's personal assistant. Why? Does she have it wrong?"

"Fuck, yeah, she has it wrong, all wrong. But I'm not surprised that she was clueless; Todd and Dana kept things in the dark. Given Dana's situation, the job and everything, they had no choice but to keep their relationship quiet. And Dana did have some real concerns."

"So the relationship didn't end after a couple of dates?"

"Man, they were head over heels in love with each other," Jon stated. "They were together the night before Dana was killed. Todd was devastated when he heard that she had been killed. He's still devastated, still grieving. As for the supposed drugs and PTSD problems, that's total bullshit. Todd never drinks alcohol, and emotionally he's one of the more stable men I know."

"Earlier, you mentioned Dana's job. Were you referring to her position as a United States senator, or to the position of Ambassador to Russia that she had recently been offered?"

"The Russian gig was supposed to be a big secret, but you know about it, so I guess the secret is out. Those concerns I mentioned had to do with the job in Russia. Dana was afraid that a long-distance relationship would never work out, and she was worried that if Todd did follow her over there at some point, he might end up being miserable. She wanted to be with Todd, but she wasn't sure how to make it work. Dana also worried that some would see her jumping into a serious relationship so soon after her husband's death as a real negative. She was fearful that her critics would accuse her of having the relationship while her husband was still alive, which wasn't even close to being true. Dana's been a widow for more than three years now. There's nothing wrong or inappropriate about her wanting to move on with her life. But . . . it was an issue that troubled her."

"When did Dana and Todd meet?" Dantzler asked.

"Less than a year ago. Eight, nine months would be about right."

"How well did you know Dana?"

"Not that well. She came to my place a few times, spent the night here with Todd on several occasions, and we had a few nice, long talks. Mainly, what I know about Dana, I heard from Todd."

"What's your relationship with Todd?"

"He and I are old college roommates. Arizona State University. We hit it off back then, we're still close today."

"Give him a call, ask him to contact me. It's imperative that I speak with him."

"All I can do is pass along your request. Whether or not he calls, that will be up to him."

"One last question, Jon. Have you ever met Todd's father?"

"Karl? Sure, I met him once when Todd and I were still in college. He's quite a character, too. Why are you asking about him? He and Todd aren't close."

"What does Karl do for a living?"

"He's a big movie producer out in Los Angeles."

*Bingo*!

"Thanks for talking with me, Jon. When you make that call to Todd, please implore him to get in touch with me."

---

DANTZLER SPENT the next ninety minutes on the computer researching Karl Holland. After coming up empty using "Carl" as a first name, he went with the alternate spelling of "Karl." That's when he struck gold.

There was plenty to be found, both positive and negative. Karl was, in fact, the founder and president of Holland Productions, although based on the quality and type of films he's rolled out for the viewing public, calling him a "big movie producer" was something of a stretch. The majority of his movies were low-budget, slasher-type genre flicks featuring dozens of scantily clad, well-endowed young women being pursued by a maniacal killer. Most of those movies went straight to video without ever showing up on the big screen. There were a handful of legitimate films that had done fairly well, both critically and at the box office. However, those movies had been co-produced in partnership with larger, more prominent studios. Seems Karl had little interest in putting out a high-quality product.

That was the positive. The negative dealt primarily with the strange death of his fourth wife—she drowned in their Beverly Hills pool although she had at one time been an alternate on the U.S. Olympic swim team—and the dozen-plus lawsuits filed against him for sexual harassment and/or sexual assault. In each case the charges had been dropped, which told Dantzler that Karl Holland either paid the accusers to shut up and go away, or he gave them roles in his movies.

A bad guy no matter how you sized it up.

DANTZLER SHUT OFF THE COMPUTER, trudged down the stairs, and went into the big room where Maggie and Mary-Louise were sorting through a stack of pizza coupons. Digging into his pants pocket, Dantzler took out his money clip, peeled off three twenties, and tossed them onto the table.

"Use that to pay for the pizzas," he said. "It's past time that I chip in and buy the grub."

"That's way too much," Maggie said, holding up one of the twenties and offering it back to Dantzler. "Forty dollars is more than enough."

"Buy an extra one, a large, and take it to Danny this afternoon. I'm sure he would appreciate getting some decent food. If nothing else, a good pizza pie might help lift his spirits."

"All right, if you insist," Maggie said, putting the twenty back in with the other two.

Dantzler was in the kitchen getting a can of Diet Pepsi when his phone buzzed. Checking the number, he realized the call was coming from Jon Crofford's phone. That was a disappointment. A call from Jon, one this quick, likely meant he'd contacted Todd Holland, and Todd wasn't interested in communicating with Dantzler. If that were the case, it was bad news. But it wasn't bad news—it was much worse than bad.

"Am I speaking with Jack Dantzler?" the caller inquired before Dantzler had time to say hello. The man's voice was gruff, his speech hurried. "Are you Jack Dantzler?"

"Yes, I am. And who is asking?"

"Detective Barry Rhodes, Arlington, Virginia, homicide."

"Okay, Detective, you have my attention. What do you need?"

"Did you recently speak with Jon Crofford?"

"Yeah, maybe three hours ago."

"What was the nature of that conversation?"

"I'm a private investigator working a murder case," Dantzler responded. "I needed to locate and speak with an individual, to gather some information, and I felt Jon could get me in touch with him."

"By any chance is Todd Holland that individual?"

"That's correct. Have you been in touch with him, Detective?"

"Not yet. The last call Jon Crofford made was to Todd Holland. I rang the number, got a recording. You were the next-to-last call Mr. Crofford made. That's how I got your number."

"I was a homicide detective for twenty-seven years, so I have a pretty good idea why you are calling me. Jon Crofford is dead, isn't he?"

"He is."

"Let me venture a guess. He was tied to a chair, tortured, then shot in the back of his head, most likely with a twenty-two pistol. Is that close?"

"That's not just close—it's accurate down to the last detail. Makes me wonder if you might be the shooter."

"Never met the man, Detective Rhodes, only spoke to him that one time. Plus, I'm in Chicago, which means the distance and the timeline rule me out as the shooter."

"Then share with me how you knew the details surrounding Jon Crofford's death."

Dantzler said, "I'm sure you've read about the murder of Dana Shapiro, the U.S. senator."

"Yeah, she was killed by that kid who was a war hero. That's the case you're working?"

"Danny Kafka is innocent, Detective Rhodes. He was framed for the murder."

"Hell, the kid confessed."

"All part of an elaborate plan. Anyway, back to your question. Danny was an actor in Manhattan. I went there to speak with his agent, a guy named Abe Pearlstein. A few hours after I left, Abe was bound to a chair, tortured horribly, and then shot in the back of his head. That's how I knew. Obviously, Abe and Jon Crofford were killed by the same people."

"People? You suspect there is more than one killer?"

"In Abe's case, yes. Cameras caught two men entering and leaving his office. New York detectives were unable to identify either man. Since two men murdered Abe, I'm assuming the same two took out Jon Crofford."

"What reason did they have to murder Abe Pearlstein?"

"For the same reason they killed Jon Crofford. To extract information."

"What information?"

"Names. Mine, the first time around, Todd Holland's in this instance."

"Why would they want Todd Holland's name?"

"I have no idea," Dantzler answered, knowing he'd just lied to a fellow detective.

"Let me get this straight," Detective Rhodes said. "Two men are murdered in identical ways, you were the last person to meet with the first one, and the last person to speak with the second victim. If nothing else, you've got the Angel of Death riding on your shoulder. Remind me to keep my distance from you."

"Mind if I ask you a question, Detective?"

"Over the phone, yes," Rhodes answered, chuckling. "But not face to face."

"When you phoned Todd Holland, did you leave a message?"

"No."

"Because he might be a suspect, correct?"

"Right. Also, if he's not the killer, and I doubt that he is, and he's close with the deceased, I didn't want to break the news to him over the phone. If he had answered, I would have told him I wanted to speak with him about another matter. That way I could break the news to him face to face."

"That's exactly how I would have played it," Dantzler said, thankful Todd wasn't aware that his friend was dead. "But I agree with you. Todd isn't the shooter."

"Who do you see as the shooter? Or the shooters?"

"Still working on it, Detective Rhodes. But if I do find out anything valuable, I'll share it with you."

"That would be nice. Oh, and I do have a final question for you. Did Jon Crofford say where Todd was heading?"

"He said Todd was on his way to visit an army buddy. He gave me no name, no city."

"I'll take you as man of your word, Mr. Dantzler. That if you uncover anything I might find useful, you won't hesitate to give me a call."

"You have my promise, Detective Rhodes."

Dantzler ended the call and put his phone on the table just as four pizzas arrived. They were steaming and looked delicious. The strong smell of garlic drifted through the room. After setting aside a pizza for Danny, Team West tore into the others like a pack of hyenas going after a dead carcass. Not Dantzler, who stood and watched.

His appetite had deserted him.

# Chapter Twenty-Three

At four in the morning, Sergei Lazarov was sitting in a truck stop just off Interstate 70 somewhere in Ohio. He was tired, half-asleep, and three cups of coffee weren't doing anything to perk him up. The smart thing to do, he knew, was to go back outside, climb in his car, and catch a few hours of sleep. At least until sunrise. Then he could go back into the truck stop and eat a big breakfast. Rest and food would help refuel the engine.

But Sergei wasn't going to sleep, nor was he going to grab some food. He had too much on his mind to do either of those things. Sitting there, half comatose, he signaled for the waitress, and ordered a fourth cup of coffee.

And thought about what had transpired earlier in Arlington.

He had arrived at his destination at dusk, a nice three-bedroom brick house at the center of a cul-de-sac. A single vehicle, a blue BMW, sat in the driveway. Sergei waited in his car until darkness blanketed the area. After observing no one entering or leaving the house, and the lights inside being turned on, he decided it was time to make his move. Keeping his head down while putting on his gloves, he exited his car, walked up to the front door, and rang the doorbell. When a man opened the door, Sergei, his pistol down by his side, quickly stepped inside the house and slammed the butt of his weapon hard against the stunned man's head. The blow sent him crashing to the floor, blood dripping from his wound. Sergei closed and locked the door, flipped the man onto his stomach, took out a roll of duct tape, ripped off a piece, and covered the man's mouth. Next, he taped the man's hands behind him. With the man now silenced and secured, Sergei dragged him into the kitchen, lifted him into a chair, bound his upper torso to the chair, and then taped his ankles together.

Sergei didn't know who the man was, only that he wasn't the intended target. But based on information gleaned from several letters and bills lying on the kitchen table, Sergei learned that the man's name was Jon Crofford.

Following a quick search of the house to make sure no one else was present, Sergei then spent the next hour alternating between asking Jon Crofford questions and torturing him to get answers. Sergei would ask the question, remove the tape from Jon's mouth, and wait for a reply. When Sergei didn't like what he heard, the tape was placed over Jon's mouth, and the inflicting of pain—hard punches to the stomach, knife cuts, cigarette burns—began all over again.

Finally convinced that Jon Crofford had been truthful, and had nothing else worthwhile to reveal, Sergei stepped behind the man, screwed the suppressor onto his pistol, and shot the bruised and battered man in the back of his head.

Now, sitting in the truck stop, staring at his new cup of coffee, Sergei wondered what he should do next. He had two options, one that would be terribly unpleasant, and one that would have to be carefully finessed. Neither option did much to lift his spirits.

The first option was to phone his father and tell him what he'd learned, which really wasn't very much. Jon Crofford didn't know where the intended target was at the present time, only that he was on his way to Milwaukee to visit an old army buddy. The old man was sure to scream at him for not gathering firmer information, for not continuing the torture until all information had been collected. But the old man wasn't in the room during the torture session;

Sergei was. And he was fully confident that Jon Crofford had given up everything he knew. No matter how much pain he was enduring, Jon never veered from his original statement that the target was heading to Milwaukee, and that he didn't have a specific address.

The target? Even now, Sergei was having a difficult time believing that his father wanted this man killed.

Todd Holland.

What possible reason could his father have for ordering a hit on Karl's oldest son? His father and Karl were business associates who worked together on dozens of jobs big and small, raking in millions of dollars along the way. Why would his father risk losing such a lucrative partnership, which would be the outcome if Karl got word that Yuri Lazarov was behind the murder of Todd Holland? Unlike Yuri, Karl didn't have the muscle of the Russian mob behind him. However, if Todd was killed, and if Karl found out Yuri was behind it, blood was sure to be spilled.

None of this made any sense whatsoever to Sergei.

His second option, though extremely delicate, was preferable to the first. Calling Yuri and getting yelled at was never a good first choice. And that's what would happen if he made that call. No, option number two was the one he settled on.

He would wait until he was back in Chicago, speak with Brad, and try to persuade him to call his older brother. But what reason could Sergei give that would entice Brad to make the call? Brad was sure to be suspicious and ask a bunch of questions. After all, Todd and Brad had never been close. Todd, eight years older than Brad, moved out of the house about an hour after graduating high school. He joined the army, served in Operation Desert Storm, left the military, and went to college at Arizona State University. After getting his degree, Todd went to work in the Pentagon, serving as a liaison between various Intelligence agencies. He had no time for his father or his brother, both of whom he regarded as second-rate criminals.

Given the distance between brothers, how could Sergei persuade Brad to give Todd a call? Whatever the reason, it had to be legitimate and believable. Sergei tossed around a few possibilities before finally coming to the realization that none of them had a remote chance of working.

When he had been inside the house, he found Jon Crofford's phone, scrolled down the Contacts list until he came to Todd's name and number. He thought about punching in the number, then ripping the tape off Jon's mouth and letting him speak with Todd. But he judged that plan to be too risky. Jon probably knew he was going to die, so what did he have to lose by yelling out a warning to his friend? And there was no way Sergei could make the call and try to pass himself off as Jon; his Russian accent would give him away in about two seconds. That also ruled out his leaving a message.

Bottom line: Having Jon Crofford's phone wasn't going to be of any use. Sergei concluded that he might as well toss the damn thing into the garbage, which he did after putting his gloves back on and carefully wiping the phone clean of his fingerprints.

Finished with his coffee, he paid the bill, went back out to his car, and started the engine. He would drive back to Chicago and hook up with Brad. Maybe, somewhere along the way, he would conjure up a plan that might work, although deep down inside he doubted that he would. There was, however, one thing he didn't doubt, and that caused him to cringe.

The inevitable phone call from his father.

---

AT SEVEN THE NEXT MORNING, Todd Holland made his fifth call to Jon Crofford. None of those calls were answered by Jon, nor did he advise the caller to leave a message. Each call ended abruptly, as though the phone had been turned off, or the battery was running low. Todd wasn't overly concerned; Jon was, after all, something of an odd duck. He was no stranger to peculiar behavior.

Todd scrolled through his message box and listened to the one Jon left late yesterday afternoon. In the message, Jon was adamant that Todd call a private investigator named Jack Dantzler. Jon gave Todd the number, then urged him once again to make the call.

What Jon hadn't done was give Todd a reason why he should contact this Dantzler guy.

*Thanks, Jon, for making this so cryptic, so mysterious.*

A private investigator wanting to speak with me certainly qualified as a mystery, Todd thought, as he punched in Dantzler's number. Dantzler answered immediately and identified himself.

Todd Holland said, "Yes, a friend of mine named Jon Crofford left a message saying I should give you a call. Said you're a private investigator. My question is why would a private investigator have any reason to speak with me?"

"Because I'm working for the attorney representing the man accused of murdering Dana Shapiro, and I think you can help me find some answers I'm looking for."

"The answer is simple—Dana was killed by Danny Kafka."

"No, Danny is innocent," Dantzler replied. Then: "Where are you right now?"

"Milwaukee."

"That's music to my ears, Todd."

"Why?"

"Because you're not that far from Chicago. Listen, Todd, here's what I want you to do. I'm going to give you the address for a condo in downtown Chicago. Get in your car and drive there immediately. I will be there when you arrive. Okay?"

"No, it's not okay," Todd answered. "First, I'm going to phone Jon and get his take on you. Then . . ."

"When was the last time you spoke with Jon?"

"Yesterday afternoon. I've called him several times since then, but he hasn't answered. I will keep trying until he does."

"He won't answer, Todd. He can't. I hate to break this news to you, but Jon is dead. He was murdered sometime last night."

"Jon's dead?"

"Yes."

"Why would anyone want to kill Jon? He never harmed a fly."

"Jon was tortured before he was killed. There is only one reason why—the killer was trying to find out where you are. That's why I'm convinced your life is in danger."

"Jon couldn't have told them anything. He didn't know my friend, or my friend's address. All Jon knew was that I was heading to Milwaukee."

"Write down this address, Todd. Then get in your car and get there as fast as possible. Don't phone anyone, and don't answer any calls."

"Wait. How do I know you didn't kill Jon? Maybe you did, and now you're trying to lure me to my death."

"I'll tell you the same thing I told Jon—Google me. Jack Dantzler, Lexington, Kentucky, police. You'll see that I was a homicide detective for twenty-seven years. The only thing I ask is that you do it quickly, then get on the highway. I can keep you safe once you get to Chicago."

"Safe from who? And why am I in danger?"

"The same people who murdered Dana want you dead. Why? Dana died for a reason, probably because she had information that could harm someone in our government. You had a close relationship with Dana. The people behind this plan have to be worried that she shared that information with you. Therefore, you're a loose end that needs to be eliminated."

"Dana didn't share any business or political information with me," Todd said.

"They don't know that. And they can't take the chance that she didn't share it with you. Rather than leave you alone and have to worry about what you may or may not know, they'll hunt you down and put a bullet in the back of your head. That way, your silence is assured."

"You're sure Jon is dead?"

"Yes. I spoke with the detective working the case. He told me."

"Okay, I have a pen and paper. Tell me where you want me to go."

Dantzler gave Todd the address, then said, "I will be at the condo when you get there. And remember what I said—don't make or answer any calls."

"One final question before I leave. If Danny Kafka didn't murder Dana, who did?"

"The Russians."

"The Russians? Are you sure about that?"

"We can discuss it when you're here, Todd. But right now I want you in your car and on the way to Chicago. Your safety is my immediate concern."

"I'm on my way," Todd announced, ending the call.

Dantzler tossed his phone onto the big table, and for the first time in days he actually smiled. At last, he thought, answers to some key questions were about to be uncovered.

SERGEI WAS about an hour away from Chicago when he received the call he'd been dreading. It was his father, and the old man didn't waste any time getting straight to the point. Offering no preamble, he asked Sergei if things went according to plan in Arlington.

Sergei spoke softly, offering complete details of what had taken place inside Jon Crofford's house, all the while bracing for his father's inevitable explosion, that moment when he would again label his son as either an idiot or an imbecile, or perhaps both. But to Sergei's great surprise, his father listened quietly, didn't interrupt with questions or comments, while keeping the lid on his volcanic temper. It was only after Sergei had completed his discourse that the old man finally broke his silence.

"And you are positive that this man told you all that he knew?" Yuri asked.

"Yes. With what I put him through, if he knew more he would have given it up."

"Did you make sure to leave no evidence behind?"

"Yes," Sergei answered, both surprised and bewildered that his father was behaving in such a civil manner. "I left nothing that could be traced to me."

"Well, the major task still remains. Todd Holland has to be eliminated. Do you have any idea where he might be?"

"On his way to Milwaukee."

"That's all you have? No address?"

"No," Sergei said, then quickly added, "but I have a plan that I think might help us locate him."

"Let me hear it."

"I will have Brad give him a call. During their conversation he can ask Todd where he is. Once Brad knows, I know."

"What reason would Brad have to phone his brother? They detest each other."

"That's what I'm working on right now. I have two or three possible scenarios that might do the trick." This was a lie—in fact Sergei didn't have a clue how to entice Brad to make the call. "I just have to settle on the one I think Brad will go for without asking too many questions."

Yuri was silent for a long period. Sergei could hear his father breathing, his own heart pumping hard, certain that the explosion of rage was about to occur. But for the second time in a matter of minutes, Sergei was surprised by his father's response.

"That's not a bad plan," Yuri said before adding this codicil, "just make sure you get it done."

# Chapter Twenty-Four

Dantzler needed to phone Grace but was informed by Maggie that she would be in court for most of the day. When Dantzler said he would send a text, Maggie quickly nixed that as well, saying Grace would have her cell phone turned off while court was in session. Then Maggie asked Dantzler why the urgent need to get in touch with Grace.

"I need a key to her condo," Dantzler said.

Maggie opened a desk drawer, reached inside, and pulled out a single key attached to a silver chain. "*Voila*," Maggie said, gleaming. "Ask and it shall be given."

"You're a true saint, Maggie," Dantzler said, taking the key from her. "And don't let anyone tell you otherwise."

"Do you know how to get there?"

"I have the address. My GPS can do the rest."

"When I do speak with Grace, do you want me to let her know you're there?" Maggie asked.

Dantzler nodded, said, "Tell her Todd Holland is on his way to the condo. She should join us when she can."

"Will do."

Thanks to his GPS directions, Dantzler had no trouble finding the huge structure that was home to Grace's condo. He drove into the underground parking structure, found an empty Visitor's Parking space, pulled in, and killed the motor. He got out, locked the doors, and walked over to the elevators. Only then did he check the key to see which floor Grace lived on. He wasn't shocked by what he saw; Grace lived in a penthouse condo. Of course she did. Where else would someone like Grace West reside but in one of the best and most-expensive places in all of Chicago? Nothing but high end and upscale for that lady.

Dantzler rode the elevator to the top floor, got off, and stepped into an open area. There were only two condos at the penthouse level, one to his left, one to his right. Grace lived in the one to his left.

He opened the door, stepped inside, and couldn't believe what he was seeing. He felt as though he had just entered into a make-believe world, a majestic set constructed for a glamorous Hollywood love story. The place was beyond opulent, beyond spectacular. This was no ordinary condo. Nor was it a luxury apartment. This was a palace, the kind of place Dantzler figured those ultra-wealthy Saudi sheiks and princes lived in courtesy of all the oil we purchased from them. The square footage was enormous. He wouldn't even begin to guess what Grace paid for this place. It had to be in the eight-figure ballpark. The furnishings alone, most of which were either all black or all white, were worth a major fortune. Many of the walls were home to paintings, and although Dantzler was by no means an art expert he suspected that at least a few were originals. Then there was the spacious balcony that looked out at Lake Michigan. After giving the huge place a quick run-through, he determined that nothing in this entire condo, from the sterling silver knives, forks and spoons, to the glasses and coffee cups cost less than two-hundred bucks apiece.

He knew Grace was successful, but he had no idea she was *this* successful.

Standing in the living room, Dantzler recalled the first time he became aware of Grace West. This was years before they actually met. She was being interviewed on the old Larry King Live program on CNN a few days after successfully defending a client accused of murder. It was one of those high-profile trials that captured the public's attention. Dantzler remembered having two immediate and opposing impressions of Grace as he watched the interview—she was equal parts beautiful and arrogant. By the time the interview was finished he had settled on arrogant as leaving the strongest impression.

He didn't much care for her then, and his feelings held true when she first arrived in Lexington three years ago to defend a woman named Morgan Ballard who was accused of murdering her husband while he slept. But the situation changed, and soon Dantzler and Grace were involved in an intense, albeit brief affair. When the trial was concluded, during which Grace proudly boasted that she "eviscerated" him on the witness stand (a charge he vehemently disagreed with), she left Lexington faster than a gazelle running away from a cheetah. Dantzler had no illusions that their relationship would be long-lasting or permanent, but her quick and silent exit left him with negative feelings toward her. Not to worry, he felt at the time, because it was unlikely that the two would ever cross paths again.

And now here he was waltzing through her multimillion-dollar penthouse condo searching for the liquor cabinet. Three years ago, any of this would have been unimaginable. Grace was gone, out of his life, in the rear-view mirror. On top of that, there was no way he, a life-long homicide detective, would ever agree to work for a defense attorney. Yet that's exactly what he was doing. If he needed proof that life can throw curveballs at you, he now had it.

Dantzler located the liquor cabinet and opened it. Standing front and center was an unopened bottle of Pernod. He smiled when he saw it, remembering from the time he spent with Grace in Lexington that she once tabbed Pernod as "easily the most foul-smelling alcohol on the planet." Its presence in the liquor cabinet meant she had gone out of her way to purchase it for him. Realizing this made him feel bad for not accepting Grace's invitation to spend his nights here in the condo. He made a promise to do just that once he had Danny Kafka out of jail.

He thought about mixing a drink but decided not to. He needed to be clear-headed and thinking straight when Todd Holland showed up. Closing the liquor cabinet, he went into the den, sat on the sofa—it was so soft he felt as though he was melting into it—and took out his cell phone. Scrolling through the Contacts list, he found the name he was searching for—his old friend Bobby Brennan, the NYC detective—and punched in the numbers. Bobby answered before the first ring ended.

"A call from Jack Dantzler, legendary ex-homicide detective from the Bluegrass State," Bobby said, laughing. "To what do I owe this unexpected pleasure?"

"Bobby, have you ever uttered one word that wasn't dripping with bullshit?"

"What you call bullshit, I call gold."

"See, that's exactly what I'm talking about. Bobby, if bullshit was gold, you'd have more money than Bill Gates and Warren Buffett combined."

"A guy as handsome, suave, and debonair as me has no need for all that money."

"Hate to tell you this, Bobby, but suave and debonair mean pretty much the same thing. Using two words when one will suffice is what's known as a redundancy."

"Damn, I had no idea someone from Kentucky could be so familiar with the English language. I thought all you folks spoke hillbilly."

"Now, now, Bobby. Your New York arrogance is coming through."

"Nah, I'm just ragging on you, Dantzler. I know you're about ten times more intelligent than I am."

"Only ten? I'd say that's definitely on the low end of the scale."

"Okay, twenty. Does that make you feel better?" Bobby said, again chuckling. "Now, down to business. What's your reason for this call?"

"I need your help."

"Name it."

"That tape of the two men leaving Abe Pearlstein's building, can you get that to me?" Dantzler asked.

"No problem. I'll download it, then send it to you on your cell phone. But I have to warn you that I'm not sure how much use it will be. Making a facial ID is going to be difficult. One of the guys has his head down and turned away, while the other guy, the taller one, has his right hand up to the side of his face. Why do you need the tape now?"

"A guy is on his way to see me, and I want him to take a look at it. I doubt he can shed any light on who those dudes are, but, who knows, maybe we'll get lucky."

"I'll send you the camera feed that shows them entering Abe's building," Bobby said. "That's when they are closest to a camera. It's not great, but it is better than the one showing them leaving."

"Great. Shoot that to me when you get time."

"You'll have it in less than thirty minutes. And should your guy come through with an ID, let me know."

"You got it. And thanks, Bobby."

Bobby was a man of his word, and twenty minutes after ending his conversation with the New York City detective, Dantzler was sitting at a table studying the tape of Abe Pearlstein's two killers as they entered the building. Bobby was right; the film was grainy, and the two men made a concerted effort to conceal their faces from the camera. Dantzler watched the film several times, then paused it at the moment the two men were nearest the camera. Once again, he harbored strong doubts that Todd Holland could ID either man. But he had to give it a shot.

As one of his early tennis coaches used to say, "You can't win if you don't play."

Todd Holland showed up about an hour later looking tired, weary, and stressed. He stepped inside and looked the place over, but unlike Dantzler he displayed no sign that he was overly impressed. Somehow this didn't surprise Dantzler. As the son of a movie producer, Todd had likely frequented some massive Hollywood mansions during his younger days. In Dantzler's eyes, this place was a palace. To Todd, it might seem little more than ordinary.

Todd was certainly not an ordinary looking man. He was almost beyond handsome. It was easy to see why Dana Shapiro—or any lady for that matter—would fall head over heels for this guy. He was Dantzler's height (six-three), with Paul Newman-type blue eyes, sandy-colored hair, chiseled facial features, and a lean, muscular physique that provided testimony to an extreme fitness regime. His physique was accentuated by the clothes he was wearing—black slacks, a black T-shirt with a picture of Einstein on it, and black Sketchers shoes. Todd Holland was a man who took care of his body and he wasn't ashamed to advertise it.

"Look, Mr. Dantzler, I . . ."

"Jack."

"Man, I'm about to explode. I really need to take a leak. Can you point me to the bathroom?"

"Just take off walking, Todd. I've seen about five, and I haven't even been through the entire place."

"Thanks," Todd said as he headed for a hallway to his right.

"You hungry?" Dantzler asked.

"Starved."

"How about a ham and cheese sandwich? I saw some in the fridge."

"That'll work."

"You a mustard or mayo guy?"

"Mustard."

Dantzler wandered into the kitchen, grabbed a couple plates (how much did they cost?), looked around until he found a loaf of wheat bread, then began the process of throwing together a glorified make-shift snack consisting of ham, cheese, mustard, sweet pickles, and potato chips. By the time Dantzler finished preparing their repast Todd was sitting on a stool at the bar.

"What do you want to drink?" Dantzler said, placing the food in front of Todd. "There's Diet Pepsi, water, or if you're in need of something stronger, I can get you a beer."

"Diet Pepsi will do," Todd said, taking a bite of his sandwich. "Damn, this is delicious. You make a mean ham and cheese sandwich."

Dantzler opened two cans of Diet Pepsi, handed one to Todd, and said. "Jon Crofford told me that you never drink alcohol. I should've remembered that before asking if you wanted a beer."

"Alcohol has never been my thing. Same goes for drugs. Growing up where I did, I saw first-hand the damage caused by alcohol and drug abuse. I wanted no part of that shit. Life is tough enough without carrying a monkey on your back."

Todd took another bite of his sandwich, then followed it by scarfing down several potato chips. After taking a drink of Diet Pepsi, he said, "On the drive here I listened to several messages on my phone. Two were left by Barry Rhodes. He identified himself as an Arlington detective. Said he wanted me to contact him but he never told me why."

"He didn't want to break the news to you about Jon's death over the phone," Dantzler said. "I hated having to tell you in that manner, but I really had no choice. I wanted you here, knowing you were safe."

"Thanks. But this is all so bizarre."

"You didn't phone anyone, or take any calls, did you?"

"No, I did as you instructed."

"Let me say how sorry I am for the loss of your friend. And for what happened to Dana Shapiro. I never met her, but I did speak with Jon. He came across as a really good guy."

"Good doesn't begin to describe Jon," Todd said, smiling at the thought of his friend. "He was funny, kind, caring . . . just an all-around gentle soul. Truly one of a kind."

The smile morphed into something akin to a grimace. "You said Jon was tortured," Todd said. "What did they do to him?'

"I really don't know," Dantzler lied. If Todd wanted the gory details, he'd have to get them from another source. "Detective Rhodes didn't share any of that information with me. All he said was that Jon didn't have an easy death. I took that to mean he was tortured in some way. My advice would be to not dwell on any of that. Hang on to your best memories of Jon."

"Do you know who killed Jon?"

"Not yet, but I'm working on it."

"You said it was the Russians. Why are you so sure they did it?"

"I'm only sure of one thing," Dantzler corrected, "that Danny Kafka is innocent. He didn't murder Dana, and we do know for certain that he didn't kill Jon Crofford. As for the Russians, certain facts have led me in their direction. I don't know how involved they are, but I feel certain they had a hand in what has happened."

"If Danny Kafka didn't kill Dana, then who did?"

"The actual shooter was a guy named Bobby Conrad."

"What reason did he have for murdering Dana?"

"No reason. In fact, he had no idea he was actually killing her."

Todd shook his head, said, "You've lost me. I'm totally confused."

Dantzler had no choice but to lay it all out for Todd.

"When Danny said those words on the tape, announcing that he was going to eliminate Dana, he thought he was auditioning for a role in a big movie starring Nicole Kidman and Tom Hardy," Dantzler said. "Same goes for Bobby Conrad, who happened to be a world-class military sniper. He thought he was taking part in a scene being filmed for the movie. When he pulled the trigger he had no idea that the bullets weren't blanks, and that the person being shot was Dana Shapiro, not an actor. After the scene was finished, he walked away thinking he might have a brief moment on the big screen. He was wrong; two hours later he was murdered. So was his girlfriend. Danny was immediately arrested and charged with Dana's murder. The actual shooter was silenced forever, the patsy was in custody, and the ones behind the plan rode off into the sunset. Every part of the plan worked to perfection."

"That's pretty damn devious," Todd said, finishing the last drops of his Diet Pepsi. "And you suspect that this plan was concocted by someone in the movie business, right? That's why you want to speak with me."

Dantzler nodded, said, "Tell me about your father."

"Karl is an asshole and a scumbag. Next question."

"Come on, Todd, I need more than that."

"Look, I've seen my father exactly twice since I graduated from high school," Todd related. "I have no use for the man, not after what he did to my mother. He's just a reprehensible person, that's about all I can tell you."

"What did he do to your mother?"

"Same thing he does with all the women he marries or lives with —he trades them in for a younger model. They might as well be automobiles for all he cares. My mom was nineteen when she married him, fourteen years younger than he was at the time. She was his third wife. When she turned thirty, he gave her a nice settlement, and then tossed her, me, and my younger brother to the curb. It's what he'd done with his first two wives, so no one should have been too shocked."

"I saw on the Internet that one of his wives died under mysterious circumstances," Dantzler said. "That wasn't your mom, obviously."

"That was wife number four or five. Who the hell can keep count?"

"Where is your mother now?"

"She died nine years ago. Pancreatic cancer."

"Sorry. What's the story with your brother?"

"Much different than mine, that's for sure. Brad got back in touch with Karl not long after we were sent packing. For some unknown reason Brad wanted to remain close to Karl. Why? I can't even begin to answer that question. The last time I spoke with Brad, which was five years ago, he told me he was working for our father."

Dantzler said, "Do you think Karl has the capability to put together a complicated plan like the one involving Danny Kafka and the death of Dana Shapiro?"

Todd thought about the question for a few moments before finally responding. "By capabilities, if you're asking me whether I believe he could pull off the movie aspect part of the plan, my answer is yes. But the actual killing? That aspect, I'm not so sure of."

"You ever heard of a man named Carson Welles?"

"No. Why? Who's he?"

"It's the name given by one of the two men who went to Danny's apartment to film the audition scene. He claimed to be a producer or a director, which was a lie. I searched the Internet for him, couldn't find a match. It was a bogus name."

"What about the second guy?"

"According to Danny, the man never uttered a word."

"What led you in the direction of the Russians?" Todd inquired.

"Danny's agent in New York was an old guy named Abe Pearlstein. The day after Danny's audition, Abe received a call informing him that Danny got the role, that the movie was to be filmed in Chicago, and that Danny was to fly there the following Friday. Abe told me the caller spoke with a heavy Russian accent."

Dantzler pulled his phone close and tapped the screen, bringing it to life. The paused picture of the two men entering Abe's building filled the screen. Positioning the phone so Todd could get a better look, Dantzler said, "I want you to look at this and tell me if you recognize anyone. I doubt that you will, but take a look anyway."

After Todd gave a quick glance at the two figures on the phone, he looked at Dantzler, and said, "Why are you asking me about these two?"

"Because they are only minutes away from torturing and murdering Abe Pearlstein."

Todd pointed to the taller of the two men, the one who had his right hand covering most of his face. "That's my brother Brad," he said, moving his finger to the second man. "And this one is Sergei Lazarov. Seems your hunch about the Russians wasn't too far off the mark."

"Sergei is Russian? You're positive about that?"

"Yeah."

"What can you tell me about him?"

"Nothing. I only met him once, briefly, the last time I saw Brad. I do know his father's name is Yuri." A thought suddenly shot through Todd's head. "Wait a minute. If these two murdered this Abe guy, does that mean you think they also killed Jon?"

"I'd have to say yes."

"And Dana?"

"Neither one pulled the trigger, but they helped execute the plan."

"Goddammit, I'll strangle both of these bastards if I get my hands on them," Todd practically screamed. "And I will find them. They have to pay for what they did to Dana, and to Jon."

"Oh, they'll pay," Dantzler agreed. "But a lot of dots have to be connected before that happens. Connecting them is my job, not yours. What you need to do is stay here out of harm's way. You can't do anything to help if you're dead. And Todd, you will be dead if you don't remain under the radar."

"Listen, I work in the Pentagon, in Military Intelligence," Todd pleaded. "I also saw combat overseas. Don't put me on the sidelines. I'm not some soft pansy from California. I can help."

"You will, Todd, I promise. But only at the proper time, after I've connected some of those dots." Dantzler collected his thoughts before continuing. "Do you know James Weatherford?"

"The attorney general? Well, I can't say I really know the man, but I have met him on several occasions."

"Did Dana know him?"

"Yeah, she knew everyone, all the way up to the Oval Office. Why are you asking about Jim Weatherford?"

"He did something really strange, something I can't shake free of. It's a key part of the puzzle, but I can't figure it out."

"What did he do?"

"He ordered the FBI to stand down, thus handing the investigation into Dana's murder over to Chicago PD. That makes no sense. Dana was a U.S. senator who was soon to become our ambassador to Russia. That's two reasons why the FBI should have been in charge."

"Dana met with Jim Weatherford several times in the weeks prior to her death. I would think he'd be all over the case."

"Why did they meet?"

Todd shrugged, said, "Couldn't tell you. Dana never shared details of her work with me."

"How long before Dana died did they have their last meeting?"

"Let me think about that. I'd say two weeks, three, maybe."

"We're gonna get to the bottom of this, Todd," Dantzler said just as Grace entered the condo. "Here's the boss. Stay on your toes. She's tough."

"Don't believe a word the man says," Grace said, extending her hand to Todd. "Todd Holland, I presume."

"You presume correctly," he answered, coming off the stool and shaking her hand. "It's an honor to meet you."

Grace shifted her eyes to Dantzler, and said, "Not only is he much more handsome than you, Jack, he's also more polite."

Dantzler nudged Todd in the ribs, said, "She's only praising you because you said it was an honor to meet her. Grace never met a compliment she didn't embrace."

"Diet Pepsi? Is that the best two macho men can do?" Grace asked. "How about something with a real kick to it?"

"I'll have a Pernod and orange juice," Dantzler said. "As for our young friend here, he does not imbibe."

"You don't drink at all?" Grace said, looking skeptically at Todd. "I mean, it's great to have a clean soul, but you really need to do some damage to your liver."

"I'll stick with Diet Pepsi or water," Todd said.

"Well, Jack, at least we know who will serve as our designated driver." Grace picked up their two empty plates and headed for the kitchen. "What did you two find to eat?"

"Ham and cheese sandwich, chips, and a sweet pickle," Dantzler answered.

"Gentlemen, let me make our drinks, then I'll whip us up something a lot more substantial than a ham sandwich." Opening the liquor cabinet, she held up the bottle of Pernod. "I paid big bucks to buy this nasty, foul-smelling stuff just for you, Jack. It's about time you drank some of it."

"In case you haven't already picked up on it, Todd," Dantzler said, "Grace is quite the lecturer."

After mixing Dantzler's drink, Grace made a Scotch and soda

for herself. Handing Dantzler his glass, she said, "Okay, boys, what's the plan?"

"Starting first thing tomorrow we're gonna hunt down some killers," Dantzler said, clicking his glass against hers. "And we're gonna go after them with Old Testament vengeance."

# Chapter Twenty-Five

Yuri Lazarov's blood pressure spiked considerably when he heard the caller's voice on his cell phone. The late-afternoon call was from the man who set the Dana Shapiro plan in motion, a man Yuri had not expected to hear from again anytime soon. Or, maybe forever.

Ivan Bershov.

Yuri had spoken many times with Ivan over the phone but had only met him face to face on a single occasion. But Ivan's reputation was well-known among Russians living throughout the United States. He was a Washington-based attorney, and the top lobbyist for Russian interests in the U.S. As such he was very influential both here and in his home country. He was also one of Russia's wealthiest oligarchs, and a close friend and business partner of Vladimir Putin.

Anyone with close ties to the top dog in the Kremlin was someone with immense power. A man like Ivan could have someone killed with the simple nod of his head. Yuri had no doubt that just such a thing had happened many times in the past. After all, Ivan, like Putin, had once ranked high up in the old KGB. And those guys didn't mess around. They'd kill you without so much as blinking twice.

Yuri wondered what the call was about, then realized that Ivan was probably calling to inquire how things had gone in Arlington. This caused Yuri's blood pressure to shoot up even higher. What answer could he possibly give? None that would satisfy Ivan, that much he knew for certain. Yuri could lie and say that Sergei had eliminated the target. But that would be a foolish thing to do. At some point, if the falsehood was revealed, and it most certainly would be, Ivan would have both Yuri and Sergei eliminated instead.

No, Yuri decided, it was best to tell the truth, to acknowledge that Sergei had eliminated one man, and was now in the process of trying to track down the intended target. He'd tell the truth and hope that Ivan would give him a pass. What other option did he have?

But Ivan didn't call to ask about Arlington or the status of the intended victim, Todd Holland. Rather, he gave Yuri an address on Mulholland Drive, and ordered him to be there within the hour. Ivan ended the call before Yuri had a chance to ask any questions.

Now, Yuri's BP was at massive-stroke level.

What could this meeting possibly be about? he asked himself as he left the house and headed for his car. Couldn't be good, that was the only answer he came up with. He wasn't invited or asked to be there; he was given a direct order. Implicit in that order was *be there or else*. Was Yuri walking toward his death? His own execution? Had Ivan somehow found out that Sergei failed on his mission to Arlington? Was Sergei already dead? Should he phone Sergei, and pray that his son answered, and if he did, then tell him to go into hiding?

Should he . . . No, Yuri decided, rather than worry so much, it was wiser to be prepared.

He quickly got out of his car, raced back inside the house, went into the den, and removed his forty-five from a drawer. After securing it behind his back, he untucked his shirt and let it cover the weapon. Chances are he wouldn't have a need to use it, but it was better to be prepared than to go into the meeting unarmed. Feeling slightly more secure, he ran back to his car, started the engine, and began the trek to Mulholland.

Fifty minutes later he arrived at his destination.

Which was a big house located behind an iron gate that sat near the very top of Mulholland, within shouting distance of where Jack Nicholson resided, and where the late Marlon Brando had lived. Yuri pulled in, stopped at the gate, and pressed the button on the speaker. Above him he could hear the whirring of a camera as it shifted and zeroed in on him. Several seconds later, someone from inside the house, security in all probability, instructed Yuri to identify himself, which he did. As the gate began to swing open, the man ordered Yuri to follow the driveway up to the house and park out front. Once Yuri arrived, the man said, someone would be there to escort him inside.

Translation: *Someone would be there to search you for weapons.*

Yuri would have to ditch the forty-five and leave it in the car. This meant he would be entering the house unarmed. A lamb to the slaughter if Ivan was intent on killing him. But Yuri had no other option. If he showed up with the weapon, and if it was discovered, he might die on the spot. Reaching behind him he took the forty-five and placed it in the glove box.

The area in front of the house looked like a parking lot for high-end SUVs, convertibles, sedans, and sports cars. The vehicle Yuri parked directly behind was a black Escalade. A sleek silver Maserati sat in front of the Escalade. Beyond the Maserati sat another sleek car that looked to be even pricier than the two parked behind it. Yuri quickly concluded that his three-year-old Prius was the cheapest vehicle among this group.

Once Yuri had exited his car he saw a solidly built man dressed in all black walk briskly in his direction. The man said nothing but indicated that he wanted Yuri to raise his arms above his head and spread his legs. Yuri knew the drill; he'd been through it in the past. He was being searched. The man knew what he was doing, giving Yuri a thorough pat-down, front and back. Had Yuri decided to take his chances and bring his weapon, he would probably be dead by now.

When the man was satisfied that the visitor posed no threat, he silently motioned for Yuri to follow him into the house. Yuri started to ask who was inside awaiting him, but he chose not to. Anyway, he doubted the man would have answered. He clearly wasn't the chatty type.

Yuri was led through the house, out to the back deck, where four men sat at a table next to the swimming pool. *Oh, shit, they are going to drown me*, was Yuri's first thought when he saw the quartet sitting near shimmering water brightly lit by underwater lights. Of the four men, he only knew one—Ivan.

Two were complete strangers to Yuri, but he did recognize the man sitting directly in the middle. Although Yuri had never met the man in person, he had seen many pictures of him. And, of course, Yuri was well aware of the man's reputation.

Yevgeny Voronov.

The second-most powerful and influential man in Russia.

If Ivan was a close confidant of Putin's, then Yevgeny Voronov was like the Russian leader's brother. If Ivan was worth twenty-billion dollars, Yevgeny was worth at least twice that much. If Ivan could have a man killed by nodding his head, Yevgeny could have it done with the raising of an eyebrow.

His power in Russia was second only to Putin's. The two men were the same age, and had known each other since the days prior to their time in the KGB. Trust was not a sacred commodity in the Soviet Union, not at any level of government, but if it did exist anywhere, it existed between Putin and Yevgeny Voronov.

*Why in the hell is that man here?* Yuri said to himself as he joined the four men at the table.

None of the men spoke, nor did they offer any hint that they were about to. They simply sat and stared at Yuri, each man with a hard and cold expression on his face. This was it, Yuri knew, this was his time to die, and this was his execution squad. He could bolt, make a dash for it, and try to escape before the four men could react. But that plan had no chance of being successful, not with those two dressed-in-black goons standing fifteen feet behind him. They'd chase him down and have him back at the table before he could get ten feet away. And beat him to a pulp along the way. No, it's better to sit still and see what transpires rather than make a move that could only end in disaster.

One of the men Yuri didn't know broke the silence. "You look nervous," he said. "Any reason why?"

Yuri was surprised that the man spoke with an American accent. He fully expected all four men to be Russian.

"Not nervous, only curious," Yuri responded.

"Curious about what?" the man asked.

"What this meeting pertains to and why I'm here."

"You are here because you were ordered to be here," Ivan said, sternly.

"Yeah, yeah, I get that," Yuri said. "But what's this meeting about?"

Ivan pointed at Yevgeny, and said, "Do you recognize this gentleman?"

"Sure."

"Nyet," Yevgeny said, slicing his hand through the air.

Yuri got the message. Shaking his head, he said, "No, I don't recognize him."

Clearly pleased with Yuri's response, Yevgeny almost smiled, nodded, and indicated that he wanted Ivan to pick up the conversation.

"Now, a question for you," Ivan began.

"I know, you want to hear how things went in Arlington," Yuri interrupted. I . . ."

"We are not concerned with Arlington," Ivan corrected. "We are more interested in how things are going with this private investigator. This man named Dantzler."

"Nothing, really. We have him under constant surveillance. Thus far, he has done nothing that poses a threat to us."

"I wouldn't be so sure of that if I were you," said the man with the American accent. "He's done more than you are aware of. Much more."

"I don't see how that's possible. All he's done is talk to a few people."

"Yes, and that's what has us concerned."

"Okay, what do you suggest I do?"

"You have to ask?" Ivan said.

No, Yuri didn't have to ask. He knew exactly what Ivan was saying. They wanted Dantzler dead.

"Is there a time frame?" he wanted to know, picking up on the hint.

"Tomorrow, at the latest."

"I will inform Sergei and Brad immediately. They will get it done."

"This is top priority, Yuri," the American intoned.

"What about Todd Holland?" Yuri asked Ivan.

"Dantzler first," Ivan answered. "Then we worry about Todd Holland."

Ivan picked up a bottle, filled four glasses with vodka, then nodded at Yuri. Ivan's message was clear: no fifth glass means it is time for you to leave. He was not being invited to the party. Standing, he turned and walked toward the door, flanked on both sides by the two sullen-faced dressed-in-black goons.

Puzzled by what had just transpired, Yuri climbed into the Prius, started the engine, put it in gear, curled around the parking area, and headed away from the house. He drove a few hundred feet until he reached the iron gate, waited until it opened, proceeded to Mulholland, made a right, and began the long journey home on the famous—and dangerous—two-lane highway that offered glorious views of the bright dream factory city below.

Unfamiliar with the winding road, and driving in darkness, he traveled at an unusually cautious speed. Twice, he was passed by drivers who were in a hurry, and who had more courage than he did. He continued on to Woodrow Wilson Drive, made a right, went a short distance, and made another right onto Cahuenga Boulevard. Not far past the Hollywood Bowl, Cahuenga became Highland Avenue. Seeing the lights from a Walgreens Pharmacy, Yuri ducked into the parking lot and picked up his cell phone from the passenger's seat. He needed to give Sergei a call.

With the motor idling, he started to punch in Sergei's number, and then he hesitated. The previous meeting still had him puzzled. Not so much what was said, but rather who was in attendance. Ivan, sure, he knew Ivan would be present. But the other three? That's what had him baffled.

Why was Yevgeny Voronov there? Thinking about it, Yuri concluded that the answer to that question was simple: Yevgeny was the mastermind behind the plan to assassinate Dana Shapiro. That's the only possible explanation. Ivan was taking orders from someone, and that individual was Yevgeny Voronov. That begged an additional question: Did someone else order Yevgeny to put the plan in motion? If so, that person could only be the top man himself.

Russia's president.

And even if he didn't give the direct order, he surely gave his okay. No way does the murder of a U.S. senator happen without his approval.

Yuri shifted his thoughts to the other two men at the meeting. Who were they, and why were they present? What role did they play in the killing of a United States senator? Their mere presence at the meeting meant they had to be involved in some capacity. Although neither man was introduced to Yuri, one did speak, and he was an American. The second man remained silent during the meeting, but Yuri got the feeling that he was also an American. So the killing of Dana Shapiro wasn't a Russia-only job. Americans were involved.

Yuri finally punched in Sergei's number. He listened through half-a-dozen rings before he heard his son's voice instructing the caller to leave a message. Yuri grunted his displeasure, ended the call, and began searching for Brad Holland's number. Once located, he punched in the correct numbers. Brad answered almost immediately.

"Yeah, what's up, Yuri?" he said, sounding sleepy.

"Have you heard from Sergei?"

"Nah, not since he left to go visit you. Said you weren't feeling well. You okay now?"

Remembering that's the excuse Sergei was going to use to separate from Brad, Yuri answered, "Feeling much better now. Thanks for asking."

"How long ago did he leave you?"

"Yesterday," Yuri lied. "He should be getting back to Chicago fairly soon."

"That's good. I miss my Russian bro."

Yuri rolled his eyes, and said, "Where are you right now?"

"Sitting on my ass down the street from the lawyer's house on Sheffield. Why?"

"Is that where the private investigator is at the moment?"

Brad had been asleep for nearly four hours, so he wasn't sure if Dantzler had returned from wherever it was he went earlier in the afternoon, or if he was still gone. In the darkness, and parked on the same side of the street as Dantzler's Mercedes had been, Brad couldn't tell if Dantzler's vehicle was there or not. But there was no way he was going to say any of that to Yuri.

"Yeah, the investigator is inside the house," Brad finally said.

"There has been a change in our plan," Yuri said. "He is no longer to be followed. He is to be eliminated."

"Shit. When?"

"Tomorrow is as good a day as any."

"Do you want me to wait for Sergei?"

Yuri pondered that question for a few moments, then answered, "Yes. But if Sergei doesn't arrive by late tomorrow afternoon, you have the green light to get it done yourself. Can you handle it, if it comes to that?"

"Without a doubt."

"Excellent. And keep in mind what I always say—leave no witnesses and no evidence that can be traced back to you."

"What should I do if the lady lawyer happens to be in the house?"

"Do you really have to ask that question, Brad? If she's there, she dies."

"Got it," Brad said, closing his phone as a shot of adrenalin flooded his insides.

THE REASON YURI could not reach Sergei was because his son was indisposed at the moment. Meaning: He was with a woman.

When he was only a few miles from Chicago, Sergei decided that he was in no hurry to hook up with Brad. He was horny as hell, and sitting around on his dead ass in the car with Brad wasn't going to take care of that issue. But he knew someone who could —Shantay.

Shantay was black, or mixed, or Hispanic, but Sergei didn't care. She was an animal in bed, and that's what really mattered. Yuri would raise hell, of course, if he knew his son was with a woman of color. The old man didn't think his son should screw any woman whose skin wasn't white. But the old man had never been in the sack with Shantay. If he had, he might just change his way of thinking. Shantay could do things most women didn't even know about.

"Is that you, baby?" Shantay said when she answered Sergei's call. "My favorite Russian boy?"

"You up for some fun tonight?" Sergei asked.

"Depends on how much you're willing to pay for that fun."

"How about a hundred bucks?"

"Aw, baby, I've already got plans for tonight. Now, if you can up that dollar amount, I just might be able to change those plans."

"Two-hundred."

"Make it two-fifty, throw in a bottle of Grand Marnier, and Shantay is all yours, baby."

"I'm on my way."

Shantay lived on West Garfield in one of the most-dangerous neighborhoods on the South Side. People were gunned down in that area on a daily basis. It was as much a combat zone as a neighborhood. But none of that dissuaded Sergei from paying her a visit. Shantay was worth the risk. Most definitely.

Grinning, he drove off in search of the first liquor store he could find.

# Chapter Twenty-Six

Dantzler made love to Grace that night, thus breaking his promise to keep sex out of their relationship until Danny Kafka walked out of jail, free of the murder charge he was facing. But he, Grace, and Todd stayed up talking deep into the night, during which he consumed more Pernod than he should have. At some point, Grace decided it was time for the chat and the drinking to end. She led the two men upstairs, then directed Todd toward a bedroom at the end of a hall that Dantzler judged to be the length of a football field.

After Todd was in his room and the door was closed, she and Dantzler went into the master bedroom. Less than a minute later they were both naked and in the bed. The lovemaking went better than either one would have predicted. They took it slow (the second time), there was no hesitation or awkwardness, no apparent drop off from the time when they were together in Lexington. All things considered, a pleasurable night for both.

Dantzler awoke the next morning and looked at the clock on the table next to the bed. It was six-thirty, meaning he'd been asleep for just three hours. He groaned. Between the late-night chat that lasted until well after two, and his consuming too much Pernod, he felt like death times two. Rolling over, he realized that Grace was not lying next to him. She was probably taking a shower, a fact confirmed when he heard water running in the bathroom. Closing his eyes, he was sound asleep within a minute.

A kiss on his lips woke him up. Not a bad way to be jarred out of a deep sleep. Grace was standing above him, fully dressed, and smiling. She leaned down and gave him a second kiss.

"I'm off to the office," she said, walking toward the door. "Get some sleep. You need the rest."

"Is Todd up yet?" Dantzler asked. His throat was dry, his voice scratchy.

"No, and I doubt he'll be up for a while. He was really beat." Grace walked back to the bed, leaned down, and gave him a third kiss. "Last night was fun, Jack. You were great."

"Does that mean I wasn't eviscerated?"

"You were not, smartass. Now go back to sleep."

Which he did. He was out like a light twenty seconds after Grace was gone. And didn't wake up until it was almost noon. He couldn't recall the last time he slept this late. He felt good and rested, but at the same time somewhat guilty. A healthy adult male shouldn't stay in bed sleeping half the day away.

He got up, straightened the covers in an I'd-be-a-lousy-housekeeper manner, went to the bathroom, brushed his teeth, and took a hot shower. After getting dressed, he opened the door and looked down the long hallway toward Todd's room. His door was still closed. Sleep-wise, he was getting his money's worth.

Dantzler trudged down the stairs and headed straight for the kitchen. Opening the refrigerator, he grabbed a bottle of water and downed the contents in two long gulps. He searched the kitchen until he found a pantry that had two cans, one for garbage and one for recycle. He tossed the empty water bottle into the recycle can, went back to the fridge, and took out a second bottle of water. After taking a quick drink, he left the kitchen, and went into Grace's office.

It was time to find out all he could about Yuri Lazarov.

Which didn't turn out to be much. If Yuri was a master criminal, he certainly knew how to keep it out of the public eye. The extent of information Dantzler gleaned from his search amounted to almost nothing. Certainly nothing of consequence. Yuri was born in what is now Saint Petersburg but was known as Leningrad at the time of his birth sixty-six years ago. He came to the United States when he was in his late teens, presumably with one or both parents, although that information was not in the file. According to what was in the file, Yuri was the sole owner of several body shops in and around the Los Angeles area. This didn't tell Dantzler anything. What, exactly, was considered several? Was it three, was it ten? And were they legitimate businesses, or chop shops? Legal or criminal?

Dantzler shifted focus and began searching through past editions of the Los Angeles Times, hoping that long-established publication might provide more information. It didn't. All he found were three brief mentions, none of which tied Yuri to criminal activities, or to Karl Holland. Simply stated, there wasn't a single hint that Yuri Lazarov was anything but a law-abiding citizen.

And yet someone had sent Yuri's son and Karl's son to kill Abe Pearlstein. And that person had also dispatched the two killers to find and murder Todd Holland. To find Todd, they had to torture and kill Jon Crofford. Maybe Karl was that person. Maybe Dantzler's premise was all wrong. Maybe his belief that Russians were involved really only meant a single Russian—Sergei Lazarov.

But that simply didn't compute for Dantzler. Didn't feel right. If Karl gave the order, that meant he dispatched two men, one of whom was his son, to murder another son. Could Karl Holland be that cold, that vicious? Could any father harbor enough hatred that he would order the death of his own flesh and blood? No doubt, it had been done in the past, but was that the case in this instance? Dantzler had a difficult time accepting that it was.

But . . . Sergei Lazarov and Brad Holland didn't just decide to take off on a murderous rampage. Someone sent them. In Dantzler's mind, it had to be Yuri.

Up above, Dantzler heard the toilet flush and the unmistakable sounds of footsteps walking across the floor. Todd had finally risen from the dead. His period of hibernation was over. Dantzler checked his watch. It was now almost three-thirty. He left the office and went back into the kitchen. He'd been so involved with his Yuri Lazarov search that only now did he remember that he hadn't eaten a thing since getting out of bed. He was starving. There was probably plenty of food on hand, but he decided to wait until Todd came downstairs, and then ask him if he wanted to eat here, or go find a restaurant. Dantzler was hoping Todd would opt for the restaurant.

---

BRAD HOLLAND still hadn't heard a peep from Sergei. This told Brad that his friend was probably drunk and shacked up with some chick. He had phoned a half-dozen times, but Sergei hadn't picked up. Brad was now officially pissed off. Here he was, stuck in a damn car, his ass hurting like a son-of-a-bitch, while Sergei was downing booze and getting his rocks off. Somehow, none of this seemed fair to Brad. More important, unless Sergei showed up soon, Brad would have to take out the private detective by himself.

Brad had been watching the house all day. There had been no sighting of the intended target. The only ones he had seen were the five women who were there every day, one he recognized as the attorney, four he assumed worked for her in some capacity. He knew that one male worked there, the big guy, but Brad had seen neither hide nor hair of him. Maybe it was his day off.

Darkness was beginning to descend. In another hour the light would be completely gone. Brad was getting hungry, having had nothing to eat but some cold chicken from KFC at noon. He thought about leaving his spot and driving to the nearest fast-food joint he could find. But he didn't. Instead, he closed his eyes and dozed off. A few minutes later the slamming of a car door startled him awake. He wiped his eyes and looked up just in time to see Dantzler entering the house. Another man was in front of him, but he was already too far inside the house for Brad to identify him. He assumed it had to be the big man who worked for the lady attorney.

Not long after the two men entered the house, three women

came outside and began walking to their cars. One was the attorney. She was flanked by a black women and one who appeared to be an Oriental. They said goodbye, the attorney got into her car, and the other two got into a separate vehicle. Both cars drove away, heading in the same direction down Sheffield. Only minutes after they had departed, two more women, both younger than the first three, came outside, got into a blue Nissan Sentra, and drove off.

Brad saw his opportunity. With or without Sergei, it was time to make his move. He'd wait a few more minutes to see if anyone else emerged from the house, and to let darkness cover the area, and then he would go inside and take care of the private investigator and that big guy. By his calculation, not having to torture either man, he could be in and out within five minutes. Put two bullets in each man, then vamoose.

Nothing to it.

# Chapter Twenty-Seven

They entered the house single file, Todd peeling off to head for the bathroom, Dantzler walking straight into the big room. The liquor cabinet was his ultimate destination. He was standing at the end of the long table when he heard the front door open. The sound startled him. There was something in the way the door was opened, a louder-than-usual noise that alerted his senses to possible danger. It was a feeling honed by his many years in law enforcement.

Turning, he saw a man moving swiftly in his direction. Arm raised, pistol in hand, intensity in his eyes, ready to fire. Dantzler yelled "Gun!" and dove to the floor just as a bullet slammed into the bookcase above his head, sending pieces of book covers, paper, and wood fluttering down onto the table and the floor. Dantzler scrambled to find cover behind a chair while reaching for his Glock. But he wasn't going to get it out in time. The shooter was now no farther than ten feet away, smiling, pistol up, ready to finish the job.

Then he was gone. Disappeared. Out of sight in the blink of an eye. Removed and neutralized by—

Edward.

Hearing Dantzler's "Gun!" warning, Edward rushed out of his

office, and with no hesitation or fear for his own safety, he crashed into the shooter's blind side with the force of a two-ton truck. The sound of the impact was enormous. Edward landed on top of the shooter, the gun flying from his hand, the air in his lungs gone in a loud whoosh.

The man did not know what hit him.

Dantzler got to his feet and put his Glock away. There was no longer a need for it; Edward had taken care of the threat. He walked over and picked up the shooter's weapon. And felt a twinge of disappointment. The gun was a thirty-eight, not a twenty-two, the caliber used to murder Abe Pearlstein and Jon Crofford. This meant the shooter either had another weapon, or there was a second gunman. Or, just as likely, this wasn't one of the men who killed Abe and Jon.

As Edward disengaged from the shooter and lifted himself up, Dantzler said, "Nice take-down, Edward. Perfect technique. I'm sure your Illini coaches would be proud of you."

"Had a sudden flashback," Edward noted, not even breathing hard. "Thought he was an Ohio State quarterback."

"Let's get this asshole into a chair."

Dantzler grabbed the shooter under one arm, Edward got him under the other arm, and they picked him and sat him in one of the chairs. The shooter groaned, and his eyes rolled like someone had pulled the lever on a Vegas slot machine. He shook his head, trying to focus. Looking to his right, he saw Dantzler. Focusing more, he looked straight ahead at Edward. Then, his eyes now almost completely focused, he glanced to his left, and . . . blinked several times, his brow wrinkled, and a confused look swept over his face. After doing a double-take and shaking his head, he finally managed to speak.

"Is that you, Todd?" he mumbled. "What the hell are you doing here?"

Rather than answer, Todd had a question of his own. "Why the hell did you kill Jon Crofford? Tell me, Brad, why did you torture and murder him?"

Seeing Todd begin to inch forward, Dantzler eased in front of

Edward and positioned himself between the two Holland boys. He knew that if he didn't block the advance, Todd was ready to rip his younger brother to shreds. His anger and hatred were palpable.

"Let me at that little bastard," Todd yelled, angling to work around Dantzler. "I want to hear him tell me why he went to Arlington and did what he did to Jon."

"I didn't kill anyone named Jon," Brad protested. "Hell, I never killed nobody. And I ain't never been to Arlington. I don't even know where that is."

"I don't believe you, Brad," countered Todd, who was still continuing to get at his brother.

"I've got this, Todd," Dantzler said, using his forearm to keep Todd at bay. "Let me handle it."

Dantzler took out his cell phone, held it up, and snapped a photo of Brad Holland. Then he began typing a text message:

**Wait five minutes and then send back a single-word reply: "Yes." Will explain later.**

He continued fake typing for another minute, then said, "Brad, I just sent a message to Grace West. She's Danny Kafka's attorney, and she just happens to be with him at the Cook County Jail. I told her to show your picture to Danny, and ask him if he recognizes you as Carson Welles. Wanna bet that he says yes?"

Brad responded by rattling off chapter one, verse one of the criminal's manual:

"I want a lawyer."

"Well, it's your lucky day, Brad. You're in an attorney's office, so you won't have to travel far to find one. However, this is also an unlucky day for you. See, I'm not a cop, which means I don't have to give you a damn thing."

Dantzler's phone dinged. He looked at Grace's one-word reply, smiled, and turned the phone so Brad could read the message.

Brad barely glanced at the phone, snarled, and defiantly turned his head away.

"Okay, Brad, now we know where things stand," Dantzler said. "You're in to this up to your eyeballs, involved in at least four homicides, and you are going to sit here and give me all the details. And I don't want to hear the words attorney or lawyer come out of your mouth. You'd only be wasting your breath and my time if you do. So . . . don't."

"Fuck you and fuck a lawyer," Brad sneered. "I ain't saying nothin' to nobody."

"Here's the deal, Brad," Dantzler said. "You have two options. Option A, I pull up a chair and we have a civil question-and-answer talk. Just a couple of guys shooting the breeze."

"That's not happening."

"Well, you haven't heard Option B yet. Option B, Edward takes you into one of the offices and beats you senseless."

"Are you so sure he can do that?"

"He's an ex-NFL linebacker, Brad. So yeah, I'm sure he can handle a squirt like you."

Brad looked up at Edward, genuine admiration on his face. "For real, you were in the NFL?" he asked. "Which team?"

Edward didn't answer, only continued to stare hard at Brad.

Dantzler said, "Decision-time, Brad. Which option do you choose?"

"Think I'll take Option B. Know why? Cause I think you're bluffing."

"Option B, it is." Dantzler turned to Edward. "Which room, Edward?"

"Better do it in my office," Edward replied. "If we get blood in either of the women's offices, they'll be pissed. Probably make us clean up the mess."

"Stand up, Brad," Dantzler ordered.

Brad did as he was told. At six-one, he was the shortest of the quartet. The runt of the litter. This realization hit home quickest when standing next to Edward, who towered above him. Brad didn't know much about animals, but he did know that runts normally don't survive for very long. They are casualties, usually the first to go.

"All right, all right," Brad said, sitting back down. "I'll go with Option A."

"See, Todd, your brother is more intelligent than he looks."

Dantzler turned a chair around and sat down facing Brad, their knees not more than two inches apart. "Here's how this works, Brad. I ask questions, you answer truthfully. The first bullshit answer you give me, you go into that room with Edward. We clear on that?"

Todd said, "Ask him why he killed Jon Crofford. Make that your first question."

"I keep telling you, I didn't kill anyone named Jon. That's the gospel." Brad twisted his upper body slightly, and groaned. "Man, I'm hurting real bad. I think my ribs are broken. Got anything for the pain?"

"Yeah, honest answers," Dantzler said, "beginning with who was behind the plot to assassinate Dana Shapiro?"

"I don't know who was behind it," Brad said, wincing in pain. "We just followed the orders we were given."

"We, meaning you and Sergei Lazarov?"

Brad nodded.

"Okay, who did give you and Sergei your orders?" Dantzler asked.

"Which time?"

"Let's begin with Danny Kafka's audition for his part in that phony movie?"

Brad glanced up at Todd, hesitated, then answered, "Our father. Karl Holland."

"Why did your father want to kill a United States senator?"

"I don't know. Ask him."

"I intend to. Now, tell me about Bobby Conrad. Who recruited him for this plan?"

"Karl."

"Who provided the rifle used to kill Dana?"

"Karl."

"Did you kill Bobby and Molly Jackson?"

"No, I've never killed anyone," Brad said, clearly becoming exasperated.

"Who did?"

"Sergei, I suppose."

"Suppose? You weren't with him at the time?"

"No, he went ahead to that abandoned apartment building to wait for Bobby to show up. Bobby thought that's where he was to be paid. I stayed behind to get the rifle once Bobby fired the shot. Then I took it down the alley and hid it behind a Dumpster."

"Did Bobby know what was happening?"

"No, the poor sap really thought he was filming a scene for the movie."

"So, Bobby shows up and Sergei shoots him in the back of the head, right?"

Brad nodded.

"Why did he kill Molly?" Dantzler asked.

"Sergei was sitting in his car waiting for me to arrive. She showed and went inside the building. He followed her in and killed her."

"Shot her in the head, right?"

Brad shook head, said, "No, he told me he cut her throat." Then: "Can I have something for the pain? I'm really hurting bad."

"As soon as we finish talking."

"Damn, man, this is unfair."

"Why did you kill Abe Pearlstein?" Dantzler asked, ignoring Brad's whining.

"Who?"

"The old guy in Manhattan."

"Oh, him. Yeah, well, Karl found out a private investigator was snooping around. He suspected that you were the guy. When we informed him that you'd gone into the building, he said for us to wait until you left, go inside, find out what the old guy told you, and then make sure he stayed quiet forever. That's what we did. We made him talk, then Sergei shot him."

"How did Karl find out that I was, in your words, 'snooping around'?"

Brad shrugged, said, "I don't know. I'm just a low man on the totem pole. Karl has answers to your really important questions."

"Where is Sergei?" Dantzler inquired.

"I don't know. I haven't seen him for a couple of days. He told me his father was ill, and he needed to go check up on him. That may or may not be true. My guess is he's somewhere shacked up with a chick."

"Yuri is his father, right?"

"Yeah, I'm sure Todd told you that."

"Does Karl have a connection with anyone high up in our government? Maybe someone in the Justice Department?"

"Hell, how would I know that?"

"Final question, Brad. Who gave the order for you to come in here tonight and kill me?"

"No one."

"You just took it upon yourself, found the initiative, and made the decision to come in here and take me out? Is that what you want me to believe?"

"It's the truth."

"Brad, I doubt you've ever made a serious decision in your life," Dantzler said. "You strike me as a guy who acts at the behest of others, not someone who makes command decisions."

"Believe me or don't believe me, I don't give a shit. I've told you the truth."

"Brad, you really want me to believe that Karl Holland, a second-rate movie producer, has the smarts, the means, and the wherewithal to put together and pull off a plan that has so many moving parts? I'll believe that when one of his movies wins an Academy Award, which, we all know will never happen. It's all Karl, right? You're sticking with that? Yuri is not involved in any way? That's what you're telling me?"

Brad was silent as he let some things filter through his mind. He'd not once mentioned Yuri, instead laying all the blame on Karl. Maybe it wasn't right going against family, but it felt like the wise thing to do. There was no reason to piss off the Russian. After all, he might need Yuri's help in the future. Yuri appreciated strength, obedience, and loyalty above all else, and when he finds out that Brad clammed up while being interrogated, he might be more inclined to offer his help.

"Karl is the man you want," Brad finally said, officially throwing his father under the bus.

Dantzler dug into his pants pocket and pulled out his car keys. Handing them to Todd, he said, "Go out to my car, open the trunk, and bring me two sets of handcuffs."

Todd took the keys and headed for the door.

"What car are you in, and where is it parked?" Dantzler asked Brad.

"Black Audi down the street."

Dantzler fished through Brad's pants pockets until he found a set of car keys. Then to Edward, he said, "We need to hide Brad's car. Any idea where we can park it?"

"Sure, behind the house," Edward said. "No one will see it there."

"Will you do it?" Dantzler said, as Todd returned with the handcuffs.

"Not a problem. But aren't you going to turn Brad over to Sly Douglas or Brooke Mason? I'll make the call if you want me to."

"Not yet."

"Why not? They need to have him in custody."

"Think about it, Edward. If we turn him over to Chicago PD, he'll have that lawyer he's been asking for in less than an hour. If that happens, he'll get bail, or worse, he'll be cut loose. We can't allow that to happen."

"With what he's admitted, there is no way he walks out of there," Edward said.

"He'll either deny everything, or he'll say we beat a confession out of him. And with the way you took him down, he just might have a couple of cracked ribs. Definitely, a few bruises. Even a cut-rate defense attorney could spin that into solid gold. No, we'll keep him here until I decide how I want to play this."

"Okay, you're calling the shots."

As Edward turned to leave, Dantzler said, "How much do you think that bookcase weighs?"

"If you include all the books, I'd say fifteen-hundred pounds," Edward replied. "Maybe even a ton."

"Yeah, I'd say that's about right. Bottom line, it's not going anywhere, is it?"

"It would take a crane to move it."

When Edward was gone, Dantzler took one set of cuffs from Todd and ordered Brad to stand. "Where is your phone?" he asked.

"I left it in the car."

Dantzler said, "Can I trust you to be a good boy, Brad? If you can make that promise, I'll cuff your hands in front of you rather than in the back. Normally, I would never do that, but since you do seem to be in genuine pain, I'll make that concession. But only after you give me your word that you'll behave."

"Yeah, yeah, I promise."

Dantzler put the cuffs on, took the second pair from Todd, then walked Brad over to the side of the bookcase. After helping ease him down to a sitting position on the floor, Dantzler put one cuff around Brad's right ankle, and then secured the second cuff to one of the bookcase legs.

"Come on, man, you've got me sitting on this hard-ass floor," Brad said. "My butt's already killing me, and my ribs are hurting like a son of a bitch."

"You're a tough guy, Brad. You can handle it."

"At least get me some water. I'm dying of thirst. And maybe some Tylenol or Aleve. Something to knock this damn pain."

Dantzler looked at Todd, said, "Can you do that without killing him?"

"It'll be difficult, but I'll restrain myself," Todd replied.

Outside, Dantzler could see headlights as Edward moved Brad's Audi behind the house. His cell phone buzzed. The call was from Grace.

"Where are you guys?" Grace asked.

"At the office on Sheffield."

"Just you and Todd?"

"No, Edward is here. We also have a special guest . . . Brad Holland."

"Todd's brother? Why is here there?"

"He came in, gun blazing, fully intent on killing me."

"What?" Grace screamed. "Are you okay? What about Edward and Todd? Are they all right?"

"We are all fine, thanks to Edward. You should have seen the big guy, Grace. He moved like a blur, took Brad down like he was a feather. The NFL pinheads screwed up by taking a pass on that guy."

"And you are both okay, right?"

"A lot better than some of the books in the corner of your bookcase. Unfortunately, they took a direct hit."

"You mean he actually shot at you?"

"That's what guns blazing means, Grace."

"Jesus, I need a drink. No, let me amend that. I need several drinks, strong ones."

"I know the feeling."

"Have you contacted Sly Douglas and Brooke Mason?" Grace said.

Dantzler gave her the same speech he'd given to Edward. She listened to his spiel, and to his surprise offered no resistance.

"What is your next step?" she wanted to know.

"I'm going to spend the rest of the night trying to hatch a plan that might work. If I can't, then we will have to bring in Chicago PD. But I'm hoping we don't have to do that until sometime down the road. I'm still convinced someone in our government is involved in all this. I want the chance to find that individual without any interference or hindrance from local law enforcement. Bringing them in is a last resort."

"What if it's more than a single individual?"

"Then I'll find them all."

"Is there anything I can do?"

"Yes, Grace, there is. You can start by giving Edward a big raise. We would not be having this conversation were it not for him. The man absolutely saved my hide."

# Chapter Twenty-Eight

D antzler knew he had to do something, and he needed to do it fast. The status quo couldn't hold for much longer. The clock was ticking. Time was his enemy. So was his own sense of guilt, his belief that he was behaving in an unprofessional manner.

He was essentially holding hostage a man who had confessed to being involved in four homicides. That was not only wrong, it went against his own personal code of conduct. If Sly Douglas or Brooke Mason were keeping a confessed killer from him, he'd be royally pissed. And he would have every right to be. Just as Sly and Brooke would have every right to be pissed at him should they learn that he had Brad Holland handcuffed to a bookcase in a house on Sheffield Avenue. He was not treating them with professional courtesy.

It was almost ten, and he was sitting at the table across from Todd Holland, who still had that I-could-kill-you-Brad look in his eyes. Dantzler had a plan he thought might work, one he wanted to run past Todd first. He considered it a longshot at best, but it was the only thing he could come up with in such a short time frame.

"Hey, I'm starving. What about some food?" Brad said. "Hell, if you're gonna keep me chained up like an animal, the least you can do is feed me."

Edward came into the room in time to hear Brad's plea for food.

Dantzler said, "What about it, Edward? Think you could rustle us up something to eat?"

"As you know, I'm famous for my omelets. I can also throw in some hash browns and toast. Will that work?"

"I'm all in," Dantzler answered. "What about you, Todd?"

"Sounds good."

"Omelets?" Brad said. "Who eats omelets at this hour of the night? That's a breakfast food."

"You get an omelet, or you get nothing," Dantzler said.

"You're a heartless prick, you know that?" countered Brad.

"I'll make him one," Edward said. "Either he eats it, or he doesn't."

"Can you put cheese and onions on it?"

"Anything to make you happy, Brad."

When Edward had departed for the kitchen, Dantzler began to lay out his plan to Todd. Todd listened, kept his eyes directly on Dantzler, but didn't interrupt with questions or observations. Fifteen minutes later, when Dantzler concluded his talk, Todd remained quiet for a long moment before responding.

"That's a pretty good plan," he finally said. "But I have a better one."

"Let me hear it."

This time Todd spoke and Dantzler listened. Todd's explanation was brief, taking less than five minutes. When he finished, he leaned back and waited for Dantzler's judgment. He didn't have a long wait.

"You're right, Todd, it is a better plan," Dantzler's responded. "Do you think we can pull it off?"

"Absolutely."

"You're gonna have to be persuasive."

"Not a problem."

Edward came in carrying two plates of food. He placed one in front of Todd, then looked at Dantzler, and said, "What about the mutt? Where do you want him to sit?"

Dantzler got out of his chair, went over to Brad, bent down, and undid the cuff that was connected to the bookcase leg. After gingerly helping Brad to his feet, Dantzler pointed to the chair he had been sitting in. Brad slowly walked to the chair and took a seat.

"You right-handed or a lefty?" Dantzler asked him.

"Right."

Dantzler unhooked the cuffs on Brad's wrists, then took Brad's left arm and cuffed it to the side of his chair.

When Edward set the plate on the table, Brad said, "Hey, I use both hands when I eat."

"Shut up and eat, Brad," Dantzler snapped. "I'm tired of hearing you whine. You're worse than a five-year-old."

Edward came back out and handed Dantzler his plate. The food smelled delicious. An omelet, hash browns, sliced tomatoes, and wheat toast. Only then did Dantzler realize how hungry he was. He attacked the food with a vengeance. So did the Holland brothers, both of whom ate in silence. Although Brad Holland was a constant complainer, he knew excellent food when it came his way. Good enough, in fact, to shut him up.

When Dantzler finished eating, he took his plate into the kitchen, placed it in the sink, praised Edward for the good grub, and then went back into the big room. Despite the late hour, he needed to make a phone call. But first he had to figure out what to do with Brad once he had finished eating. Dantzler mentally ran through a couple of possible scenarios before deciding to do nothing at all. Not now, anyway. Later, he would lock Brad in one of the upstairs bedrooms. For now, though, Brad wasn't going anywhere. Not with massive Edward and still-pissed-off Todd hovering in the room like a pair of lions just waiting for a reason to attack their prey.

Dantzler went into the front room and took a seat at Mary-Louise's desk. He scrolled through the Contacts list until he found the name he was looking for. Taking a deep breath, he punched in the numbers, and waited. The call was answered by a woman who did not sound particularly pleased.

"Hello."

"Kate?"

"Who is this?"

"Jack Dantzler."

"Dantzler? Do you have any idea what time it is?"

"It's Jack, remember?"

"Dantzler, I repeat: Do you know what time it is?"

"Yeah, almost midnight."

"Why in God's name are you calling me at this hour of night?"

"We need to talk."

"Then phone my office tomorrow morning and I'll work you into my schedule. Now, goodnight."

"This can't wait until tomorrow. We need to talk now."

"Talk about what, specifically?"

"The murder of Dana Shapiro, for starters."

"Are you nuts, Dantzler? I have no interest in listening to you spew more of your cockamamie theories about Dana's death. We've traveled that road before. It didn't interest me then, and I doubt it will interest me now."

"You were close friends with Dana, right?"

"Yes."

"'Very' close, if I recall correctly. Surely, you want to know the truth about the murder of a 'very close' friend."

"And you are in possession of that truth? Is that what you're saying, Dantzler?"

"It's sitting right here in front of me."

"Have you shared this truth with Sly Douglas or Brooke Mason?"

"No."

"You should," Kate said. "It's their case, not mine."

"Forget whose case it is. That can all be sorted out later on. Tonight, it's just the two of us, Kate. You really need to come see me."

"Where are you?"

"Grace's office on Sheffield Avenue."

"And you want me to come there? At midnight?"

"Yes."

"Can't this wait until tomorrow?"

"Yes, Kate, it could wait. But it would be best if you came here tonight, right now. You won't be disappointed, that I can promise you."

Kate paused for a moment, then finally said, "I'm sure I'll regret this, but . . . all right. I'll be there in about an hour."

She ended the call before Dantzler could respond.

SERGEI SLOWLY DROVE UP SHEFFIELD, his eyes scanning both sides of the street, searching for Brad's car. He didn't see it. No big deal, he thought. After all, it was pitch dark, thus rendering the black Audi as practically invisible. He drove ahead, turned, and made a second slow pass back down the street. Still no sign of Brad or the Audi.

Sergei decided to park and wait for Brad to show up. He figured Brad, tired of sitting on his ass, had probably gone to get something to eat. If that were the case, then he should be back fairly soon. However, there was a second possibility that had to be considered—with the private investigator's car parked in its usual spot, and with nothing suspicious or out of the ordinary happening in the house, Brad might have chosen to leave his post and check into a motel room. Who could blame him if he did? Sleeping in a bed was far more comfortable than sleeping in the front seat of a car.

Leaving for any reason was a bad decision on Brad's part, Sergei suddenly realized, because just at that moment a dark sedan pulled up in front of the house, and a woman exited the car. She locked the car, then walked briskly up to the front door, and knocked. She was immediately allowed inside.

Sergei took out his phone and punched in his father's number. It was late—almost eleven o'clock on the West Coast—but he didn't care. He had to speak with his old man.

"Where the hell have you been for the past two days?" were the first words out of Yuri's mouth. "Hanging out with whores?"

"No, I've been on my way back from Arlington," Sergei answered.

"Did you go by way of Canada?"

"What does that mean?"

"It means you should have been back in Chicago yesterday."

"Well, I'm in Chicago now, down the street from the lawyer's house, and Brad is not here. Do you have any idea where he might be?"

"Perhaps I do," Yuri said. "There was a slight change in plans, and I ordered Brad to handle it."

"What change?"

"Observing the private investigator was no longer an option. He needed to be eliminated."

"And you sent Brad in to do it? That was a big mistake."

"I couldn't send you in, could I, Sergei? No one knew where the hell you were."

"You should've waited until I got back, no matter how long it took."

"Waiting was out of the question."

"Have you heard from Brad since you gave the order?" Sergei asked.

"No."

"So you have no idea if he got the job done, or if something bad happened?"

"Is there any activity at the house?"

"As a matter of fact, there is. I just saw a woman park out front and enter the house."

"The lawyer lady?"

"No, it wasn't her."

"Any idea who she might be?"

"No, but she has government plates on her car."

"Sergei, get away from there right now. I'm afraid you're right— some bad shit must've happened. You need to go."

"What about Brad?"

"Forget about him. Just leave. Ditch all your weapons where they can never be found. Are you in a rental?"

"Yes."

"Did you give a phony name when you rented it?"

"Of course."

"Get to the airport, wipe the car clean of prints, and leave it in long-term parking. Then catch the first flight back to Los Angeles. Text me your TOA, and I'll have someone at LAX to pick you up."

"What do you think happened?"

"I don't know, Sergei, but whatever it was, it can't be good. That's why you need to get out of Chicago."

"Maybe it's not so bad," Sergei countered. "Could be the private investigator has a late-night booty call."

"With someone driving a government vehicle? Are you willing to take that chance? I'm not. Do what I said, Sergei. Get your ass back to L.A."

Sergei started the engine, pulled away from the curb, and drove several hundred feet before turning on the headlights. Once they were on, he mashed down on the gas pedal and sped away, looking for the first place where he could safely ditch his two pistols. As the car picked up speed, Sergei realized that for one of the few times in his life he felt genuinely fearful of what lay ahead. As the lights from downtown Chicago lit up the night, his father's words echoed in his head:

*Whatever it was, it can't be good.*

# Chapter Twenty-Nine

Kate Flanagan was let into the house by Edward, who then escorted her into the big room. She was dressed in faded Levis, a blue sweatshirt, and sneakers. Her hair was tied back in a ponytail, and she wore no make-up. She would have described herself as a plain-Jane; Dantzler thought she looked gorgeous.

Dantzler stood at the far end of the table. Kate gave him a hard stare then shifted her attention to her right, where Todd was sitting. Then, looking to her left, she saw Brad, his head down on the table, looking like he was sound asleep. He wasn't; raising his head he grinned, and then tried to lift his left arm, the one handcuffed to the chair. The cuffs made a loud rattling sound.

"Who is this man, and why is he in handcuffs?" Kate said to Dantzler. "What the hell is going on here?"

"That young man is Brad Holland. He's the person who is going to unveil the truth for you."

"Are you a lawyer?" Brad asked Kate.

"No, she isn't," Dantzler said before Kate could answer. He wasn't sure if she was an attorney or not, but in the event she was, he didn't want her answering Brad's question. For her part, Kate, sensing Dantzler was up to something, remained silent.

"Any chance she's a doctor or a nurse?" Brad said, grimacing in pain. "I need one. I'm not kidding about having some cracked ribs. They hurt like a son of a bitch. I need painkillers, something much stronger than Aleve or Tylenol."

"Take slow breaths and don't make any sudden movement," Dantzler advised. "You'll be all right."

"Why is this man in pain?" Kate inquired.

"Because he got creamed by a Big Ten linebacker," Dantzler answered.

"Why was he creamed?"

"Because he came in shooting at me," Dantzler said, pointing over his right shoulder at the bookcase. "He missed with his first shot, but he would not have missed with the second one. However, before he had a chance to pull the trigger, he got blown away by a rather violent wind. In fact, let me introduce you to my savior. This is Edward, one of Grace's paralegals. Our other guest is Todd Holland."

"Todd?" Kate said. "Are you Dana's Todd?"

Todd nodded.

"Dana talked about you a lot. She said . . . Dana loved you very much."

"Trust me, the feeling was mutual," Todd whispered.

Kate looked quizzically at Dantzler, and said, "Brad Holland, Todd Holland—are they related?"

"Brothers. But different as night and day." Dantzler shifted focus from Kate to Edward, said, "Did you find it?"

Edward stepped forward and placed a tape recorder on the table. Dantzler scooted it closer to Brad, and pushed the Play and Record buttons. Then he gave his name, the time, date, location, and his intention to interview Brad. After that, he identified the others assembled around the table. Once all that was out of the way, he began the questioning.

For the next ninety minutes, Brad answered Dantzler's questions, repeating most of the earlier responses almost verbatim. There were a couple of times when he veered slightly off-course, either to embellish his previous answer, or to conveniently overlook a certain detail. On those occasions, Dantzler quickly challenged Brad, who immediately got back on track and answered accordingly.

As Brad related his story, Dantzler kept a close eye on Kate. He was curious to see how she responded to the tale Brad was unveiling. Initially, Kate appeared to be skeptical, perhaps even indifferent to what was being said. But that quickly changed when Brad began revealing the details that led up to—and subsequently followed—the cold-blooded murder of Dana Shapiro. Kate's look went from indifference, to disbelief, to an anger that was a match for Todd's. At one point during Brad's revelation Dantzler worried that either Kate or Todd might leap across the table and attack Brad. Deep down, he wouldn't have blamed them if they did.

When Brad answered the last question, Dantzler said, "Anything else you want to say?"

"Yeah, when can I get some sleep?"

Dantzler said, "Anything you want to ask him, Kate?"

"I want to do a lot more than ask him questions," Kate replied. "I want to put him in a cold grave, send his ass to hell. Unfortunately, I can't do that."

"Hell, lady, why are you so angry at me?" Brad said, innocently. "None of this was my idea. And for the record, I've never killed anyone."

Dantzler unlocked the cuff and ordered Brad to stand. Then he tapped Brad on the shoulder and pointed toward the stairs. Brad slowly climbed the steps with Dantzler close behind. When they reached the top, Dantzler motioned for Brad to take the middle bedroom. Brad entered, went straight to the bed, and flopped down.

"Hate to do this to you, Brad," Dantzler said, "but I can't trust you to be a good boy. Put your hands together."

"You're going to put those damn things on me? How am I supposed to sleep when I'm shackled like a wild animal?"

Dantzler cuffed Brad's hands in front, went to the end of the bed, and removed Brad's shoes and socks. "Put your legs together," he ordered.

"Not my feet, too. Come on, man, give me a break."

"You'll manage," Dantzler said, turning out the light. Brad was snoring before Dantzler closed the door.

"I want to murder that little sleaze ball," Kate said, once Dantzler had descended the stairs.

"You're FBI, Kate, not a vigilante, so get that thought out of your head." Dantzler sat at the table across from her. "Are you now willing to acknowledge that I wasn't pitching a cockamamie theory after all? That what I was saying had the ring of truth to it?"

"Okay, Dantzler, you're brilliant. But what . . ."

"Jack."

"Oaky, *Jack*, where do we go from here?"

"We start climbing the ladder all the way to the top. We don't stop until we bring down the people who set this plan in motion."

"Before you take this a step further, let me straighten you out on a few things. First, Brad needs to have his rights read to him, then arrested. Second, you have to bring Brooke Mason and Sly Douglas into this. They have a right to know what's going on."

"We can do all that, Kate. But let's hold off for a day or two."

"You seem to be conveniently ignoring the fact that I'm a federal agent. I have a sworn duty to apprehend someone suspected of committing a homicide, especially one involving the murder of a United States senator."

"You seem to be conveniently ignoring the fact that you were ordered to stand down and let Chicago PD handle the case."

"Fair enough, Jack. But considering the facts I learned tonight, I can safely say that the previous order is no longer valid. As for Chicago PD, you just made my case that Brooke and Sly should be notified and brought into the investigation."

Dantzler said, "Tell me, Kate. Do you seriously believe Karl Holland is such a criminal mastermind that he could pull off a plan this intricate, this wide-ranging without help? I certainly don't. And neither does Todd, Karl's own son. There is someone far above Karl's pay grade who is pulling the strings."

"Yuri Lazarov?" Kate asked.

"Maybe. But I doubt it. This is going to go much higher up than either of those guys. And I have a strong feeling that you won't like who's sitting at the top of that ladder."

"I know what you are going to say, Dantzler. Don't."

"I hope I'm wrong, Kate, because it'll cause a real shit storm if I'm right."

"If Karl Holland is the next rung on the ladder, how do you plan to get him? Are we going to L.A.?"

"No, we're going to lure him to Chicago."

"How do you plan to do that?"

"The same way Karl lured Danny Kafka and Bobby Conrad into participating in a phony movie."

"What? With another phony movie?"

"Exactly."

"That's your plan?"

"Actually, Kate, it was Todd's plan. And he thinks it can work."

"Let me hear it."

Todd cleared his throat, took a sip of water, and then began.

"Karl has always been fascinated by the JFK assassination. He's studied it for decades, really broken it down and taken it apart piece by piece. It's an obsession for him. He's convinced that the Mob was involved, that Carlos Marcello, the New Orleans Godfather, was the true architect of the plot to get rid of the president. He did it because of his hatred for Bobby Kennedy, who repeatedly went after the Mob, and who once had Marcello deported and dropped off in the jungles of Guatemala. Marcello knew that if the president was taken down, then Bobby Kennedy, the attorney general, would lose his power once Johnson became president. And that would ease the pressure on the Mob."

Todd took a second drink before continuing.

"But for Karl, the most-intriguing character of all was Jack Ruby. Everyone knew Ruby was a Mob guy, first here in Chicago, then in Dallas. He was in with all the top guys, Marcello, Sam Giancana, Santo Trafficante, Johnny Roselli . . . Ruby ran errands for all of them. And then he shoots Lee Harvey Oswald. Guns him down in front of television cameras, FBI agents, Dallas cops, and Secret Service agents. Do you really believe Ruby did that on the spur of the moment? Of course not. He was ordered by the Mob to silence Oswald."

"You're giving me a history lesson, Todd, not a plan to lure your father to Chicago," Kate pointed out. "Why not leave the past and bring us to the present?"

"For decades, ever since I can remember, Karl has dreamed of making a movie about Jack Ruby. Think about it. There never has been one. They've made movies about Kennedy, Oswald, that district attorney in New Orleans, but never one that featured Ruby as the lead guy. In those movies, he's always a peripheral character, just the low-life strip-club owner who shot Oswald. If Karl thinks he can make a serious movie about Jack Ruby, he'll jump at the chance."

"How do you make that happen?" Kate asked.

"I'll call Karl and tell him that I work with a guy in the Pentagon whose father grew up with Ruby in Chicago. I'll let Karl know that this man has a story to tell, but he's too old to travel all the way to Los Angeles. If Karl wants to hear what the man has to say, he'll have to come to Chicago. Trust me, Karl will be on the first plane heading this way."

"You haven't spoken to Karl in years," Dantzler pointed out. "Don't you think he'll be suspicious if you call him out of the blue?"

"Any suspicion he might have will melt away when he hears about the Ruby angle," Todd replied. "You have no idea how badly he wants to make that movie."

Kate looked at Dantzler, said, "Let's say it does work. Do you bring Karl here?"

"No, Todd will pick him up at the airport and take him to Grace's condo downtown. Once he's there, we let him listen to Brad's confession, then start grilling him."

"He'll ask for an attorney," Kate said.

"If he does, well, Grace will be right there."

"Jack, I will agree to this plan on one condition. And it's non-negotiable."

"I know what you're going to say, Kate."

"Brooke Mason and Sly Douglas have to be in that room when

we brace Karl Holland. Disagree and I'll go upstairs, wake up Brad, read him his rights, and arrest him."

"Have it your way, Kate. I'll contact Brooke and Sly first thing in the morning."

"When do you plan to phone Karl?" Kate said to Todd.

"Around ten. That's eight on the West Coast."

"Okay, I guess we wait until then," Kate said.

---

BY EIGHT A.M., the office was buzzing with activity and curiosity. Mostly, the Team West tribe focused their attention on the bullet hole in the bookcase, and on the heroics performed by Edward when he saved Dantzler's ass. Maggie and Mary-Louise seemed more interested in Todd than in what had taken place the previous evening. They rarely took their eyes off him. Seems Dantzler had been replaced as their golden boy.

The only person not present was Brad, who was still asleep in the upstairs bedroom.

By nine, the population had expanded by two. Brooke Mason and Sly Douglas, having been contacted by Dantzler an hour earlier, were now on the premises, sitting at the table, listening to the question-and-answer session recorded in the middle of the night. If they were angry or upset with Dantzler, they kept it to themselves. They were both professionals, Dantzler knew, and as such, if they wanted to register a complaint, they would do it privately and not in front of a crowd.

When the interview with Brad ended, Dantzler asked the two Chicago detectives if they needed to hear it again. Both declined. Then Dantzler spent the next few minutes filling them in on the plan Todd had concocted to lure Karl Holland to Chicago. Neither Brooke nor Sly registered any complaints or offered suggestions. They both agreed that the plan had merit.

At ten-fifteen, Todd left the room, climbed the stairs, and went into the bedroom to his right. It was time to make the call to his father. Closing the door, he sat on the bed and punched in Karl's number. It was now or never, time for him to give the performance of a lifetime.

Downstairs, the crowd spoke in whispers, anxious, waiting to learn if the first part of Todd's plan—the crucial part—was going to be successful. Everything seemed to hinge on the outcome of that one phone call.

It didn't take long before they had their answer.

Todd came down the stairs, smiling. Before reaching the bottom of the steps, he gave a big thumbs-up.

"He was all over it," Todd related. "Just like I knew he would be. He can't wait to meet the man who was good friends with Jack Ruby. Said he'd pick the guy's brain clean, then go back to Hollywood and make an Oscar-caliber movie. Poor shmuck has no idea what he's in for."

"When is he planning to come here?" Kate asked.

"Today, first flight he can get. He'll call and let me know when he's arriving."

"Did he inquire about Brad?" Dantzler said.

"Yeah, near the end of our conversation he wanted to know if I had heard from Brad. I told him I hadn't."

"So the plan is off to a good beginning," Brooke Mason said. "Maybe it will work."

Todd said, "I'm confident it will."

"But it's only a first step," Kate pointed out.

"Yeah, but a thousand-mile journey begins with . . . you know the rest," Sly reminded.

"Get your game faces on, guys," Dantzler advised. "It's time to start putting away some very bad individuals."

# Chapter Thirty

K arl Holland's plane arrived at O'Hare a few minutes before six in the evening. Todd had told his father that they would meet at the Baggage Claim area. He was sitting in one of the chairs lined along the wall when he saw his father riding down on the escalator. Todd stood and went to greet Karl, who seemed genuinely pleased to see his oldest son for the first time in more than five years. Not pleased enough for a hug, though; a handshake was the best he had to offer.

"How many bags did you bring?" Todd asked.

"Just one," Karl replied. "There, that brown one."

Todd grabbed it off the carousel. Then he led Karl outside and toward the Short-Term Parking area. Neither man spoke during that brief trip. When they located the car—Todd was driving (it was Grace's)—he put Karl's bag into the trunk. Once they were in the car and buckled up, Todd fired up the engine and drove away from the massive airport.

"Are you hungry?" Todd said. "If you are, we can stop for a bite to eat before we get to the condo."

"No, I'm not hungry at all," Karl replied. "I'm just anxious to meet the man who can give me real insight into the mind of Jack Ruby. You know how much I've always wanted to make a movie about Ruby. Hell, I was talking to you about it when you weren't any bigger than a small turd."

"Yeah, I remember."

"How old is this guy, anyway?"

"Oh, I don't know. In his late eighties, for sure."

"And he knew Jack Ruby? I mean, he really knew the guy?"

"Yes, he knew Ruby."

"What's your opinion of Sean Penn as Ruby?" Karl said. "Think he could pull it off?"

"Sean Penn can do anything, Karl, so, yes I have no doubt that he can be a very real Jack Ruby. But do you really think you can land Sean Penn for that role?"

"Hell, I'll offer him so much money he won't be able to refuse."

"Are you positive that you don't want something to eat? This could be a long night."

"That's what I'm hoping for. A long night filled with hours of information about Jack Ruby."

"I'm fairly certain that plenty of information will be shared tonight," Todd said.

Those were the last words either man spoke for the remainder of the ride into town. Todd was surprised by his father's silence; he figured the old man would continue gabbing about a movie that was never going to be made, much less seen by a single person. But Karl didn't mention it. He also didn't inquire if Todd had heard from Brad, or if he knew of his whereabouts. Apparently, Karl chose to ride silently, lost in his own thoughts. The silence didn't bother Todd at all.

When they arrived at the condo, Todd pulled into the underground garage and parked in one of Grace's designated spaces. After locking the car and getting Karl's bag out of the trunk, father and son walked over to the elevators. Todd punched the Penthouse button.

"The penthouse, huh?' Karl said. "The old man must've done

well for himself, living at the top of a joint like this. I'm surprised by that."

"Yeah, life is full of surprises," Todd answered.

Stepping off the elevator, Todd pointed to a door on the left. He walked ahead, opened the door, used his right arm to usher the older man inside, and then moved behind his father. He did so in case Karl tried to bolt once he realized that he wasn't there to talk about Jack Ruby, or a movie about the infamous gangster.

Once inside, Karl was immediately confronted by Kate. She nodded and smiled, but there was nothing remotely friendly in her look or her demeanor. She was deadly serious, all business, and she wanted to convey that to Karl.

Karl, half-turning, said, "What the hell is going on here, Todd? Where is the old man who knew Jack Ruby? Who are these two broads?"

The second of the "two broads" was Grace, who was sitting on a sofa, a smile on her face.

Kate said, "Karl, my name is Kate Flanagan. I'm an FBI agent. You are going to be here a while, so you need to pay close attention to what I'm about to say. My advice to you is, don't say a single word until I tell you that it's okay to speak. We are going to sit down and listen to a tape recording. Once that's finished, your first instinct will be to ask for an attorney. You may do so if you wish; that's your right. But in my professional opinion, that would be a mistake on your part. If you do ask for an attorney, I will read you your rights, handcuff you, and place you under arrest. What happens to you after that is out of my hands. You will be just one small piece in a very large legal machine. However, if after hearing what's on the tape, you elect to answer my questions, I'll have some leeway with the district attorney. I can tell him you cooperated, which he might factor in when it comes time to recommend sentencing."

"Wait a minute," Karl protested. "You've already got me tried and convicted. That's . . ."

Kate silenced him with a firm wave of her arm. "Remember my advice, Karl," she said. "Don't say anything until I give you my okay. We clear on that?"

Karl nodded but didn't speak.

"Good. Now follow me."

Kate led him into the big dining area. Stopping at the doorway, Karl began to survey the room with great interest, his eyes scanning left to right, seeing faces of individuals he did not know or recognize. His search ended when he saw Brad. Seeing his youngest son in handcuffs sent Karl's spirits plummeting. For that split-second, his thoughts shifted from Jack Ruby to Lee Harvey Oswald. Like Oswald, Karl realized, he was about to be assassinated.

Kate said, "The two individuals to your immediate right are Brooke Mason and Sly Douglas. They are both Chicago homicide detectives. The man next to me is Jack Dantzler, an ex-cop turned private investigator. I think you already know the young man sitting at the table."

Sly slid a chair back and motioned for Karl to take a seat, one directly across the table from Brad. Brooke and Sly sat at opposite ends of the table, while Dantzler and Todd sat flanking Brad. Kate hovered over Karl like the angel of death. Without saying a word, she punched the Play button on the tape recorder.

Karl did his best to act calm and unaffected, a façade that failed to last more than a minute once he began hearing Brad's answers to the many questions hurled his way. Karl's face tightened, his jaw clenched, and his breathing became heavier. And each time Brad laid the blame solely on his father Karl's eyes became darts aimed at his traitorous offspring.

When the conversation ended and Kate turned off the recorder, Karl looked first at Brad, then at Todd, and said, "My two boys. One's a rat, the other one is Judas. You're living proof why abortion should be legal. I should've had both of you cut out of your mother's belly like a rotten tooth."

Kate said, "Decision time, Karl. Attorney, or answer our questions? What's it gonna be?"

"Say I do talk to you. How much goodwill can I expect from the district attorney?"

"I can't answer that, Karl. A lot depends on the information you give us, and whether or not it helps solve the case. What I can do is promise you that I will put in a good word with the D.A. I'll tell him you helped us out. What he does will be up to him. But I can assure you that district attorneys and juries tend to have a favorable opinion of cooperating witnesses."

"What the hell?" Karl said after thinking about things for a moment. "Thanks to my two sons I'm already screwed. Might as well help. What questions do you have for me?"

Kate ejected the old tape from the recorder and replaced it with a new one. Then, after taking a seat next to Karl, she punched the Play/Record buttons and scooted the recorder closer to Karl. Next, she gave a preamble similar to the one Dantzler had given prior to questioning Brad, reeling off the time, date, location, purpose of the interview, and the names of those present. Once that was taken care of, the questioning got underway.

"According to Brad, you were the lone genius behind the plot to murder a United States senator," Kate began. "No one at this table believes that to be the truth. But for the record, I'll ask anyway. Is it true?"

Karl stared at Brad, shook his head, and said, "I don't know why my moron son told you that nonsense. He knows it's not true."

"Who was behind it?" Dantzler asked.

"Hold on a minute," Karl said, pointing at Dantzler. "Who's asking the questions?"

"Anyone who wants to ask one," Kate replied. "Don't worry about where the question comes from, Karl. Just answer each one truthfully and honestly, beginning with the question Jack asked you. Who was behind it?"

"If you don't believe it was me, then who do you think it was?"

"Yuri Lazarov," Kate answered.

"Well, you're wrong. It wasn't Yuri."

"So, Yuri played no part in the plot. Is that what you're saying?"

"No, that's not what I'm saying. Sure, Yuri was involved. Hell, he's the one who brought me into it."

"Explain that for us."

"Yuri approached me and said an important individual had to be eliminated. He gave me some details, told me how much money we were to be paid if we successfully pulled it off, and then asked me if I had any idea how we could do it. I told him to give me a day or two to think about it. It didn't take that long; the phony movie idea came to me almost immediately. When I informed Yuri, he said let's do it. And we did."

"You needed a patsy, and you needed an actual shooter," Dantzler pointed out. "Let's start with Danny Kafka. How did you find him?"

"Hell, everyone in the movie business knew about the war hero who was in New York studying to be an actor. He was easy to find, even easier to set up."

Sly Douglas said, "What about Bobby Conrad? How did you recruit him?"

"Read about him in a Time magazine article, about how he was this great and deadly sniper over there in the war. The article said he was living and working in the Chicago area. Tracking him down was easy. So was luring him into the plan. You have to understand, everybody wants to be in the movies."

"Who secured the rifles?" Kate said.

"Yuri."

"Who did he get them from?"

"Couldn't tell you."

"Who gave the order to murder Bobby Conrad and Molly Jackson?"

"Wasn't me, so it must've been Yuri. Either that, or Sergei and Brad took it upon themselves to kill them."

"I never killed anyone," Brad practically screamed. "It was Sergei."

Dantzler said, "What about Abe Pearlstein? Did Yuri also give that order?"

Karl nodded, said, "When Yuri heard that a private investigator had met with the old Jew, he told Sergei to find out what information had been revealed, and then to silence him for good. He was what you call collateral damage."

Todd said, "Why was Jon Crofford murdered? He was no threat to you, or to Yuri."

"I have no idea what you are talking about," Karl said. "I'm going to tell you the same thing Brad did: I never heard of anyone named Jon Crofford. If he was killed, I had nothing to do with it. Probably, it was Sergei acting on Yuri's orders."

"Now for the biggest question of all," Kate said. "What was Yuri's reason for killing a United States senator?"

"He didn't have one; he was simply following orders. There is no way Yuri Lazarov or Karl Holland would ever come up with a dangerous plan like that on our own. We never dreamed of taking on something that big. Over the years we've pulled off dozens of jobs but none of that magnitude. We're middle-of-the-road guys, not major players. But this was a once-in-a-lifetime opportunity to make more cash with this single deal than with all other jobs combined. I doubt Yuri had any choice but to say yes. Me, I wasn't going to say no to thirty-million bucks."

"Why do you think Yuri had no choice but to go along with the plan?" Dantzler said.

"Because a very powerful Russian gave him a direct order, that's why. And trust me those damn Russians don't play around. They'll kill you in a second."

"What's that powerful Russian's name?" Kate inquired.

"Only Yuri can answer that one for you."

"And Yuri never told you why the person giving the order wanted Dana Shapiro eliminated?"

"No, he didn't say, and I never asked. Truthfully, I didn't want to know. Sometimes it's better to be ignorant than informed, especially when dealing with those crazy fucking Russians."

Kate looked around the table, and said, "Anyone have more questions for him?"

"Yeah, I have one," Dantzler answered. "During any of your conversations with Yuri, did the name James Weatherford ever come up?"

"No."

Kate turned off the tape recorder, then said, "Stand up, Karl and put your hands behind your back." When he complied, she recited the Miranda warning, placed the bracelets on, and told him that he was under arrest for conspiracy to commit murder. "Do you understand everything I've just told you?"

"Yeah, I've seen it done a million times in the movies."

"This isn't make-believe, Karl. It's very real."

"How much did I help myself with the district attorney?"

"Like I said, that will be up to him," Kate answered. To Brooke and Sly, she said, "Karl and Brad are all yours for the time being. I'll communicate all this with my SAC, and see how he wants to proceed. We'll sort this out once I get his input."

After Brooke and Sly escorted the two prisoners out of the condo, Grace came into the room, opened a cabinet, took down a bottle of Scotch, and began making drinks for everyone except Todd. As always, he asked for and was given two bottles of water.

Kate took a drink, and then said to Dantzler, "What did you think of Karl's responses, Jack?"

"He was being truthful. He told us all he knows."

"I agree," Kate said, adding, "And that brings us to Yuri Lazarov. He's next in line for a serious come-to-Jesus meeting."

"I think you should let me be the one to question him."

"You mean, send you to Los Angeles? Come on, Jack, you know I can't do that. This is about to become a Federal investigation. You're not even a cop anymore. You don't have the authority to question Yuri Lazarov. Just sit back, relax, and take comfort in knowing that none of this would have happened were it not for your efforts."

"What if I go on my own?"

"Then I'll handcuff you myself, lock you up, and lose the key."

Dantzler laughed, said, "I'll make a deal with you, Kate. I won't go to Los Angeles if you'll promise me that when you question Yuri or Sergei, I can be in the room with whoever is conducting the interrogation. Do I have your word on it?"

"I'm not in the business of handing out promises. Sorry."

"Are you in the business of keeping an innocent man locked up behind bars, Kate? Because from where I'm sitting, you have more than enough evidence to have all charges against Danny Kafka dropped. Why not make that happen?"

"Is he always like this, Grace?" Kate said.

"Pretty much."

"How do you put up with him?"

Grace held up her glass, said, "By consuming massive quantities of alcohol."

# Chapter Thirty-One

W ith or without Kate's promise it was not in Dantzler's nature to sit on the sidelines and watch the action unfold from a distance. He was a participant, not a spectator. From his perspective, there was still work to be done, a job to finish, and he had no intention of watching that work performed by others. If this were a tennis match, he would remain one-hundred percent involved until the outcome was decided. That's what he would do in this situation.

Yes, there would come a time when the case moved beyond him, when it was out of his reach. He understood this to be an undeniable fact. But that time had not yet arrived. There was still work left for him to do, and a brief window of opportunity in which to do it.

Bureaucratic red tape, which he had always despised, was now his ally. The larger and more-structured the organization, the slower its wheels turned. Chicago PD certainly ranked in that category, but even that massive organization was nothing compared to the size and complexity of the Federal Bureau of Investigation. Regardless of how proficient those organizations were—and no one doubted their capabilities—rarely did matters move up the ladder with great alacrity.

Kate Flanagan, now actively involved in the investigation, would have to share her knowledge of the case with her Special Agent in Charge. Together, they would plan their next step, which would be to inform someone higher up the food chain. That person would either give them permission to go ahead and move forward, or order them to hold back and let Chicago PD handle it. If ordered to take charge, their first step would be to contact the Los Angeles office, inform the SAC what was happening, and have his agents locate and apprehend Yuri and Sergei Lazarov, and then escort them to Chicago.

For Chicago PD the situation might be even more complex and time consuming. There, you had two agents—Brooke Mason and Sly Douglas—working two separate-but-connected cases. That required them to get with their superiors and coordinate how they planned to proceed. And in all likelihood, Brooke and Sly would be told by their bosses that nobody was doing anything without first conferring with the FBI. If the brass ordered the two detectives to get with the Feds, it would mean an even slower grinding of the wheels.

In Dantzler's calculation, he had one day, maybe two, in which to do what he knew had to be done.

Get his ass out to Los Angeles.

Grace, of course, was against his decision to head west. This surprised Dantzler. Normally, Grace was something of a renegade, a gutsy lady willing to defy orders handed down by those in high places. In this particular instance, that individual was a bossy FBI agent. But that wasn't the case tonight. Following Kate's lead, Grace advised Dantzler to stick around and let the Feds do their thing.

"You're making a bad move, Jack," Grace said. "You don't want to buck the FBI. Right now, Kate is on our side. You go to L.A., she might not be."

"Kate's not my boss, Grace. You are. And the way I see it, I'm not bucking anyone. I'm a private investigator hired to get Danny Kafka out of jail, and that's all I'm trying to do. Yuri Lazarov is the next step in that direction. I need to question him, he lives in L.A., so that's where I'm going."

"When?"

"The first flight out of O'Hare."

Dantzler went into the kitchen, made the call, and booked a seat on a seven-thirty departure. The Delta flight, which included an hour-long layover in Dallas, was scheduled to arrive at ten-fifteen Los Angeles time. Dantzler checked his watch; it was now nearly five a.m., barely two-and-a-half hours until his plane departed. Certainly not enough time to get any sleep. Therefore, he might as well go ahead and get to the airport early. He went upstairs, took a shower, dressed, and packed his Glock in a locked metal case, a requirement when carrying a weapon on a commercial flight.

Grace was asleep on the couch when Dantzler came downstairs. Todd was in the office, sitting at the desk, waiting as the printer spit out a single piece of paper. Dantzler entered the office just as Todd was removing the paper from the printer's tray.

"Here is Yuri's address," Todd said, handing the paper to Dantzler.

"Santa Monica, Twenty-Fifth Street. Is that far from LAX?"

"Not at all. Shouldn't take you much more than thirty minutes, depending, of course, on the traffic."

"Isn't traffic in L.A. always brutal?"

"You could say that." Todd picked up a bottle of water from the desk and took a sip. "You really think it is wise going out there alone? Those are some dangerous folks you're talking about."

Dantzler held up the metal case, said, "That's why I'm taking this."

Grace, bleary-eyed, tired-looking and barely awake, stood in the doorway. "You sure I can't persuade you to take a pass on this trip?" she asked.

Dantzler shook his head.

"What do I tell Kate if she contacts me?"

"The truth always works best, Grace."

"She won't be happy."

"What's she gonna do, Grace, fire me?"

Dantzler folded the paper Todd had given him and put it in his coat pocket. He nodded at Todd, gave Grace a quick peck on the cheek, and headed out into the night's cool darkness. This was a dreadful hour for a bone-weary man to be on the road, but it was the perfect time to be traveling through one of this country's largest and most-populated cities. With virtually no traffic to slow him down, he was parked and inside O'Hare fifty minutes after leaving Grace's place.

At the check-in counter he declared that he had the Glock then filled out the required paperwork. When that was taken care of he made his way to the Delta terminal, slid down into a seat, and began the wait until boarding time.

He was snoozing when the call came. Shaking himself awake, he boarded the plane, found his window seat in first class, buckled up, and immediately fell into a sound slumber. And stayed asleep until being jarred awake by the plane's rough landing. Seeing evidence that the plane was in LAX, he realized he had slept straight through the layover in Dallas. He looked at his watch; it was eleven forty-five, meaning it was nine forty-five in Los Angeles. He calculated that once he departed the plane, secured his weapon and rented a car, he should be on his way to Santa Monica within the next hour. If Todd's prediction was accurate, that the trip from LAX to the Santa Monica address could be made in thirty minutes, it would put Dantzler at Yuri's house somewhere around eleven-thirty.

He beat that prediction by two minutes. At eleven twenty-eight he was on 25th Street, parked in front of Yuri's place. The house, though certainly impressive enough, wasn't anything truly special. Dantzler considered it to be little more than a glorified bungalow. There were dozens of much larger houses up and down the street. Located in Santa Monica, it probably cost Yuri six-million bucks to purchase. In Lexington, far from an ocean and a beach, this same house located in a nice neighborhood might go for a million-five. Funny how an endless view of water can be so expensive.

Dantzler exited the rental and walked up to the front of the house. He fully expected some type of alarm system to warn of his presence, but nothing happened. There were a couple of security cameras at various places high up on the house, but if they were operating, and if he was being watched, no one inside seemed to be particularly concerned. He did think this was odd, especially given that the house was not in a gated community. The wealthy typically go to great lengths to provide protection from potential enemies, and to distance themselves from those considered to be riff-raff. If someone was inside, that individual should be inquiring who Dantzler was, and what reason he had for approaching the house. Conversely, if the house was empty, some type of alarm system should be blaring. Of course, there was always the possibility that it was a silent alarm, in which case the cops might be showing up at any moment.

If that happened his mission would be a failure even before it began.

Undeterred, Dantzler walked up to the front door, reached out to ring the doorbell, stopped, and let his arm drop to the side. There was no need to ring the bell; the door was open maybe six inches. This was never a good sign. If his many years as a homicide detective taught him one lesson, it was this: finding a door slightly ajar tended to mean things hadn't gone well for those on the inside. With that in mind he took out his Glock and clicked the safety off.

His instinct that something bad had taken place inside the house was on the money. And he realized this almost immediately. After moving through a small foyer, he went into the den where the body of a man was sitting partially upright on a sofa. Judging by the deceased's youthful face and the clothes he was wearing, Dantzler guessed the dead man was Sergei Lazarov. He was the victim of a gunshot to his right temple. His body was slumped slightly to his left, his hands were in front of him, and the pistol, a forty-five, rested in his lap.

Dantzler quickly checked other first-floor rooms for more victims. There were none. Then he went through the same routine on the second floor. Once again the rooms were empty. He then came back downstairs and headed for the pool area out back. And that's where he found victim number two, an older man, one he assumed was Yuri Lazarov.

The dead man was sitting in a chair by the pool, blood running down from the back of his head, collecting in a puddle on the teak deck. Like his son, Yuri had been killed by a gunshot to the head, one that probably came as a surprise while he was relaxing and taking life easy on a nice Los Angeles evening. Dantzler didn't even bother feeling for a pulse; he could tell that Yuri had been dead for several hours.

Dantzler had no choice but to call Kate. She needed to be alerted to what he had found. And he would call her. But not just yet, not until after he had a quick look around. He went back into the house, making sure to avoid touching anything that might disturb a potential crime scene. His main objective was to see if Yuri had an office. He did; it was down a narrow hallway off to the left of the den.

The office was small and sparsely furnished, with much of the space taken up by a sofa, two chairs, and a file cabinet. An oak desk sat against the far wall opposite the sofa. Resting on the desk was a laptop, which Dantzler had no intention of touching. To do so would most certainly be altering potential evidence. He wasn't going to do anything that might hinder a homicide investigation. That would be violating one of his long-established cardinal rules.

Lying next to the laptop was an expensive leather-bound appointment book/weekly planner. It was open to yesterday's date. There were no notations on that page. Dantzler removed a pen from a cup and placed it in the crease between pages, his way of not losing his place while also not touching the book. Next, he took a second pen and began carefully flipping through the pages. As he did so, one name kept popping up—Ivan. Four notations on four different dates.

Just Ivan. No last name, no details. However, one notation, made two weeks ago, did catch his eye.

*Ivan, YV, Mulholland.*

Dantzler took out his cell phone and snapped a picture of that notation. Then, once again using the pen, he continued looking through the planner. Several pages had one or two entries, but most were blank. Apparently, Yuri was not a social guy. But just when he was about to call it quits, he came across an entry dated ten days prior to the murder of Dana Shapiro. It was short and cryptic, but it spoke volumes.

*Call Ivan Bershov, plan is a go, thirty million.*

This was all Dantzler needed to know.

He used the pen to flip the pages back to their original place, wiped the pen on his handkerchief, and put it back in the cup. He followed the same fingerprint-removing routine with the first pen, and then holding it by the handkerchief, he returned it to the cup. There was nothing left to do now but call Kate. His work here was finished.

Stepping outside, he punched in Kate's number. She answered immediately, and Dantzler could tell from the tone of her voice that she had indeed spoken with Grace.

"Seriously, Dantzler, are you really in Los Angeles?" she barked.

"Yes, I'm standing in front of Yuri Lazarov's house on Twenty-Fifth Street in Santa Monica. And you need to send agents here ASAP."

"Why do I need to send agents?"

"Because Yuri and Sergei are dead. Both were shot in the head. The shooter tried to make it look like a murder/suicide, but it wasn't. The scene was staged. Your guys will recognize the fake set-up just as quickly as I did. Oh yeah, you might want to alert LAPD as well."

"You're an asshole, Dantzler. Has anyone ever told you that?"

"A few times, sure. But come on, Kate. Are you really pissed at me, or could it be that you're upset because I keep solving your damn cases for you?"

"I repeat—you are an asshole."

"Let's be friends, Kate. It makes life so much better."

"I will put in a call to the SAC in Los Angeles. He'll inform the local authorities. You stay put until my guys show up. Can you follow that one order?"

"Oh, almost forgot. I have another name you need to check out. Ivan Bershov."

"Ivan Bershov? The Washington, D.C. attorney?"

"You know him?" Dantzler asked.

"Not personally, no. But I've heard of him. Why are you bringing up his name?"

"Because he's in this up to his eyelids."

"How do you know?"

"He was mentioned several times in Yuri's appointment book."

"Sweet Jesus Christ, Dantzler . . . you meddled with potential evidence?"

"Don't worry, Kate. Your crime scene is as pristine as Eden on that first morning."

"Just stay put asshole. We'll talk when you get back to Chicago."

"Be sure to let your people know that I'm on your side. We don't want any accidental shootings, do we?"

"It wouldn't be an accident if I had my way," Kate said before punching off.

# Chapter Thirty-Two

D antzler spent most of the next two days in bed catching up on much-needed sleep. Except for trips to answer nature's call he was one step from a dead man. Back from L.A., he'd opted to stay in the house on Sheffield rather than Grace's condo, yet all the normal activity and noise from below had not disturbed his slumber. He could have slept through a tornado.

He awoke at two in the afternoon and decided it was time to re-join the living. He checked his phone to see if he had slept through any calls, or if he had any messages. There were none. This was both a surprise and a disappointment. Why hadn't Kate contacted him? he wondered. By now she surely had information to share with him regarding the Ivan Bershov situation. But she hadn't made contact. Why? Was it because she was still miffed at him, or could it be that the FBI's investigation had hit a snag somewhere along the way? Perhaps it had gotten bogged down in red tape. Whatever the reason, he viewed not hearing from Kate as a bad omen.

Dantzler shaved, showered, dressed, and headed downstairs. The front room where Maggie and Mary-Louise sat was empty. Everyone was gathered in the dining area, standing like statues in front of the big TV screen. As Dantzler drew closer and stood next to Todd he realized that Grace was absent. Thinking she was probably in her office he started to head for the hallway, only to be stopped by something Todd whispered.

"Some crazy shit is going on in our nation's capital," Todd said, pointing at the TV. "Who would've believed this would happen?"

Dantzler focused his attention on the TV screen, where CNN, with its ubiquitous Breaking News logo, was informing viewers that James Weatherford had abruptly resigned his position as attorney general. Several CNN field correspondents, when questioned by Brooke Baldwin, offered plenty of speculation as to why Weatherford was leaving, but none of them offered hard facts. Possible reasons for his stepping down included health problems, family issues, and his well-documented disagreements with the current administration. But in the end they all agreed that Weatherford's leaving was a mystery that required further examination.

Dantzler caught what was on the news crawl at the bottom of the screen a second or two before Team West noticed it. Once they saw it, silence gave way to a loud cheer, hugs, and a few tears.

*Danny Kafka, the Medal of Honor war hero arrested for the murder of Sen. Dana Shapiro two weeks ago has officially been cleared of all charges. He is scheduled to be released from jail sometime today.*

This was the news they had all been waiting to hear.

Thirty minutes later, Grace came into the house, followed by Danny. He was immediately set upon by Team West, getting long hugs from the ladies and a firm handshake from Edward, who then introduced Danny to Todd. Dantzler watched it while standing next to Grace. He pretended not to notice when she wiped tears from her eyes. Like most folks, she was only tough on the outside. Inside, she was softer than a kitten.

Dantzler thought Danny had weathered his stay behind bars far better than most men would have. His hair was long, he had a full beard, and he'd dropped a few pounds, but all things considered he was none the worse for wear. True, he'd only been incarcerated for a couple of weeks, but that was more than enough to cause a weak man to crash and burn. Fortunately, Danny Kafka was anything but weak.

Danny approached Grace, said, "I really don't know what to say, or how to thank you for what you did. What *all* you guys did. I mean, I really thought I'd be locked up forever. Now I'm free."

"This is who you really need to thank, Danny," Grace said, touching Dantzler's arm. "More than anyone else, Jack is responsible for your freedom. He did the heavy lifting."

"Thanks, man," Danny said. "Grace told me you were the best, that if anyone could figure things out, it was you. Turns out she was right. Anyway, thanks for always believing in my innocence."

"All in a day's work, Danny," Dantzler said. "I'm just relieved things worked out in our favor. That doesn't always happen."

Grace nudged Dantzler, indicating she wanted him to follow her to the office. Once inside, she sat behind the desk, opened a drawer, and removed a checkbook.

"How much do I owe you for your services, Jack?" she asked. "And please don't cheat yourself."

"Nothing. If you worked this case pro bono, then I worked it pro bono."

"Get real, Jack. You can afford to be magnanimous now, but when all those credit card bills start arriving you might have a change of heart. Besides, I'm going to rake in a windfall from this case. I've already had invitations to be a guest on evening shows on CNN and MSNBC, and morning shows on ABC and CBS. And in case you're thinking Danny will be left out, don't. Within the next few days he'll have every legitimate movie producer in Hollywood banging on his door. Same goes for agents. He and I will make out like bandits. So should you."

"Write the damn check, Grace, but spare me the sermon. Just know that you don't have to."

Grace filled out the check, tore it from the checkbook, and handed it to Dantzler. The amount was fifty-thousand.

"That's too much, Grace. How about you cut it by half?"

"No way, Jack. Truth is, that's not even close to what you deserve."

Grace gave Dantzler a hug and walked out of the office. Dantzler was about to follow her when his cell phone buzzed. He looked at the screen. Finally, a call from Kate Flanagan.

"Looks like you have a chaotic shit storm in D.C.," Dantzler said.

"God, it's a friggin' nightmare," Kate replied. "As you can imagine, all hell has broken loose."

"Seems I must've been right about Jim Weatherford."

"It's a friggin' nightmare," Kate repeated.

"Care to fill me in on the details?"

"Where are you?"

"Grace's office on Sheffield."

"Stay there," Kate ordered. "I'm leaving D.C. in a few minutes, should be back in Chicago by five or five-thirty. I'll plan on being at Grace's office around eight. We can all sit down, and I'll fill you in on the details. Does that work for you?"

"See you at eight, Kate."

# Chapter Thirty-Three

S inatra launching into "My Kind of Town" alerted Dantzler to the arrival of the expected guest. Checking his watch he saw that it was only seven-thirty. This could only mean Kate's plane had arrived early, and she was running ahead of schedule. He left the big room, where Danny and Todd were glued to CNN's continuing coverage of James Weatherford's sudden resignation, went to the front door and opened it, fully expecting to see Kate Flanagan. Only it wasn't Kate. Standing there, shoulder to shoulder, were Brooke Mason and Sly Douglas. Both appeared to be sagging from fatigue and lack of sleep.

Seeing the surprised look on Dantzler's face, Brooke said, "Kate sent us a text saying she would be here at eight. She suggested that we should also be here."

Dantzler led them into the big room and asked if they wanted something to drink. Both detectives quickly said they'd love a cold beer. As Dantzler left for the kitchen, Brooke and Sly introduced themselves to Danny, took a seat at the big table, and quickly shifted their attention to the TV screen.

Grace came out of the kitchen first, followed by Dantzler, who had two bottles of beer in hand. He gave one to each of the detectives, neither of whom wasted any time taking a drink. The quick hit of cold beer seemed to provide them both with an energy boost.

"Are either of you hungry?" Grace asked. "If you are I can whip up something for you to eat. Might not be great, but at least it will be filling."

"Nah, this cold beer is all I need," Sly said.

"Same here," echoed Brooke.

"Well, there are plenty more in the fridge," Grace informed them. "Feel free to help yourself."

For the next twenty minutes, the only ones speaking were the folks on CNN. The show's anchor, the correspondents out in the field, and those on the panel in the studio continued to discuss and debate the many rumors and unsubstantiated theories that swirled around the Jim Weatherford situation like Hollywood gossip. Despite all the verbiage, what it all boiled down to was that none of them had a clue what was really going on.

What those sitting at Grace's table knew—or at least hoped for —was that within the next hour or so, courtesy of Kate Flanagan, they would know far more than what the CNN tribe knew.

They would know the truth.

AT PRECISELY EIGHT o'clock Sinatra announced Kate's arrival.

Grace went to the door, let Kate in, and led her into the big room. Her eyes scanned around the table until they finally settled on Danny Kafka. She smiled and nodded, sending him a silent message that she was happy he was free and out from under the dark cloud that had been hanging over him for almost three weeks.

Dantzler studied Kate closely. If Brooke and Sly looked fatigued, Kate appeared to be completely exhausted. Like she hadn't slept in days, which was likely true. She wore a navy pants suit, white blouse, and tennis shoes. The suit was rumpled, meaning she'd probably had it on for a while. There were dark circles under her eyes, her hair was loosely tied back in a ponytail, and any make-up she'd been wearing was long gone. She would have described herself as a total wreck; Dantzler thought she was beautiful.

"You look like you could use a drink," Grace said. "What'll you have?"

"Bourbon, straight," answered Kate, taking a seat at the end of the table.

"Coming right up."

Grace went to the liquor cabinet, grabbed a glass and a bottle of Maker's Mark, filled the glass, and set it in front of Kate. "Nectar of the gods," Grace said.

Kate took a sip, then said, "If we were in one of those old cowboy movies, this is when I would order you to leave the bottle. But you'd better not do that, Grace. I'm so weary that too much of this stuff would probably knock me out."

"You look beyond weary," Brooke noted.

"These last forty-eight hours . . . you have no idea." Kate glanced at Dantzler, said, "You did good Dantzler, getting Danny out of jail. But damn if you didn't stir up a hornet's nest."

"Maybe those hornets needed stirring up," Dantzler replied.

Kate took another sip of bourbon, this one bigger than the previous sip, and said, "I'm sure none of you care to hear about hornets, or how weary I am. Nor do I have the strength or energy to prolong this conversation any longer than necessary. So . . . here goes."

She set the empty glass on the table, briefly collected her thoughts, then finally said, "Let me begin by informing you that Ivan Bershov was taken into custody two nights ago, and that I and another agent have been questioning him for the past eight hours. He . . ."

"Eight hours?" Brooke interrupted. "What? Didn't his attorney advise him to shut up?"

Dantzler could see from Kate's expression that she wasn't pleased with being interrupted by Brooke. He'd been in Kate's position numerous times, many more times than a near-novice like Brooke had, and he understood that the story came first, questions later. It was a lesson Brooke would learn over time and with more experience.

"No, he did not at any time ask for legal representation," Kate continued. "This came as a surprise to all of us, but the more he talked the less surprised we were. And trust me when I say the man talked. He spoke faster and said more words than an auctioneer on speed. He couldn't get them out fast enough. And according to Ivan, he was the sole mastermind behind the murder of Dana Shapiro. He decided she had to go—for reasons I'll get to momentarily—then he contacted Yuri Lazarov, and ordered him to see that the mission was carried out. Yuri recruited Karl Holland, who came up with the fake movie idea. Not long after that, poor Bobby Conrad, thinking he's shooting a movie scene, fires the bullet that killed Dana. We pressed Ivan on this for the full eight hours, hoping to catch inconsistencies, but he never once varied his story. If Ivan is to be believed, he is the person who conceived and set the plan in motion."

Kate paused and glanced around the table, waiting for the question she knew was coming. And it was Dantzler who posed it.

"And do you believe Ivan?" he asked.

"Not for a second," Kate said, shaking her head. "He's obviously a bright guy, but the notion that he did this on his own is just not credible. No, Ivan is falling on his sword for someone else."

"Why would he do that?" Brooke said.

"Simple. Because he is more afraid of that individual than he is of our judicial system," Kate answered. "Ivan knows that if he rats on the real mastermind, his family will be killed, and then at some point, even if he's behind bars, he'll get a bullet to the brain. Compared with seeing his family wiped out, spending the rest of his life in prison isn't such a bad deal."

"Any idea who that someone is?" Sly inquired.

Kate nodded, said, "We're not one-hundred percent certain, but we do have a pretty good idea."

"Let me guess," Dantzler said. "His initials are YV."

"You got it. Yevgeny Voronov."

"Who is Yevgeny Voronov?" Brooke said.

"The second wealthiest, most-powerful, most-influential man in Russia," Kate answered. "Voronov is a close and long-time ally of the top man himself. Very little happens in Russia that isn't approved by those two men. Given the power they wield, it's easy to see why Ivan was only too willing to fall on his sword."

"Any chance this Yevgeny dude can be held accountable for the senator's death?" Sly said.

"Not really. He's almost certainly back in Moscow by now, and I doubt he'll ever set foot in the United States again. This is destined to be one of those situations where the true villain gets away with his crime."

Dantzler said, "You still haven't answered the big question—why was Dana Shapiro murdered?"

Ignoring her earlier admonition against more booze, Kate poured bourbon into her glass, took a drink, and then said, "Are any of you familiar with the Magnitsky Act?"

"Vaguely," Grace answered. "Doesn't it have something to do with adoption and human rights?"

"Broadly speaking, yes," Kate said. "It was named for a Russian tax guy who was sent to prison for investigating fraud involving Russian tax officials. While in prison he got sick, was refused medical treatment, and then he was ultimately beaten to death. Our government used this incident to place more sanctions on the Russians, primarily by prohibiting those officials responsible for Magnitsky's death from entering our country, and their use of our banking system. Both the House and Senate conducted investigations. Also, Dana headed a committee that looked into human rights abuses around the globe, with Russia topping the list of offenders. As you might expect, the Russians didn't take too kindly to these new sanctions. They countered by putting out their own list of U.S. personnel prohibited from entering Russia. In addition to that, Russia banned the adoption of Russian children by United States families. And that brings us to why Dana Shapiro was involved."

Before continuing, Dana excused herself and went to the bathroom. While she was away, Grace asked if anyone needed anything. Brooke and Sly both said they could use another beer. By the time

Grace returned with the drinks, Kate was seated and ready to continue.

"This all began when Dana overheard two Russians talking during one of those typical diplomatic social functions someone is always having in D.C. Of course, the two men had no idea Dana was fluent in Russian. What she overheard isn't exactly clear at this point, but it must've had to do with the Magnitsky Act, and in particular, something involving adoption. Whatever it was, she was concerned enough to take what she heard to Jim Weatherford, the attorney general, and to recommend that he open an investigation. He said he'd look into it before deciding if an investigation was warranted. But he didn't look into it. Instead, he went to the Russians and alerted them to what Dana had relayed to him. Ivan Bershov says he's the individual Jim Weatherford contacted, but none of us believe him. We're convinced Jim met with Yevgeny Voronov."

"Why would our attorney general be in cahoots with a powerful Russian like Yevgeny Voronov?" Sly asked.

"Because he had previously been involved with him," Kate replied. "And it all goes back to the adoption thing. The Russians may have publicly banned U.S. families from adopting children from their country, but secretly, for a hefty sum of money, it could be done. So an undercover pipeline was set-up. Families who desperately wanted a child, and who had the financial resources to meet the asking price, which ranged between two-hundred-fifty thousand and half-a-million per child, could in essence purchase the youngster. Once the asking price was deposited into a D.C. bank, the families traveled to Montreal where the child was given to them. It is estimated that more than a hundred children were bought and paid for by Americans desperate to have a child. That adds up to a lot of money for the Russians."

"But what was Jim Weatherford's involvement?" Brooke asked.

"The money that went into the bank was then transferred to an organization whose primary objective, ostensibly, was to monitor human trafficking in the Middle East. But that organization was essentially a front for what amounted to a dummy corporation the

Russians used to launder money. While some funds were used legally, most ended up in the Cayman Islands, or in Swiss bank accounts. The individual in charge of the organization was Emily Weatherford, the attorney general's wife. When Jim told Emily what Dana had overheard, and that Dana sought permission to open an investigation, they both knew the Russians had to be informed. That's when Jim or Emily, or perhaps both, got word to Yevgeny Voronov. Once that happened Dana's fate was sealed."

"How did Jim and Emily Weatherford get involved with the Russians in the first place?" Sly asked.

"Their daughter Wendy was married but couldn't have children," Kate said. "So she and her husband decided to adopt. This was in twenty-ten, two years before the Magnitsky Act went into effect. Wendy and her husband decided to adopt a child from Russia. It was perfectly legal, so no harm, no foul, right? Jim Weatherford had met Yevgeny Voronov on several occasions in the past, a fact he conveniently neglected to acknowledge during his Senate confirmation hearing, or in the paperwork he was required to fill out, both oversights punishable by jail time. Voronov helped expedite the adoption process, for which the Weatherford clan was extremely grateful. Following the implementation of the Magnitsky Act, when the Russians realized a fortune could be made via their underground railroad, and knowing Emily was in charge of the organization monitoring human trafficking abuses, they approached her to act as the financial go-between. She had no choice but to say yes."

"Why would she do that, knowing the potential jeopardy she was putting her husband in?" Brooke said. "He's the United States Attorney General, for Christ sakes."

"An attorney general who had committed perjury by not disclosing those previous meetings with Yevgeny Voronov," Dantzler pointed out. "Emily was trapped, boxed in. Either she agrees to work for the Russians, or her husband faces perjury charges. She was hostage to his past transgressions."

Kate nodded, said, "Exactly. And the sad thing is he's now facing a lot worse charges than perjury, including conspiracy to commit murder, money laundering, and fraud, just for starters. Both Jim and Emily are looking at doing serious prison time, not to mention the absolute public humiliation and disgrace that goes along with it. I wouldn't want to be in their shoes right about now."

"Have they been arrested?" Grace said.

"No, they've both made arrangements to turn themselves in tomorrow at noon." Kate took a drink, put the glass down, and rubbed her tired eyes. "Folks, it goes without saying that tomorrow will be a sad day for our country and for all of us sitting at this table. Law enforcement doesn't need any more black eyes. We've had too many already."

Kate stood, then quickly sat back down, and said, "Something you need to know about your father, Todd. Brad made a deal for leniency by informing the D.A. that your father murdered a young woman named Renee Lynn Munroe. Brad said Karl broke her neck, then had the body taken to a funeral home, where she was cremated. Then a couple of his men drove up the Pacific Coast Highway and dumped her ashes into the ocean. All three of those individuals have been taken into custody. That ends any hope Karl had of cutting a deal with the authorities. He's going away for life."

"And Brad? What about him?"

"Not knowing the details of the deal he cut, I can't say. But I do feel comfortable in predicting that he'll be behind bars for a long time."

"They're my family," Todd said, "and I hate to say it, but if you dance too close to the flames there's a good chance you'll get burned. I'd say they deserve whatever comes their way."

"Well, folks, I'm out of here," Kate said, moving slowly toward the front door. "The next few days are going to be long and exhausting. And very sad. No way could I have ever envisioned sitting down and questioning the attorney general and his wife about a crime that led to the death of a U.S. senator. God, I dread having to do that."

"You'll do fine," Grace said, giving Kate a hug. "Just remember that you're on the side of the angels."

"Thanks to all of you for your help," Kate said as Grace opened the door. "Maybe we can all get together in the future and share a few drinks. Hopefully, under better circumstances."

After Kate was gone, and Brooke and Sly had said their good-byes, Grace asked Dantzler, "What now, Jack?"

"I'm going upstairs, pack my things, and then hit the sack. Tomorrow morning, Todd and I are driving to Lexington. Not sure what Danny's plans are. I invited him to come with us, but he said there were some things he needed to do. I have a feeling he'll meet with Bobby Conrad's family and give them all the details of what transpired. He'll make sure they understand that Bobby was inno-cent. No doubt these past few weeks have been really difficult for them, thinking their son might have committed murder. Danny will disabuse them of that notion."

Grace leaned up and gave Dantzler a kiss. "Don't you guys dare leave without saying goodbye to the gang in the morning," she ordered. "They are all crazy about you and Todd. They'll miss you both, of that I'm quite certain."

"Todd more than me," Dantzler noted.

"Yeah, that goes without saying."

# Chapter Thirty-Four

Lindsey Anderson muttered "shit" under her breath seconds after her backhand shot sailed long at the far end of the court. Realizing she had acted in an unprofessional manner, and worse, that her utterance was far from silent, she glanced first at Dantzler, then at her mother, Mayor Elizabeth Anderson, shrugged, and lowered her head, clearly embarrassed.

"Sorry," Lindsey whispered. "But I really thought that was a good shot. What did I do wrong?"

Her question was directed at Dantzler. Lindsey wasn't ready to look at her mother, who was obviously not impressed with her daughter's word selection. Had Lindsey made eye contact with her mother, she would have been on the receiving end of that hard parental stare every child is familiar with.

"You did everything right up until the very end," Dantzler pointed out. "Your footwork was good, your racket was ready, and your swing went from low to high, which created the topspin. But at the moment of impact you weren't fully committed to the shot. For a split-second you questioned your action. You can't succeed in tennis, or in life without total commitment to whatever it is you're doing. A half-assed effort is never a winning strategy."

"You're right," Lindsey said, sounding as though a hidden light had suddenly been switched on in her head. "I thought about hitting a drop shot instead. I wasn't fully committed."

"Next time you won't hesitate," Dantzler said, adding, "That's enough for today. I'll see you again next Tuesday."

After her daughter had departed, Elizabeth Anderson said, "I will speak with Lindsey tonight concerning her little outburst. She knows better than to behave like that."

"I wouldn't come down too hard on her," Dantzler advised. "She's a great kid. And if that's the worst thing she ever says on a tennis court, you could chalk her up as a saint."

"Obscenity aside, how is Lindsey doing?"

"She's improving. Lindsey listens, follows instructions, and puts in the effort. Those are three important qualities to have. She'll do okay."

"But not a Wimbledon champion, right?"

Dantzler laughed, said, "I think that goal is slightly beyond her reach."

"Do you think she could eventually play at the college level?"

"If she continues to work hard, if she doesn't lose her love for the sport, and if she excels in high school, sure, I could envision her earning a scholarship."

"Well, you're a saint for spending all this time with her," Elizabeth said, patting Dantzler on the arm. "She's learning from the best, no doubt about that."

Dantzler left the court, went into the locker room, undressed, and took a shower. Thirty minutes later, he was sitting in the lounge area, alone, drinking a Pepsi, and trying to figure out why he was feeling so down and funky. The voices in his head were telling him this was a time for rejoicing, not for suffering the blues. Considering what he'd just accomplished, he should be sitting on top of the world; instead, he was wandering quietly through his own private hell.

There was no legitimate reason to be so down. Yet, he was.

It had been two weeks since he'd been instrumental in bringing to justice a group of conspirators who planned and executed the assassination of a U.S. senator. That investigation had also resulted in the capture of men responsible for the murders of Bobby Conrad, Molly Jackson, Abe Pearlstein, Jon Crofford, Yuri Lazarov, and his son Sergei. A top Russian criminal was in custody, and topping it off, our country's attorney general and his wife were now facing enough charges to send them both to prison for many years. If Jim Weatherford was found guilty, and there was every reason to believe he would be, Dantzler had played a key role in bringing down the highest law enforcement official in the land. By any standard of measurement, what he had done was nothing short of outstanding.

Most important of all, though, Danny Kafka had been cleared of the murder charge, set free from jail, and had his reputation restored. He was once again a Medal of Honor war hero, not a murder suspect. A good guy had come out on top.

Danny was also a rich young man, thanks to the small fortune left to him by Abe. Upon learning that his bank account was now rather impressive, Danny said he would donate half the money to an organization committed to helping wounded veterans overcome their horrific battlefield injuries. He also offered to give Dantzler a large chunk for "saving my ass," but Dantzler refused, saying his share should go to the families of Bobby Conrad and Molly Jackson.

Grace had been right when she predicted that Danny would be inundated with offers from Hollywood producers and directors. Two days ago, during a phone conversation with Dantzler, Danny said he'd been offered roles in five movies set to go into production. But Danny turned them all down, choosing instead to audition for the role of Edmund Tyrone, the youngest son in an off-Broadway revival of O'Neill's classic *Long Day's Journey into Night*. To his great joy, he got the part. Danny told Dantzler he chose the play over a movie as a tribute to Abe's love for the theatre.

Danny wasn't the only one to land a pile of unexpected cash. Last week, Todd got word from a California attorney that Karl had agreed to give his son total control of Holland Productions. Todd flew to Los Angeles and signed the papers. Holland Productions consisted of two large buildings located on six acres of prime L.A.

real estate, furniture and equipment, and the rights to all the crappy movies Karl had produced and released, either in theaters or on video. Added up, Todd was sitting on a sum in the neighborhood of forty-million dollars. Not surprisingly, Todd immediately put everything up for sale. Two major studios had already made overtures to purchase Holland Productions. Todd said he'd sell to the first one that made a firm offer. He wanted no part of Karl's crappy movie empire.

As she had predicted, Grace was also doing well for herself. She had been a guest on so many TV talk shows that she could almost qualify for an Emmy or Golden Globe nomination. During one of those appearances, she announced that HarperCollins had signed her to write about the Danny Kafka case. Protocol prohibited Grace from talking about the amount of her advance, but Dantzler knew it would be substantial.

He had only heard from Grace once since leaving Chicago. But this wasn't what was troubling him. He had no real desire to continue a romantic relationship with her. In truth, if he was really being honest with himself, he was much more intrigued by Kate Flanagan. He'd toyed with the idea of phoning her, to gauge her interest, but chose not to. What would be the point? Exchanging one long-distance relationship for another one would inevitably result in long-distance disappointment. He didn't need that potential heartache.

Deep down, Dantzler knew why he was feeling the blues. It had to do with the way he'd behaved with Brooke Mason and Sly Douglas. He had broken the Golden Rule by not treating them the way he would have wanted—expected—to be treated. Keeping fellow detectives on the outside, not sharing information with them was unprofessional, lacking in courtesy, and downright wrong. Sure, he could shrug it off by arguing that he was a private investigator and not a detective, and that the old rules no longer applied. But that was an internal debate he would always lose. He had treated them in a shabby manner, and there was no way of getting around that fact.

Perhaps turning in his badge had been a mistake. He couldn't deny that for all the good he had accomplished working this case he was left with an empty, unfulfilled feeling. He had gotten close to the finish line, only to be pushed aside before hitting the tape. Not being a cop meant he wasn't in a position to arrest or to interrogate Ivan Bershov. His role had been to provide information and then stand down. He wasn't allowed to place the bracelets on Ivan, or to sit across from him, look him in the eye, and question him. There was nothing Dantzler liked better than going one-on-one with a scumbag. But in his new role that was no longer a possibility. Being an outsider was the main cause of those dark feelings crawling around inside him.

The choice he faced was obvious: Move on, or continue to be a slave to the past.

"Damn, Jack, you look like a man pondering the mysteries of the universe," Sean Montgomery said, sitting across from Dantzler. "I can see that something's troubling you. Come on, pal, tell Sean what's on your mind."

"Nothing, Sean. Everything is aces."

"I sense you may be regretting the decision to go from homicide detective to private investigator. Am I close to correct?"

"Nah, I'm okay with being a shamus, a gumshoe."

"You failed to mention a dick."

"That's because I didn't want to deny you the pleasure of saying it."

"You're a prince of a fellow, Jack." Sean stood, said, "You going to McCarthy's? My understanding is the gang has assembled."

"Yeah, but first I need to make a quick stop. I shouldn't be more than a few minutes behind you."

"The first round is on you."

"Sean, if you ever offer to buy the first round, that's when I'll know this planet we call home has gone completely off the rails."

"Well, we certainly don't want that to happen, do we?" Sean said as he headed for the stairs. "Therefore, in an effort to save mankind from destruction, I'll happily continue to be the tight-fisted bastard you know and love."

When Dantzler breezed into McCarthy's forty-five minutes later,

Peter, one of the pub's owners, immediately began filling a pint glass with Guinness. Dantzler nodded at Peter, and then turned his attention to the group sitting around a large barrel that served as a table. This crew consisted of regulars Sean, David Bloom, Jake Thomas, and Richard Bird, along with the lone newcomer, Danny Kafka.

Dantzler was holding a small wooden case by the handle, which he placed on the barrel just as Peter handed him his Guinness.

"What are you bringing us?" Bloom inquired.

"A battlefield," answered Dantzler after taking a drink. He then unsnapped the two locks and opened the case, revealing a chess board. "It is time to settle once and for all who reigns as the superior chess player, Jake or Danny. All bragging stops now. Today, in this hallowed place, the truth will be decided."

After choosing to play black, Jake looked across at Danny, and said, "Do you want to tell him, or should I?"

"Please, allow me," Danny replied, looking up at Dantzler. "It makes no difference which of us wins, Jack, because both of us can easily crush you. And it wouldn't even be a close match."

"Oh, yeah," Dantzler said, taking a seat between Sean and Danny. "Well, you'll get your chance, because I'm calling winners."

"Set up your pieces, gentlemen, and let the war begin," Sean said, adding, "Let's see who earns the Medal of Honor today."

Dantzler tapped Danny on the shoulder, said, "There's only one Medal of Honor guy sitting at this table. And we all know who he is."

Danny grinned, but only briefly, then looked across the table at Jake, turned stone cold serious, and said, "Pawn to King Four."

The battle had begun.

## Acknowledgments

A special thanks to retired FBI agents Clyde Graven and Phillip Doty for guidance and for the advice that helped me navigate certain law enforcement matters. If I slipped off the right track, it's my fault and certainly not theirs. I also want to thank the McCarthy's gang for allowing me to be part of the group, and for letting me use the pub in my stories. That bunch includes Roger "Roddy" O'Byrne, Peter Kiely, Bobby O'Byrne, Sean Sutton and Joe Bryant. Thanks again to all those who continue to provide me with support and encouragement. This loyal group includes Wanda Underwood, Jake Small, Chris Boggs, Scott Boggs, Christina Young, Carol Palmer, Michael Palmer, Suzanne Slinker, Denny Slinker, Bonnie Vincent, Jim Vincent, Grant Sparks, Jimmie Nell Jenkins, Joe Gillespie, John Gillespie and Kelsey Gillespie. As always, thanks to Frank Hall for bringing me into the Hydra family, and to Tony Acree, the force who keeps Hydra Publications rolling smoothly along.

# About the Author

Tom Wallace is the award-winning author of seven previous Jack Dantzler mysteries, including *Murder by Suicide*, *The Poker Game*, *The Fire of Heaven*, *The List*, *Gnosis*, *The Devil's Racket* and *What Matters Blood*. He also wrote the thriller, *Heirs of Cain*.

His novel, *Gnosis*, won the prestigious Claymore Award at the Killer Nashville Writers Conference, and *The Devil's Racket* captured the Mystery Writers top award. *Murder by Suicide* was an Amazon best-seller.

Tom, a former sportswriter, has written several successful sports-related books, including *The Kentucky Basketball Encyclopedia* (now out in its fourth edition), *So You Think You're a Kentucky Wildcats Basketball Fan?* and *Golden Glory: The History of Central City Basketball*.

Tom is a Vietnam vet who currently lives in Lexington. He is a member of Mystery Writers of America. His web site is www.tomwallacenovels.com

## Also by Tom Wallace

Murder by Suicide

The Poker Game

The Fire of Heaven

The List

Gnosis

Heirs of Cain

The Devil's Racket

What Matters Blood

Kentucky Basketball Encyclopedia

So You Think You're a Kentucky Wildcats Basketball Fan

Golden Glory: A History of Central City Basketball

Jeff Sheppard: Heart of a Champion

Embracing the Legend: Jim Harrick Revives the UCLA Mystique

Inside/Outside: A Behind the Scenes Look at Kentucky Basketball

Travis Ford: Big Blue Dream